From Second Wind Publishing by

S. M. Senden

Clara's Wish

www.secondwindpublishing.com

Clara's Wish

By

S. M. Senden

To Brad -
Thanks So much! Enjoy
S M Senden
April 2013

Dagger Books
Published by Second Wind Publishing, LLC.
Kernersville

Dagger Books
Second Wind Publishing, LLC
931-B South Main Street, Box 145
Kernersville, NC 27284

This book is a work of fiction. Names, characters, locations and events are either a product of the author's imagination, fictitious or used fictitiously. Any resemblance to any event, locale or person, living or dead, is purely coincidental.

First Dagger Books edition published
November 2012.
Dagger Books, Running Angel, and all production design are trademarks of Second Wind Publishing, used under license.

For information regarding bulk purchases of this book, digital purchase and special discounts, please contact the publisher at
www.secondwindpublishing.com

Cover design by Tracy Beltran

Manufactured in the United States of America
ISBN 978-1-938101-28-1

Dedicated to the memory of Clara Olson

PROLOGUE

October 1959

Bergin Halverson gazed at the diamond ring the sheriff had placed on the desk. He did not reach to touch it or pick it up. In the stillness, a flood of memories swept over him. Memories he had tried so hard to leave behind in the hidden places of his past.

He sighed as he ran his hand across his forehead and down over his eyes, pausing at his mouth as if it could keep him silent a little longer.

"If you can tell us anything about the diamond ring, and who it belonged to, you could help us solve this case." The sheriff shifted uneasily in his chair as he waited for the older man to reply. Silence settled uneasily about them as the dust motes drifted lazily through the bright shaft of sunlight that streamed in through the window. "It's not every day that someone unearths a skeleton on your property, Mr. Halverson."

"No, not an everyday occurrence," Bergin Halverson said in a hushed tone. He wasn't sure he wanted to bring all those memories back again. He had lived with the fear and the pain for all these years now, and it had taken some time for there to be only a dull ache instead of a sharp pain when some memory would surface unbidden into his conscious mind.

Bergin sighed and shook his head. He didn't want to remember. They had all been so young then, such fools, especially his brother; his selfish, irresponsible brother. He winced as the pain of memory grabbed at him.

"Mr. Halverson, are you all right? Can I get you something?" The sheriff sat forward in his chair.

"No, no, I'm fine." He put out his hand and moved it like he was brushing the air away from his face on a hot day. "Just an old ghost from the past—one that I would prefer to leave slumbering."

"I do wish you would tell me at least some of what you know about this. Because if I am any good at my job, and I believe that I am, I have a hunch that you not only know who this is, but how they ended up in that shallow grave."

"I didn't kill anyone, sheriff." He shut his eyes tightly as he shook his head. Flashes of memory still came even with his eyes shut tightly against them.

"Okay, I will accept that for the moment." He pulled at his lower lip as he thought about what Mr. Halverson had said. "I would bet that you know a hell of a lot about what all happened back then. I want you to tell me what you know."

"That's not so easily done." A faint smile touched his lips and he looked into the sheriff's eyes for a moment; his gaze was slowly drawn back to the ring, then he looked away again. "It was so long ago when you count the days and years and yet . . . time is a funny thing, it plays with us . . ." his words drifted into silence as he reached out to pick up the diamond ring.

His hand trembled.

It was weighty in his hand. The ring was a heavy gold band with three perfect blue-white diamonds set into it, four karats in total. It had been designed by a man named Cartier. He held it so the light flashed across the surface of the stones.

It was a ring he remembered well and hated the associations that went with it. He closed his eyes, but scenes from his past flickered through the darkness like visages from an aged, silent film.

The ring had been unearthed with a skeleton discovered in a shallow grave in a stand of oak trees on an unused piece of his land near the ruins of an old house. The skeletal remains were being analyzed by the coroner and the anthropology professor from the university. There had been a few other things that had been found with the bones that placed the burial somewhere around 1925.

Mr. Halverson opened his eyes and looked at the sheriff for a moment, then looked down at the ring again before he began to speak.

"I guess I do know most of the story. Over the years, bits and pieces have come to light, not because I was seeking them, but they came to me nonetheless. So much that I would have liked to forget." He shook his head gently.

"Help me out here, Mr. Halverson," the Sheriff stated it more as a command than a request.

"It is a story that has taken nearly thirty-five years to come to this point, and since that time there were so many secrets kept by those of us who went on living. So many things that no one talked about, questions no one asked. No one dared, maybe we didn't really want to know the answers. Maybe no one really wanted the truth back then," Bergin said to the sheriff, meeting his gaze.

"I want the truth now. I am asking for the answers and I will get them one way or another." The sheriff held Bergin Halverson's gaze.

"Yes, I am sure you will. Eventually the truth does make its way through, no matter how deeply we try to bury it or hide it from sight," his words again drifted into silence. The eight-day clock on the wall ticking away the minutes was the only sound until Halverson began to speak again. "It has taken me all these years to lay to rest those memories of what happened, and now, you want me to remember it all again."

"I don't expect it will be easy for you, but as sheriff of the county, I have a job to do and I have to get some answers. I believe this person was murdered, and the body hidden in that grave." He raised his eyebrows, pressing the matter. "Do you know who it is in that grave?"

Bergin fought back the tears that threatened to fill his eyes.

The sheriff waited.

Dust motes danced in the shaft of light, the clock on the wall ticked away the seconds, from the street the sound of an occasional car, and far off the plaintive sound of a train whistle as it came into town.

"The person in that grave was someone that I . . ." Bergin Halverson let his words drift off into silence, shrouded in painful memory. Bergin looked again into the light playing in the facets of the ring casting a shower of little rainbows about the room. He looked deeper into the stone. On one of the polished surfaces, he saw a fragment of his own reflection. He looked into his own eye as it looked back at him from the depths of the diamond's clarity.

"Maybe if I finally let go of the secrets I have been holding all these years, maybe then I can at last be free of the ghosts that haunt me," Mr. Halverson sighed from the depths of his being, speaking more to himself than to the sheriff.

The sheriff said nothing, allowing Bergin to compose himself. He had seen the struggle on the man's face as he battled with his inner demons. He knew that this time the man would begin to relate to him the events of the past.

The radiator began to hiss as the steam rose in the lines, air hammers pounded and clanked in the iron pipes. The room began to warm against the chill that had settled in about them.

Mr. Halverson placed the ring gently back on the desk.

The sheriff sat and bided his time.

At last, Bergin Halverson began to relate his tale; his voice had a soft, far away quality to it as someone sorting through a lifetime of recollections, brushing away the thick cobwebs that clung to old memories.

"I believe it all began with a wish whispered from the heart of a beautiful but lonely woman. The old adage tells us to be careful what we wish for," Bergin sighed again, closing his eyes, struggling with the shadows of his past. He could see them all again coming to life in his mind's eye. "She got her wish, in a way." He opened his eyes and looked out the window at nothing in particular.

"Who was that Mr. Halverson?"

"Clara," he smiled, seeing her again, a young and beautiful woman of twenty-three. He, of course, was only nineteen back then. "Clara Lindgren." Bergin said her name almost as if it were a caress.

BOOK ONE

NONE BUT THE LONELY HEART

by

J. W. von Goethe

None but the lonely heart
Can know my sadness
Alone and parted
Far from joy and gladness
Heaven's boundless arch I see
Spread about above me
O what a distance dear to one
Who loves me.
None but the lonely heart
Can know my sadness
Alone and parted
Far from joy and gladness
Alone and parted far
From joy and gladness
My senses fail
A burning fire
Devours me
None but the lonely heart
Can know my sadness

CHAPTER 1

December 1923

Clara Lindgren stood at the edge of the desolate field as the chilly December wind whipped about her. The fields were barren now; winter had come to the land. The broken corn stalks, once so full of potential, lay scattered in the fields, the wind tossing them about as it played in the ruins of the harvest.

She felt that the land was a metaphor for her life, barren, and the springtime of her days were far behind her. She shivered against the cold that penetrated her thick, woolen sweater as she thought about her life.

She was twenty-three now and feared that she was doomed to spend her years as a spinster, to live as a maiden aunt and help raise one of her siblings' children if one of them would be kind enough to take her in under their roof. Clara would cook, clean and do all the menial chores of a servant in exchange for her room and board.

It wasn't how she had wanted her life to turn out. Clara still held onto the tattered hopes that someday she would meet that someone special. But that dream faded more and more with each passing season. Life was passing her by, and she didn't know if there was anything she could do to change it.

She sighed, her frosty breath enveloping her for a moment before it faded.

Clara had hoped to marry and have a family one day. But there were so few men around that she liked who also liked her. She wasn't as outgoing as her older sister who had found a nice man to marry right out of high school. She was more reticent than her younger sister who still had the possibility of finding someone. Her younger sister had garnered more attention than she ever did, already she had the fellows buzzing about her like bees to honey.

A light snow began to fall. She loved the smell of snow, a cold dryness that tickled her nose. Usually the frigid fragrances of winter wafted on the wind long before the snow began to fall. Clara looked up as the flakes fell from a flat, leaden sky. She had heard someone call it Winter's Communion if you put your tongue out to catch the flakes. She watched as they fell, growing thicker in abundance from above.

She could hear the chunky flakes as they plashed into the earth, landed on her shoulders and nestled into her hair.

Soon the bleak land would be covered in a beautiful mantle of white, transforming everything into a fairyland. If only her life could transform as easily. Clara knew she was shy, but she didn't think she was ugly. She had soft brown hair that she wore in a stylish bob, dark green eyes, flawless, pale skin, an oval face and a kewpie bow mouth. These were the attributes that everyone seemed to want, so why hadn't anyone wanted her? What was wrong with her that no man had chosen her?

Her older brother was married and was starting a family. Her other two brothers were courting some local girls they had grown up with and were getting up the nerve to ask them to be their brides. She sighed, knowing she was powerless to change how things were done in her day and age. The men are the ones who get to ask, and if no one asks, then you don't get married.

Snow was beginning to accumulate in the rutted furrows, filling them up, transforming the land. Soon the fields would not look so desolate or abandoned with the remnants of that which had been once so full of life and plentiful harvest. The snow now covered the broken stalks, making them over into something wondrous, like something out of a fairy tale.

She realized that it was the first snowfall of the season. She could make a wish now. She had learned of an old French custom of making a wish the first time you did something, or, in this instance, the first of something in a year.

This was the first snowfall of winter, 1923.

She closed her eyes; she knew her wish by heart. She had wished it so often. She wondered if it would ever come true.

"I wish that this might be the last Christmas that I ever see on the farm. I wish to leave this place forever." Her whispered words took shape in the cold air and hung before her for a moment and then were lost in the frosty wind that snapped them away.

CHAPTER 2

Clara turned away from the scene before her and returned to the house. She had to get ready. Today happened to be the wedding day of a neighbor girl, Linda Swenson. She was only just seventeen and marring a man who was twenty-five. He was someone Clara grew up with. He should have asked Clara to marry him. But he had never given her a second look.

She sighed; she was too old to ever find someone now. All the men her age were already married or spoken for. She would go to the wedding and endure the happy bride, so young and pretty and so sweet. She would sit on the sidelines wondering why she had missed her chance.

The screen door screeched on its hinges as she opened it. The front door creaked a little as she pushed it open and quickly came into the house, shutting it behind her. The screen door slapped shut on the other side. She smiled at her father who was sitting in the parlor reading the newspaper. He looked up as she entered and smiled in return. Clara headed up the stairs to the room she shared with her little sister.

Ingmar was already half dressed. She had curly brown hair and eyes, and had that slim figure of a girl just entering womanhood. She had a much more outgoing personality than Clara and made friends easily. Clara smiled at her sister as she turned to greet her. She was brimming with the excitement of the day.

"I lightly pressed your party dress for you. It's hanging in the chifferobe." Ingmar didn't seem to be able to hold still. It had been two years since the last wedding in the area. She was terribly excited to go to the wedding as a young lady and not as a child. She was sixteen now, and had been told she could stay with the adults instead of being shuffled off with the children.

"Thank you." Clara looked at her sister, seeing her as the young woman she was becoming. Despite the span of years between them, they had become quite close over the last year. Clara wondered if it was because she could still remember so clearly what it was like to be sixteen and standing on the threshold of her adult life when all her hopes and dreams were fresh and new, before the years had slipped by, leaving her behind, alone and unclaimed by any boy in the county who would step forward to declare her for his sweetheart and, later, his wife. “And don’t you look pretty.”

“Do you really think I’m pretty?” Ingmar spun around happily. Clara’s approval was important to her.

“Yes, you really are very pretty. All the boys will want to dance with you.” She brushed her fingers gently against her sister’s soft cheek. She envied her sister’s youth and exuberance. But she wouldn’t take it away from her for anything. Maybe she could find some little happiness through her sister’s romances. She could sit back and watch what would happen to her sister that had never happened for her.

“I love you, Clara.” Ingmar wrapped her arms about her sister. “You are the best sister anyone could want.” She squeezed her tighter. “I really do love you. I wish I could be more like you too. You are so strong and just know so much. I mean, you are a wonder with the sewing machine; you made both our dresses for the wedding. I can’t even sew a straight seam. I just can’t get the treadle going the right speed, and I can’t keep control of the fabric as the feed dogs guide the material under the needle.”

“You’ll learn. I couldn’t always do it right either. Grandmother had to teach me, just as I am teaching you.” Clara smiled as her sister extolled her virtues. At least someone had noticed she was good at something. She hugged her sister in return.

“Oh, Clara I wish my body was more like yours, too! You are so wonderfully flat-chested and have small hips that look so good in the latest fashions. Somehow I don’t think I will ever be as flat as you. Already, I have to bind my bosom. You are so lucky, and I am so lucky to have you as my sister. Oh, I love you Clara.” Ingmar hugged her tighter slowing the flow of her adoration for a while.

“I love you, too.” Clara, a little overwhelmed, pried herself loose from her sister’s tight embrace and gazed into her eyes. “You are the best friend I’ve ever had.”

Clara took her neatly pressed party frock from the chifferobe and looked at her handiwork. She was pleased. She had been able to find a nice piece of deep green, silk velvet on sale a while back. She had saved it hoping for a special occasion to make it up into something. The wedding was a good excuse for a new dress and she would be able to wear it through the Christmas season.

She ran her fingers along the softness of the fabric, a warm green like the emerald depths of a forest in summer. It was a color that she knew would set off her eyes and it would complement the reddish undertones in her hair. She still longed to be considered beautiful by someone; she had cut her thick, long hair in hopes of not looking like she was right off the farm. Her mother had cried for days, and had made a placket of the hair, and had it in a frame on the wall of the bedroom.

"You'll look so very sophisticated in that frock. One day I hope I can look sophisticated like you do." Ingmar brought her back to the moment.

"You are such a silly goose," Clara chided her; though she doubted her sister had a clue what the word sophisticated meant. Clara pulled off her day dress and took a sponge bath before putting on clean under-things and her new gown. She took out a pair of black, clocked, silk stockings and pulled them onto her legs. They felt so soft against her skin. She slipped her feet into the black satin shoes with the French heels and stylish, slim lines. Her sister nodded approvingly with every article of clothing she donned. Then Clara pulled the silk-velvet dress over her head and let it fall about her, loving the feel of the fabric against her skin.

"If I can't get married myself, at least I can wear something wonderful," Clara teased her sister.

"Careful, you'll out shine the bride," Ingmar chided.

"Somehow I doubt that. All eyes will be on the bride and her wedding gown. She will have that look of love in her eyes, and it will melt us all. There won't be any need for the furnace to be turned on; we will all bask in the warm glow of their love." Clara allowed herself to be carried off into the world of romance she had read about in books. She wondered if it really existed.

"You really are too silly. Not turn on the furnace. In case you didn't notice, it's snowing outside," Ingmar laughed, kissing her sister on the cheek then began to dress.

Clara combed through her hair, smoothing down the stray locks. Then she took out the small vial of *Replique* a perfume by Raphael of Paris that she had purchased a few years ago with some money she had gotten for Christmas. It had a sweetly-spicy, exotic scent to it, and on warm nights it seemed to embrace her in a sensual, heady scent that carried her miles away to romantic places around the world. She dabbed the tulip shaped stopper behind her ears and at the pulse points on her wrists.

She took in a deep breath of the heady perfume and smiled, letting it go with a sigh of delight in the daydream in her imagination the fragrance created for her.

She gave herself another look in the mirror, pleased with how she looked. She opened the drawer of her jewelry box and took out the long strand of faceted, black onyx beads she had bought to go with her dress and slipped them around her neck. She decided to let them hang their full length with only a little knot just below her navel. It was all the rage, and she so wanted to be stylish, even if she was alone.

CHAPTER 3

The wedding was a romantic experience, transforming their church, usually so stark and unadorned, now full of flowers that perfumed the air like a nearly forgotten summer afternoon. The bride, in a dress of gossamer, sheer silk trimmed in ivory and gold lace, looked like a drawing of a fairy tale princess and the groom looked good, like a prince, in his black suit.

Clara had seen how they looked at one another and sighed, gently rubbing the ache in her heart.

Afterwards, the crowds gathered in the church hall for the reception. Years ago, someone had hauled an old barn in from the country and the men had remade it into a church hall, and then helped the man build a new, bigger barn on his land. The hall had a connecting passage with the church and was used for many functions, and was very spacious. Today it was decorated with flowers and bunting for the joyful wedding celebration. The snow was still falling thick and white outside. The room inside was warm in contrast to the stark-white beauty of the winter landscape.

A piano player and a fiddler were playing some old folk tunes as a number of people began to take partners and dance. Clara spotted her sister Ingmar being coaxed onto the dance floor and smiled.

Clara walked by the refreshment table piled high with cakes and cookies and so many good things to eat. Some ladies ladled punch into little cups and handed her one. She smiled and thanked them as she accepted the cup.

The punch was sweet.

So was the bride. Linda Swenson was now Mrs. Lars Hanson.

Clara sighed again, and helped herself to a slice of cake. She walked over to a chair, one of many waiting along the wall that would soon be filled with old ladies and other wallflowers. She planted herself in a chair, knowing that she would be there for the rest of the reception.

A group of three men gathered nearby, not even aware that she was there. She was used to it. Men always acted like she was no more than a picture on the wall or a table in a corner. She didn't know what it was that she lacked, and it hurt deeply that she was so insignificant. She, like every other woman, just wanted to be loved and cherished.

Clara couldn't help but overhear their conversation.

"A December wedding. Silly idea, don't you think?" spouted one man in an overly loud voice. He was about forty-five, his face was puffy and he had a large gut. His chin slid into his neck, and disappeared into his shirt collar. He shut one eye to focus better on his companions. "Do you think there might be some reason they had to get married at this time of year?" He asked with a frown.

"Couldn't say," another man replied taking a sip of his punch, his eyes wandering to where the bride stood laughing with her bridesmaids and some other friends. The man was about the same age as his companions, mostly bald and graying. Under his eyes were puffy pillows of fat. Broken capillaries stretched across his nose and cheeks. His mouth, usually turned down in a sour expression, now pulled into a lecherous half smile. "But I do envy him the task of creating their children."

"Yes, me too." He too turned to look as the new Mrs. Hanson was kissed on the forehead by her father who was tall and slim, but her father had never been gifted with good looks. His face was weathered from too many seasons in the fields.

"Fetching little thing, isn't she," the first man said with a little growl to his voice that was reminiscent of a cat in heat.

"Old man Swenson knew how to make them," the second man said laughing boisterously, nudging the other man in the ribs.

"His wife is still a fine-looking woman," the third man spoke up as he watched the bride's mother whispering to her daughter, making her blush.

"Very handsome woman, very handsome indeed," the first one agreed taking a large bite of cake. It didn't quite fit, but he stuffed it into his mouth with the back of his fork. Some of the icing smeared on his cheek. His tongue tried to find it as his eyes swept over the visage of the bride's mother as if she were another piece of delicious cake to be had at his pleasure.

"When those two put their heads together, they were able to make beautiful children," the second man nodded, also looking the woman over from head to toe.

"Linda is the prettiest of them all," the third man said looking over his punch glass rim as he greedily took another swallow.

"If I were a younger man, and had no wife to be jealous, I would sure like to bed that one." The second man smiled with a definite leer in his eyes.

Clara heard their crude talk. She wondered why they all wanted the bride, what was it about the girl that ignited their fire, even stirred the passions of the old men. She had never had anyone look at her the way these men looked at Linda. They were like the hungry wolves who hung at the edges of the fields, licking their lips, preparing to hunt some small helpless animal.

It revolted her.

The men moved away, heading for the refreshment table again, but not before they each took another longing, lustful look at the bride who was unaware of their sniggering and leering.

Clara wondered if all men were like that when they were together with no women to temper their conversations.

Ingmar came over and flopped down into the seat next to Clara. She was quite warm, and was panting. The color in her cheeks looked pretty. The hair along her forehead was damp with perspiration.

"Clara, I had to take a rest. I have been dancing almost since the music began. I needed to sit down for a moment before I passed out." She fanned herself with her hand. "Have you danced at all yet?"

"No." Clara looked down, ashamed a little that she hadn't been asked at all. "I don't think I will be dancing tonight."

"I'll dance with you," Ingmar said taking her sister's hand ready to lead her onto the dance floor.

"You are sweet, but no. It wouldn't be the same." Clara shook her head gently and smiled at her sister. Ingmar wasn't being mean at all; she just didn't know what it was like to be left at the side of the room all your life. Ingmar had never been one to sit along the side of any room. She always managed to create excitement and enjoyment wherever she went. "Besides, you are dancing enough for us both."

"Well, I'm sitting this one out. I need a rest. It's so hot in here." She slouched back into the chair and fanned herself with her hand.

Clara offered her the glass of punch. Ingmar took it and drank greedily.

It didn't take long before a pimply faced boy came up to Ingmar and asked her to dance. She looked at Clara, shrugged her shoulders and laughed, but sent him away. Soon enough another fellow came up and stood before Ingmar and Clara. He was tall, fair and seemed rather shy.

"Miss Ingmar, would you dance with me, please?" He gave her a little bit of a smile as his hands fidgeted behind his back. "My name is Bergin, Bergin Halverson. You may remember me from high school."

"Yes, I do remember who you are." She smiled at him, flattered that an older boy would pay attention to her. She turned to Clara to tell her more about him. "Bergin already graduated from school last year."

"That's right. Now I am working on our family farm," he replied.

"Wouldn't you like to dance with my sister, Clara?" Ingmar sat back and fanned herself, still feeling warm from her earlier exertions. "I am catching my breath."

He turned to Clara and gave her a little bow.

"I would be honored if you would dance with me, Clara." He smiled at her as he held out his hand for hers.

"You are too kind, but I would not deprive you of dancing with Ingmar." Clara shook her head, and waved her hand at him to underscore her refusal. She didn't want him to dance with her out of pity, or second choice to her younger sister. He was a handsome youth, and would make a fine friend to Ingmar.

"Your sister won't have me." He looked back at Ingmar and shrugged a shoulder. "So here I stand with two women who have refused to dance with me."

"We will have to do something about that then," Ingmar giggled, a smile on her lips and a twinkle in her eyes. "I will dance with you on one condition." Ingmar looked up into Bergin's face.

"Yes?" He replied with great anticipation. His hair was a soft blonde; his eyes were a faded blue like a spring sky.

"Take this glass, fill it with punch, bring it back and give it to Clara, my sister, and then, and only then will I consent to dance with you," Ingmar giggled and gave him a coy little smile.

Eager to please her, he took the proffered cup and headed off to do her bidding.

"You didn't have to—" Clara started to say.

"Nonsense, I gulped down all your punch, just like a field hand in the heat of harvest." She patted Clara's hand; then looked about the room for Bergin's tall form anticipating his speedy return. "It's the least I could do."

* * *

Bergin Halverson stood with some of his old high school classmates watching the people pair off and begin to dance. He always felt a little shy in a large assembly such as this. Many of his friends had already found the girl they were thinking about marrying, but he hadn't found the one as yet, and wondered if he ever would. It seemed as if the girls that he didn't like were all too willing and the few he did like were either taken already or completely ignored him.

His older brother had offered to pass on a few tips, but Bergin had simply laughed and told him no. His brother's sort of girl was not someone he would even want to date. He was looking for a wife, not a party girl.

He looked about the room and happened to see a girl he had liked when in school. Occasionally, he might see her at church; she was about three years younger, and he had not tried too hard to get to know her. She was too young then, and the years between them at that time were too great. But now, it wouldn't be such an obstacle.

He smiled as he gazed at her; how pretty she had become. And how popular. He noticed too that a group of boys hovered about her and would grab onto her to dance as soon as she had finished with the earlier one.

He didn't think he had the nerve to go ask her for a dance.

"Hey, Bergin, see something you like out on the dance floor?" One of his friends elbowed him.

Bergin turned to look at his friend.

"Could be," he said, not wanting to commit himself. He didn't want them giving him too hard a time about any one girl.

His friend turned to guess where he had been looking. He smiled and nodded his head in the direction of the Lindgren girl surrounded by three guys all vying for her to take them as her next dance partner.

"Are you watching little Ingmar Lindgren?" He tried to line up his sight with where he believed Bergin was looking.

Bergin blushed, but made no other reply.

"I knew it. She is very pretty, good choice," his friend laughed, giving him a friendly punch on the arm.

They watched together as Ingmar begged off from the boys and headed to the seats along the wall, joining a pretty girl who could be her sister. The seated woman looked shy, and not inclined to join into the festivities. Ingmar drank a glass of punch the woman offered and they laughed together. A pimply faced boy came up and asked Ingmar to dance, but she sent him away, and sat back in her chair.

"Go ask her now. It's a good time. She's not surrounded by other admirers," his friend encouraged him. "She might even say yes to you." He gave Bergin a gentle shove in the direction of the women across the hall.

Bergin waved off his friend's prodding encouragement, crossed the room and came to stand before Ingmar and Clara Lindgren and just a little afraid of being rejected as he made his petition to her for a dance.

* * *

Clara had no idea how her sister could do it. The boys fell all over themselves just to have a moment of Ingmar's attention.

"Thank you for trying to get me a dance partner. I could see it was you he wanted, not me. I don't want anyone to have to settle for their second choice. Not you, not me, and not that young man." Clara didn't want to settle for the young men who sought her sister. She still hoped for someone who wanted to be with her and her alone.

"I didn't want you to sit here alone all night," Ingmar said with her head down. "So many of the boys are eager and willing to do almost anything I ask them." She looked up into her sister's eyes.

"Be sure you don't abuse that willingness," Clara warned her sister.

"Oh, I won't, I promise. Sometimes it's fun to see them beg and fight among one another." She spotted Bergin making his way carefully back to where they were sitting. He carried the punch cup as if it were a holy relic.

"I think you like this one, Ingmar," Clara whispered as they watched him approach them once again. "Maybe more than the others."

"Hush now, here he comes," color rose to Ingmar's cheeks as she shushed her sister's apt observation.

"For Ingmar's sister," Bergin smiled and gave Clara a little hint of a bow and offered her the full cup of punch.

"Thank you, Bergin," Clara smiled and took the cup of punch.

"I know you have turned me down for this dance, but some day, I hope that you will allow me to dance with you." Bergin placed his hand over his heart and looked into Clara's eyes and held her gaze for a moment.

"Maybe someday." Clara gave him a wistful smile. She looked away as she felt the color rising in her cheeks. She was pleased that the room was warm, and maybe no one would notice her blushing.

"Ingmar?" He turned and held out his hand for hers.

Ingmar giggled, leaned over and gave Clara a kiss on the cheek and was gone with the tall, blonde fellow to dance once again. After his dance with Ingmar, Bergin had even come back over to be sure he couldn't entice Clara out onto the dance floor at least once. She shook her head and waved him away again with a laugh. She was pleased by the invitation.

Clara sipped her punch and settled back in her chair again to watch her sister enjoy herself some more. A succession of boys all asked Ingmar to dance until the musicians took a break to have some punch and cake as well.

In a loud voice, some man announced that it was time for the bride to throw her bouquet to the hopeful unmarried women in the room.

Ingmar came up and took Clara by the hand.

Clara tried to pull away from her.

"You must come join us for the throwing of the bouquet," she insisted.

"No, I'm too old, you go," Clara replied, feeling embarrassed. She didn't want to have people stare at her. Much as she wanted to be a part of the bouquet toss, she just couldn't join in with the others.

"I can't go alone, I would be too embarrassed. Our brothers would tease me mercilessly, and with no fields to work in winter, they would be at it all day." She tugged at her older sister. "Please, Clara. Pretty please with sugar on top?"

"All right, for you," Clara replied knowing she was blushing. She hoped no one would see. It was always so difficult to refuse Ingmar anything.

Clara reluctantly joined the group of silly younger girls all giggling and hoping to catch the bouquet so they would be the next to marry. She stood behind her little sister, at the back of the group, hoping to look more like an observer than one of the hopeful.

Clara watched the pretty, young bride who would now have a life of joy and partnership ahead of her as she looked over her shoulder to see where her cousin was standing. She turned back and threw the bouquet over her shoulder. She lobbed the flowers in a high wide arc that seemed to move slowly through the air. The pretty ribbons fluttered as they sailed up into the lofty ceiling. It traveled further than the bride had anticipated, then began to fall back to the earth.

Clara, without realizing it, raised her arms to reach for the projectile heading her way. It landed heavily in her arms. She hadn't expected it at all.

"Oh my!" She said in a surprised whisper.

"Clara!" Ingmar squealed with delight as she saw the stunned look on her sister's face. "You caught the bouquet. How wonderful for you!"

"The old one caught it," one of the girls who didn't even look old enough to think about boys commented, making a sour face. She didn't even look thirteen.

"They shouldn't let spinsters in the bridal bouquet toss," another girl who looked about the same age said with a pouty expression. She grabbed her friend by the arm and stomped off to drown their sorrows in some peach pie.

"You would think she would have kept her place along the wall instead of pushing us out of the way to grab the thing," a girl standing with the bride's cousin commented, looking over her shoulder with a disgusted look on her face.

"It's so unfair!" the bride's cousin said, looking at Clara with daggers in her eyes. "I was supposed to be the one to catch it." Everyone in the area knew that she had wanted to catch the bouquet and show her boyfriend so he might get the hint and pop the marriage question to her.

"It's amazing that Clara caught the thing, I don't know any man who would marry her," another girl spoke up with a nasty twist in her voice.

"Definitely over the hill if you ask me," her companion retorted as they looked at Clara with disgust.

"A spinster with her best years already behind her," another girl spat out, making sure Clara would hear her cruel words.

A tear welled in Clara's eye as she endured the cruel comments, at the same time her heart swelled with the unexpected luck of catching it. Maybe there was some hope for her after all. She walked slowly back to her chair, cradling the flowers like a baby. She buried her nose in the rare scent of flowers at this time of year.

The musicians took their places and began to play again.

Clara hadn't noticed him as he crossed the room, but she looked up to see a wonderfully handsome man standing before her. He smiled at her. She looked around, confused; sure he should be talking to some other younger lady at the reception.

"A very fortuitous catch." He looked into her eyes. His voice was soft and gentle like summer rain.

"Yes," she said; her words fleeing from her mind as she looked into his clear, blue eyes.

"My name is Erdman Halverson." He held out his hand for hers.

"Clara Lindgren," she stammered. She had to make herself raise her hand to his. She felt herself tremble. He grasped her hand firmly, still gazing into her eyes.

"Might I be so privileged as to dance with the girl who was so fortunate as to catch the bridal bouquet?" He was pulling her to her feet as he spoke. "I'm not a man to be denied. Say you'll dance with me?"

She didn't know what to say, no words came to mind, but she was on her feet, and he was wrapping his arm about her as he glided to the dance floor, flowers and all. He was tall, his blonde hair was like wheat at harvest, and his eyes were like the clearest summer sky. He grasped her firmly, yet gently, as if she was something special to be cared for and protected.

Clara was so confused she didn't know what to do, so she did nothing but allow herself to be swept up by this man and carried off into a new experience. She even allowed herself to smile. She breathed in the fragrance of him, clean and fresh like crisp linen and sweet soap on skin.

"I noticed you earlier, but didn't have the nerve to approach you. You provided me with just the right excuse." His gaze held hers like a magnet. A smile played on his lips. "You caught the bouquet. It was fate that you were the one who beat out all the other girls, and it allowed me to get up the courage to come over here and speak to you." He twirled her in his arms, making her even dizzier than she had felt before.

"Erdman," his name was all she could manage to say.

CHAPTER 4

"May I get you a glass of punch, Clara?" Erdman inquired, after he kept her on the dance floor for three dances in a row.

"Oh, yes, I am a little warm from the dancing, Erdman. Yes, thank you." She blushed, looking up at him through her thick eyelashes. She had to keep her head down a little and gaze up at him through her lashes because she was afraid she might start to tremble or her head would wobble with nervousness if she simply looked him in the eye.

"That perfume you are wearing confuses me." He nuzzled a little closer into her neck where she had put the perfume. She could smell its warm spiciness herself, and inhaled the fragrance. She wanted to seal the memory with the scent so she could remember this man and the dance whenever she smelled her perfume.

"Confuses you?" She didn't understand what he meant. She urged him to step away from her. She didn't want people to start gossiping about her.

"Yes, it confuses me; I don't know what you want me to do. Should I take you in my arms and make love to you? Or should I worship at the altar of your pristine beauty, for you are a goddess of chastity and virtue?"

"Maybe you better get that punch," she managed a twitch of a smile. He ran a finger down her arm; she tingled with an excitement that fluttered through her whole being, and raised goose bumps on her arms.

"Be right back," he said, giving her cheek a slight caress with his fingertips. His touch was so light she wasn't sure that he had really touched her at all.

Clara sat down before she collapsed. She watched him walk across the room until he was lost in the press of people on the dance floor. She had to pinch herself to see if she was dreaming or awake. She watched eagerly to see if he would return, fearing that it was simply a ruse to get away from her by offering to bring her some punch.

She tried not to look too anxious. She picked up the bouquet again and smelled the sweet perfume of the white roses. Through the petals, she saw that he was returning. It made her heart skip a beat.

He came back.

He was smiling at her.

"I brought you punch as well as a piece of the wedding cake. I don't think you have had a chance to have any yet." His hands full with two glasses and one plate with cake. He handed her a fork. "I hope you won't mind sharing."

"No, not at all." She gave him a nervous twitch of a smile as she took the offered cup of punch and the fork.

"I simply couldn't manage two plates and forks and full punch cups. I'm sorry." He apologized as he took a seat beside her.

"No, that's fine. I don't think I could have carried it all either." She used the fork to cut off a bite of the cake and lift it to her mouth. The cake was so good.

"Make a wish," Erdman said as he took a bite of cake.

"A wish?" She raised her eyebrows in surprise. She thought she knew everything that there was to make a wish upon in the universe.

"You must always make a wish on a piece of bridal cake, especially if you are sharing it with someone." He closed his eyes, and made a show of making his wish.

Clara followed suit.

She knew what she wanted to wish for this time. She wished for Erdman Halverson to love her and to be her husband. When she finished she opened her eyes to see him smiling at her.

"What did you wish for?" He put another section of cake on his fork.

"You're not supposed to tell wishes, or they won't come true." She shook her head at him. Clara couldn't tell him her wish. Not now. But she hoped that she might be able to in the future. *You know what I wished for that night we met* . . . she let the thought drift away. She would come back to that thought before she went to bed that night and finish the conversation that she hoped would be in her future.

"I wonder if our wishes were the same." He lifted a piece of cake on his fork and held it to her lips. She took the proffered cake and blinked at him, amazed that this was happening to her.

Clara couldn't find any words with which to respond.

CHAPTER 5

Clara set the bouquet gently on the dresser. She touched the soft rose petals tenderly. It was a night unlike any other she had ever known. She closed her eyes, remembering the gentle touch of his lips as he kissed her hand before saying goodbye. The memory sent a tingling chill of excitement through her body.

It made her smile.

She felt as if she was floating, carried away by the excitement of what had happened that night. And it happened to her, not her sister or someone else. It had happened to her. She took a deep breath and let it go.

Yes. It happened to her.

She slowly and dreamily began to remove her clothes. She would have something to dream about tonight. As she pulled her dress over her head, her sister came in the room with a big smile on her face.

"You look so beautiful," Ingmar told Clara, seeing her sister as she had never seen her before.

"With my hair all mussed from pulling my dress over my head, yes, I'm sure I do." Clara ran her hand over her hair to settle it into reasonable order again.

"No, Clara, it is the smile on your lips and the glint in your eye," Ingmar chided her sister. "I think you have a sweetheart. I wonder if my sister has fallen in love with the tall, blonde and, oh, so handsome man that swept you onto the dance floor?"

"I don't know about that." She opened the door to the chifferobe and took out a hanger for her dress. She smiled to herself, she was pleased that the feelings she had in her heart were something that others could see and recognize.

"He was so taken with you." Ingmar pulled her dress over her head and tossed it onto the floor. "He didn't pay attention to any other girl there."

"Didn't he?" A faint whiff of her perfume wafted from the folds of her dress as she straightened it on the hanger.

"No. Just you," Ingmar smiled, enjoying her sister's happiness.

Clara inhaled, trying to calm her heart. Her sister's words made her body tremble again in that terrible chill of joy that passed through her from head to foot. She hung her dress in the chifferobe, caressing the soft fabric once more, just as he had done, running his hand down her arm.

"I don't know what to say," Clara stammered. She reached down and gathered up her sister's discarded dress and hung it in the chifferobe as well. She closed the door and sat down at her dressing table. She saw her image in the glass and smiled at herself.

"Who is he?" Ingmar began to laugh. "Or did you forget to get his name?" She removed her underclothing, tossing them onto a chair and pulled on her nightdress.

"Yes, silly, I did get his name. I was not so blinded by his good looks that I forgot to ask," Clara laughed with her sister. She sat up as tall as she could and told Ingmar who he was as proudly as she could. "His name is Erdman and he is a college man."

"College? Well, aren't we grand?" Ingmar crawled onto the bed, and got in under the covers. "Where is he in college?"

"Up at Ames, the school of agriculture." Clara looked at her sister, then turned back to look at the dressing table. She didn't want her sister so see the color rising in her cheeks.

"How old is he?" Ingmar asked.

"He is a little younger than I am, but he didn't seem to care about that." Clara brushed her thick hair. She hoped her sister wouldn't be shocked because he was younger. Usually it was the men who picked younger girls. However, if he didn't mind, she wouldn't care either.

"Will you see him again?" She plumped a pillow then turned all her attention to Clara, waiting for her reply.

"He asked me to write to him." Clara didn't turn around, but looked at her sister's reflection in the mirror as she brushed her hair some more. One hundred strokes a day was her routine. "I told him it wouldn't be proper for me to write first. I told him that he should be the one to initiate that," Clara said softly, she could feel the color rising in her cheeks again. She looked away from her sister's surprised, but pleased, gaze.

"Clara, I'm so excited for you!" She tumbled out of bed, and ran to embrace Clara. She really was so pleased that the sister she loved so dearly had found someone to care for her. Someone that she liked in return. "You caught the bridal bouquet, too. That means that you will be married within the year!"

"That's just an old wife's tale," Clara said trying to dismiss the idea, at least to her sister. Secretly she wanted it to be true.

Married within the year.

Clara dared to hope for the first time in so many years.

CHAPTER 6

Bergin had watched as Clara and Ingmar Lindgren left the dance. Clara held the bouquet of flowers as if she was cradling a child; she had that painful look of exquisite happiness on her face. He knew that his brother, Erdman, had been the one who had put it there. It both angered and saddened him.

He had watched as Erdman had walked over and engaged Clara in conversation after she had caught the bouquet. Erdman danced with her, holding her close to him, a smug expression on his face that she could not see. Then he watched as Erdman had brought them cake and punch. Bergin turned away when he saw Erdman lift the fork to her lips. He couldn't watch any more of his brother's shenanigans.

Clara Lindgren was not normally the type of woman his brother pursued. Erdman liked his woman to be fast and easy. *So why had he deliberately sought her out and swathed Clara in his charm? She was a nice girl. What was he hoping to accomplish?* Bergin's thoughts rattled about in his head as he noticed Erdman looking for him, and heading his way. A good deal of the crowd had thinned out after the bride and groom had departed to begin their life as husband and wife.

"Ah, there you are Bergie. Ready to get the hell out of this boring assembly of farmer hicks and local yokels?" Erdman strode over to where Bergin was chatting with a few of his old school classmates.

"We might be boring to you, college boy, but maybe not to one another," Jacob Stanton said, taking on a defensive body posture; his fists tightly clenched. He had made it obvious over the years that he detested Erdman. It was rumored that Erdman had ruined his older sister's reputation so that she had needed to go live with family down in Montgomery County. Erdman had adamantly denied the rumors, claiming his innocence in the matter.

"People who are easily bored are in reality the one who is boring in and of themselves." Emil Sorensen stepped between Jacob and

Erdman hoping to avoid a fight at his cousin's wedding. "Since you find us all so dull, why not go home then?" He flashed an insincere smile at Erdman.

"Just what I had in mind. I'm bored to death and am in need of something to divert my attention. I know it is not to be had here in the sticks." He returned an insincere smile to Emil. "Bergin? I am in desperate need of something alcoholic, and since there is nothing here that even comes close to that sort of refreshment, I need to go elsewhere to obtain it. You ready?" He said with a distinct tone of exasperation in his voice and expression as if one more minute in such tedious company would threaten his very existence.

"I'll get the team ready," Bergin said to his brother after saying good night to his friends. He retrieved his coat and gloves before he stepped out into the cold evening. The snow that had been falling when they arrived lay thickly on everything. The skies had cleared, and the bright mantle of stars twinkled overhead. He looked up at the sky, picking a star, and made a wish; *Don't allow my brother to hurt that nice girl too much.* He whispered into the cold night air, the warm breath of his words forming like a frosty, insubstantial froth before they melted away.

Bergin sighed, checked the harness and reins on the horse and rig and climbed into the sleigh, snapping the reigns lightly on the horse's back turning her about so he could pick up Erdman and head home. He loved the winter; it was so clean, so silent. It made him feel less alone in the world.

Stars twinkled in the heavens. The moon was almost full and reflected on the mantle of snow cast everything in pale bluish hues.

Bergin settled himself into the sleigh and pulled the horse hide blanket across his knees as he watched Erdman get in beside him.

"Good thing you thought to bring the sleigh and not take my car!" Erdman snorted a laugh as Bergin snapped the reins and the horse began to pull them away from the reception hall with a slight lurch. "So, you have any luck with the locals, little brother?"

"Luck?" He looked at Erdman confused by his statement. The gentle rhythm of the horse's stride was made evident in the jingle of the sleigh bells.

"Did you make any progress with any of the local girls at the reception tonight?" Erdman jabbed his elbow into his little brother's side. "I saw you trying to get that one girl to dance with you tonight.

It really is a shame that you have no prowess with the fairer sex. I could teach you quite a lot, if you would only pay attention to the pearls of wisdom that constantly fall from my lips on the subject of women."

Bergin only grunted. He didn't want to dignify his brother's comments with an answer. Erdman was pompous, arrogant and had no clue about anyone but himself. In contrast, Bergin knew that he was himself reserved, in many ways Bergin was the exact opposite of his elder brother. He liked it that way.

"I don't know why you picked her, little brother, she really was too old for you, and though I will admit that she was not bad looking." He looked over at Bergin who simply furrowed his brow. "You really are the most impossible person. Here I am trying to help you learn about women, and all you can do is grunt and frown. I doubt you will ever find anyone to marry and start breeding with around here that is worth having. You need to get the hell out of here, explore the women of the world, and get some perspective and experience, little brother."

"There is nothing wrong with the women around here, and the Lindgren girl is someone I happen to like." Bergin had liked Ingmar Lindgren since he had met her at a church function his senior year in high school, but he had never said anything to her for the simple reason that she was too young at the time. Once he graduated from school he didn't have any reason to see her, and did not feel that he could call on her until they were reacquainted. He had been so pleased to see her at the wedding reception, and had forced himself to ask her for a dance. Bergin didn't want his brother knowing that he liked the girl for the simple reason that he didn't trust Erdman not to charm her and steal her away, ruining Bergin's chances with Ingmar Lindgren.

"Why Bergie, I didn't know that you were so interested in the girl or I would never have spoken to her," he feigned concern and remorse. "Now I know how much she means to you, and well I'm afraid it's too late to undo what was done tonight."

"Leave it be, please?" Bergin grumbled in reply to his brother's incessant egging him on. It was happening more and more, Erdman flaunting his success with the girls at the college.

"I only went over to speak to that little wallflower to show you that she could be conquered. I don't know why you couldn't get her on the dance floor at all; she was such an eager, willing little thing. In fact, I would say that she was desperate for attention from anyone male and ambulatory. So, what I mean in saying that is that, sadly, you just couldn't make the grade," he sighed as if he really felt sorry for Bergin. "Again."

They rode in silence, only the jangle of the bells and the hiss of the runners in the snow as they rode home. The chill, snow-scented air whipped across their faces. Bergin contemplated his brother's words. He recalled the scene from earlier that night, and realized that Erdman had not seen everything that had happened. He had only seen his interactions with Clara Lindgren, and took them as a failure. He wanted to laugh; his brother had gotten it all wrong.

"Are you talking about Clara Lindgren, Erdman?" He asked with a look of astonishment on his face.

"Is that her name? Sorry, I couldn't recall what she said it was. The answer is yes, I saw you head over there and speak to those girls, asking the one to dance, and even getting her a glass of punch. It was painful to see you grovel to her. Maybe you'll learn that groveling and begging are not the way to win her undying love and affection." His laugh was spiteful. "You must learn that there are times you just have to reach out and take what you want in this world."

"Erdman, you are beyond belief," Bergin could do nothing but chuckle.

"I couldn't watch anymore of that farce you were playing out. I headed out to seek liquid fortification to help me deal with the humiliation of any brother of mine being refused by some old maid," he replied in a frustrated tone.

Bergin began to laugh.

"Why are you laughing?"

"Never mind," Bergin tried to stifle his laughter, but the irony of the situation was too rich. This time the joke was on his brother for a change. He had only seen his interactions with Clara, and hadn't paid enough attention to see that it was Ingmar who was the one he wanted to dance with.

"So you approached Clara, to try to show me up because you got her to say yes to dance with you, when she refused my invitation?" He fought the smile that wanted to break out on his lips.

"That would be the gist of the situation, yes," he replied, no longer amused.

"You fool."

"I am not a fool, little brother," Erdman snapped back, angry at being the butt of some joke he didn't know about. No one laughed at him and got away with it. "Don't get your nose all out of joint because I was successful where you failed."

Bergin didn't know what to say in return. He didn't want to give himself away, yet the fact that he had bested his brother was too precious to let it pass. The only problem was that Clara Lindgren was a nice person, and he hoped his brother would grow bored and forget all about the woman before he inflicted some real damage. Bergin wondered if he should tell his brother he had made a mistake.

He listened to the rhythmic jangle of the bells as he thought about what to say, if anything.

For her sake, he could not keep quiet.

"It was not Clara Lindgren that I went to ask for a dance," his voice was soft.

"No? Then what were you doing over there?" Erdman shot an angry look at his brother. "Practicing how not to succeed with the fairer sex?"

"I had gone to ask her little sister for a dance, she asked me to request a dance from her sister, Clara, first. That was what you saw. Clara didn't want a handoff from her little sister. She wanted someone to ask her because they wanted to dance with Clara. I doubt you could understand that."

"She turned you down, I saw it," he stammered.

"Yes she did," Bergin smiled. "You thought you would play the big man and make me look bad. Well, you failed. I danced with the girl I wanted to dance with, and you made a fool of yourself. Now maybe you can forget her, and just go back to school. She is not your type anyway."

"Not my type?" He was annoyed and it showed. "What do you mean?"

"She is a nice girl, not one of the *Rosie Round Heels* you seem to favor," Bergin said, for him this conversation was bold. He had never challenged his brother before, and it was feeling good to finally express himself after so many years of putting up with all the manure his brother had been spreading.

"You mean she is still a virgin?" A sly grin spread across his face as he spoke with a licentious tone to his voice.

"Erdman, no. Don't do it, leave her be," Bergin gave his brother a cross look. He didn't like the expression on his brother's face. Even in the moonlight he could see what his brother was contemplating, and he didn't like it one little bit. "She is one of our neighbors; she lives a couple of miles from our farm, on the other side of the Albertson's old place," he pleaded.

"I don't know what you are talking about, little brother," Erdman said, affecting an innocent tone. "I have to admit, I did like the girl. Something about her intrigued me. I can't say exactly what, but there was something," he reassured his little brother.

"You will have to live here among all these people when you finish college, and you can't do anything that will mar the family reputation any more than you have done already," Bergin replied.

"If you are inferring that I had anything to do with Polly Stanton's fall from grace, then you don't really know what all happened, little brother."

"Then, the baby was not yours?" Bergin snapped back, confronting his brother with the question everyone asked. "Tell me another fairy tale. You were the only one she ever talked about. You were the only one she had ever stepped out with. Somehow I do not believe you."

"Sorry you don't believe me, Bergin," Erdman replied, giving his brother an earnest look. "It is my word against hers. I never touched the girl, not that way. I don't know who the father is."

Bergin could only give him a snort of anger in reply.

"Don't worry about the Lindgren girl, little brother," Erdman patted his brother on the arm. "She really may turn out to be the woman who tames my wicked heart."

Bergin pulled into the barnyard and pulled the reins back, stopping the horse. Erdman hopped off the sleigh and headed to the house. Over his shoulder, he called back to his brother.

"I know you'll take care of the horse and put away the sleigh, like the dutiful little brother you are."

"Right. I wouldn't expect you to lift a finger to help. After all, you are a college man," Bergin grumbled his reply as he led the horse into the barn, unhooked the sleigh and prepared to brush down the horse before covering her with a blanket for the rest of the night. As he worked, he said a little prayer for Clara.

Another thought chilled him to the bone. If Erdman hurts Clara then what are his chances of seeing her little sister, Ingmar?

"Damn you, Erdman. Mess this up for me and I swear I'll kill you," he said into the frosty night as he walked across the barnyard to the house.

CHAPTER 7

The winds came from the south, tempering the sharp edge of winter's chill air. Clara looked at the thermometer by the door of the house; tapping on it to be sure it was working. The mercury had climbed to forty-eight degrees as the sun tried to break through the clouds.

It had been in the sixties the day before and much of the snow had melted. The once pristine, white mantle was now a tattered, threadbare remnant, stained and dirty from soot, soil and dust. Patches of the moist earth, richly black, were exposed, but that soil was not quite ready to stir itself to wake the seeds buried in its bosom. Spring was still a promise that winter was not ready to give way to just yet. The January thaw teased everyone to the hope and expectation of the warmer days still to come, yet were still a few months away.

The clouds had covered the sun again. Now the pale gray of the sky was dimensionless and dull. Trees stood out as dark skeletal forms against the flat grayness. Strong winds buffeted the trees, making them dance in twisting, frantic motions. Winter was asserting herself once again. Everything looked shabby and depressing.

It fit the mood Clara found herself to be in that day.

Clara knew that Erdman had gone back to college a few days after Christmas, so he wouldn't have a chance to write until he got back to school. When he had asked for her address, she had made sure to print her name and address very carefully. She didn't want to take the chance of having his letter misdirected.

She had tried not to be too obvious about greeting the postman every day for the past two weeks since the New Year, but she was so anxious to hear from Erdman. She wondered if he would remember her when he got back to school.

She saw the postman's wagon coming up the rutted lane to their house. Hoping that today was the day the letter would come; she pulled on her boots and bundled into her jacket, and headed out to their post box at the fence. The wind was whipping through the pine trees close to the house making a hollow sound that made her look up into the green bows as they danced above her. The air smelled of cold again and of pine resin. It made her draw her coat tighter about her. The temperature was dropping rapidly. The teasing warmth was dispelled in the harsh winds that now came back from the north.

She greeted the driver with a wave of her hand. The icy wind bit into her soft skin; she had been in a hurry and had forgotten to put on her gloves. A letter from Erdman would warm her.

"Miss Clara, I swear you are waiting for a letter or a package or something. You sure don't come out here to greet an old man like me on a frosty morning like this." Mr. Swenson chuckled as he handed her the mail. "Nothing for you today, dear. Maybe tomorrow," he smiled at her. The look of disappointment on her face pained him.

"Right," she said bravely. The warmth of the day, like her hopes, had faded. A few flakes of snow had begun to fall.

"Don't worry, he'll write soon enough. He'd be a fool not to correspond with someone as pretty as you are," Mr. Swenson smiled, making his wrinkled face look like a cartoon character.

"Thank you, Mr. Swenson." Why was it the old men could say such things to her that her contemporaries could not? She turned and headed back into the house. She was completely mortified that Mr. Swenson had guessed what she was waiting for.

She left the mail on the hall table for her father to deal with when he was ready. She slipped out of her boots and hung her coat back in the closet, and headed up to her room. Softly she closed the door and sat at the dressing table.

She looked at herself in the mirror and began to weep.

"It was all a dream. Wake up, Clara; no man wants you. You are going to be an old maid for the rest of your life," she told herself through the tears that streamed down her cheeks. "He was only having a laugh at your expense."

* * *

Bergin had been told by his parents that he had to drive up to the college and deliver the clothes Erdman had left behind in his room. They were convinced he wasn't going to have anything to wear since he hadn't bothered to take anything much with him when he went back. Obviously, they didn't know their son very well. Bergin had been up to visit his brother at the college before, and his closets were full of expensive things that he never brought home for his parents to see. He had commented offhandedly that he wouldn't be caught dead in *Koveralls* and a flannel shirt.

Bergin knew it was a useless trip, but his mother had packed a basket full of food as well, so, at least that was something Erdman could make use of. She had fussed about the kitchen the day before and baked him some of his favorite pies with the peaches she had put up in the fall. It was an extravagance he knew she never would have done for anyone but Erdman.

The day was sunny and bright as Bergin pulled out of their road. Snow still covered the fields here and there, little clumps clustered in the shadowy side of the land. The sun had melted much of the most recent snowfall; the rich, black soil littered with the dried remains of the harvest. Deer meandered in the fields searching out some forgotten morsel left behind after harvest. Everything was a study in browns, blacks and white as the land slumbered before spring would awaken to new life. It was a time of rest, renewal and reflection that Bergin treasured.

The roads were not too bad, though rutted from the freezing and thawing of winter and traffic back and forth. The trip, at least, would give him a few hours to think as he drove. He wondered if Erdman had written to the Lindgren girl at all, as he said he intended to do once back at school. Bergin hoped he had forgotten her, and would allow the girl to have a short duration of pain and disappointment so she could get over Erdman and forget about him.

Bergin also wanted to see if he had a chance to get to know Ingmar a little better. He didn't want any interference from Erdman on that front. His brother had messed up a relationship for him before. He had made the mistake of saying something about having a date with the Stanton girl. Erdman managed to start seeing her and had ruined her. He then denied that he had seduced her. When she was sent away to family in another county to have the child, there was little doubt in his mind as to what Erdman had done.

For Bergin it had caused some friction between himself and her brother who was a classmate of his. When she came back, she had managed to reconcile Bergin and her brother. Erdman was the source of gossip and speculation for a while, so much so that many a father refused to allow his daughter to see him.

That was behind many of them now, and since Erdman was off at college, most people seemed to have forgotten what had happened. Bergin had learned his lesson, and was going to tell Erdman as little as possible about what was happening in his life and which of the ladies he had taken a fancy to in the area.

When he arrived at the college and inquired as to where he could find Erdman Halverson someone directed him to a pavilion on the campus where some people gathered in the afternoon. He saw a group of people lounging about, laughing and passing a bottle. He knew his brother would be in their midst. Wherever two or three were gathered together with some alcohol, Erdman probably had supplied it.

Bergin saw a woman come running up to him, giggling and waving. He didn't pay her too much attention since he knew no one at the college except his brother. Suddenly her body slammed into his in a shower of inane giggling. She wrapped her arms about him and pressed her lips to his throwing him off balance.

"What the heck do you think you're doing?" Bergin shoved her away and scrambled back to regain his balance. He wiped his mouth with the back of his hand. He looked the woman over; she was short; with a round face and bad hair that looked frazzled and fried from too much use of a curling iron. She had little to recommend her as a nice girl, her clothes were a little too revealing, and her face was plastered with a little more rouge than was comely. To Bergin she looked like a tart. He was disgusted by her.

"Kissing you, silly," she laughed some more, and then looked at him closer. "Oh! Geeze, you're not Erdman. Gadzooks, I'm sorry!" She moved away from him and began to giggle again in a high-pitched clamor of sound.

Erdman was walking over to Bergin and began to laugh. The girl ran up to him, and he opened his arms to her. She snuggled into his open arms, and they kissed.

"Manya, that was my little brother, Bergin, you were just pressing into a lip lock, my dear." He bent her backwards in another kiss and laughed. When he came up for air again, she began to giggle and wrapped her arms about his neck, wanting more. Erdman pushed her away.

"Bergie, this is Manya." Erdman patted his brother on the shoulder.

"Nice to meet 'cha," she said looking Bergin up and down, then looking from Bergin to Erdman and back again. "You two sure look alike. You should be more careful walking around pretending to be your brother. You could get in trouble if you tried to fool the wrong person." She waggled a finger at him like he was some naughty child.

"Erdman, I have some things momma sent," Bergin said, ignoring the girl.

"Oh, gads, what did she send this time?" He said to Bergin, as he motioned for Manya to get lost. She reluctantly moved off in a pout.

"You left some clothes behind, she was worried that you might be running naked across the campus." He rolled his eyes, knowing his brother would not want the clothes she sent along.

"Now there's an idea," Erdman laughed, as he contemplated the activity his brother had suggested. He snorted a laugh. "You would think she would have gotten the hint as often as I try and leave those farmer clothes behind."

"She sent some pie as well."

"At least that will be useful." Erdman slapped his brother on the back and guided him back to the car. "So how did you like Manya's little greeting, little brother? Really warm, wet and friendly." He gave Bergin a knowing smile.

"It was disgusting, she kept trying to get her tongue in between my lips, it was like having a snake trying to kiss me." Bergin wiped at his mouth again, remembering.

Erdman erupted into a burst of laughter, and nearly fell to the ground he was so taken with giddiness. When he had composed himself enough to speak again, his words were heavily punctuated with laughter.

"Calm down little brother, that is what's known as a French kiss. They say it started from the French men coming home and wanting to know if their women had been nipping into the brandy or wine, so they would swath their tongue inside their kissing partner's mouth."

"It was disgusting." He made a face.

"When you grow up, you'll find out how good it can be, little man." He had recovered from his laughter and now wiped a tear from his eye. "The kissing a snake was good, though. Sometimes Manya can wrap herself around you just like a snake, and oh! She can show a man a good time."

"I haven't time for this. Come get your clothes and the pies so I can get back to the farm." Bergin walked to the car.

"Aw, hell, the farm. I almost forgot!" Erdman slapped his forehead.

"Forgot what?" He froze in his tracks.

"That girl. Remember?" Erdman gave him an odd look like what was wrong with him suddenly.

"What girl?" His ears prickled with a touch of nervous fear. He hoped his brother didn't mean Clara Lindgren.

"You know, the one from the wedding that I danced with." Erdman scratched at his temple racking his brain for her name. "The frump who caught the bouquet."

Bergin sighed. Maybe if he hadn't been forced to come up here his brother would have forgotten her.

"Come on, I know you know who I mean." Erdman jostled him.

"Clara," Bergin said softly with a nod of his head. He felt as if he had betrayed the woman in speaking her name to Erdman. He opened the car door and took out the box their mother had packed with clothes and the pies and handed it to Erdman.

"Was that it?" Erdman tapped a finger to his lips, looking up in thought before he looked back and took the box from Bergin. "You could be right. I have her address somewhere back in my room. I will have to write to her. I'm going to be coming down for a party soon. I might just take her along."

"Leave her be. She probably wouldn't fit in with the people you know." Bergin closed the rear car door, and put his hand on the handle of the driver's door.

"Ah, the people I know. You don't have any idea of the people I know, little brother," he mused.

"Right, sleazy snake-women and booze hounds," Bergin replied, furrowing his brow. He had never liked any of the people his brother hung around with, especially since going away to college.

Erdman tossed his head back in laughter.

"Don't forget the mobsters, rumrunners and all those lowlife sort of people as well. You better be nice to me, or I could have someone wipe you out!" He teased as a wicked grin spread across his lips. "I could have you rubbed out, you know. I'm not kidding; I really do know those sorts of people." He looked down his nose at his little brother as the thought rolled around in his mind. He caressed the idea and liked the feeling of power as it filled him.

"I'll be getting back home now." He opened the car door and climbed into the driver's seat. Bergin shook his head; he had seen the expression on his brother's face change, and it chilled him somewhat. He also noticed his brother's posture change. He wanted to derail where Erdman's thoughts seemed to be taking him. "I'll let mother know you were not naked, and that you loved the pies."

"What kind of pies this time?"

"Peach."

"Oh, good! My favorite." He looked into the box with anticipation.

"Goodbye, Erdman." He waved, and closed the car door.

"Thanks, little brother. Look out for wild women and French kissing!" He broke into peals of laughter again as Bergin started up the car and drove away. "I'm on my way up to my room to write to that girl now, and eat some of momma's peach pie."

Bergin shook his head, sorry for the fact that he had reminded his brother about Clara Lindgren. He hoped that by the time Erdman got back to his room she would have slipped his mind again.

It began to snow on his way home.

CHAPTER 8

A trip to town was always considered to be a treat. There was a break in the weather after the latest snowfall and Clara's mother wanted to take advantage of it. They had to drive into Council Bluffs to get the provisions her mother had listed on the tablet that morning. She had asked Clara to accompany her in hopes of cheering her up a bit.

Bertha Lindgren was proud of her mechanical acumen in that she was able to start their old Model T Ford without help, but was always pleased to have someone to regulate the throttle and sparks settings, especially in the winter.

"Climb in, Clara, and set the throttle and sparks levers to the ten minutes to three, like I showed you last time." She could tell Clara was not paying attention to her. It was not like Clara to be so distant. It worried her.

"I'm sorry, momma, where are they?" Clara looked at her mother as if she had been called back from some faraway place.

"Reach over the steering wheel." She peeked into the automobile to see Clara locate the levers and give her a nod as Clara adjusted their settings. "I hope that the next automobile we get will have an automatic starter on it. This really is so ridiculous a set of steps in order to get the car started. Now you know if it had been a woman who had invented the automobile, things would have been a lot simpler, and made more sense," she laughed to herself as she chided the male inventors. It was something she had often teased her husband about. She took the crank in hand as she complained, knowing she was just chattering to herself.

Clara nodded to her.

"Now remember, when the crank turns and the engine catches turn those levers back to twenty-five minutes to two. Got that, old girl?" Mrs. Lindgren raised her eyebrows and watched to see if Clara was paying her any real attention.

"Yes, I remember," Clara tried to smile back to her mother.

Mrs. Lindgren took the crank in her right hand, knowing that it was important not to tempt fate by using her left hand. She didn't want to injure herself as the crank turned. One of the neighborhood boys had nearly broken his arm when he used his left hand to turn the crank, so she was always very careful. She slipped her finger through the loop of wire that controlled the choke and pulled the wire as she gave the crank a good turn.

The engine roared to life and she looked up at her daughter and smiled as she saw Clara adjust the spark and throttle levers for her. There had been times when she had not been able to get to the throttle and spark dials in time and the engine had died, and she had to start all over again. She put away the crank, and secured the choke wire and climbed in next to Clara and pulled the lap robe over her knees. She urged the vehicle forward out of the drive and turned in the direction of town. The drive would take them about an hour at ten to fifteen miles per hour. She didn't dare go any faster on the country roads since they were not very smooth, and the ride was bumpy at best.

The road was frozen into ruts from the last time it was warm enough to melt some of the ice and snow, and in the night the muddy ground had frozen again. It made steering impossible, and the car could only head along in the tracks that the previous drivers had made. The skies were a heavy leaden color and looked like they might sift out another dusting of snow before the day was through. A frosty wind blew across the barren fields blanketed once again in their mantle of winter's whiteness.

Clara remained silent as they drove past the other farms on their way. Usually Clara was a chatterbox, happy to be getting off the farm for a change and seeing the big city. Her mother grew concerned about her.

Her daughter had seemed to be out of sorts of late. She had tried to remember when things had changed. She had been very happy, skipping about the house before Christmas. As best she could remember, Clara had become sullen somewhere after the New Year, her despondency growing over the ensuing few weeks.

She tried to recall what all had happened. Clara had seemed so happy right around Christmas. Maybe it was the bouquet she caught; maybe it was the young man who had danced with her at the wedding reception. Her daughter hadn't said anything about the young man, so she had not mentioned it either. Clara was a young woman now, old enough to have been married and been running a household of her own. She didn't feel that she had the right anymore to ask her daughter questions about her private life.

"Clara, how about we take a little time and go see what's new at Beno's while we're in town?" Bertha Lindgren's voice still carried a touch of the accent from her native land of Sweden. She had come to America when she was twelve with her parents. "I know how you like that store." She knew for a fact that it was Clara's favorite store. It was on Broadway at the end of Pearl Street and was the place they liked to shop. It was one of the most popular shops in Council Bluffs.

"Do you need something there, mother?" Clara asked in a dull voice.

"You're usually so happy to go to that store. I know how you always love to walk along Broadway and be surrounded by the cars, the people, the sights and smells of the city," she said, a note of concern audible in her voice.

"I guess I'm just not in the mood today." Clara didn't look at her mother, but picked at the stitching on her gloves.

"I thought we could take a peek at what they are going to tell us are the new spring fashions. Maybe look at the new fabrics and see if there are some you would like for dressmaking," Mrs. Lindgren prodded, hoping to cheer up her daughter.

"If you would like to, that would be fine." Clara stared out of the car window not really seeing anything as the sweeping expanse of the prairie farmlands became homes and city streets. All she could think of was: W*hy hadn't Erdman written to her? What had she done? Or, even, what hadn't she done to have him forget her so easily?*

"We can look at the new hats, too," her mother still tried to find something to spark her interest. "I'm sure there will be something that will catch your eye."

Clara simply replied with a quiet *uh huh*.

Her mother parked the car on Broadway by Main Street and before she got out, she looked at her daughter, taking her hand and patting it gently. Maybe it was best to be direct. She had been pleased when she saw the young man dance with her unmarried daughter. She had prayed for Clara to find someone for years now. She too had hoped it would be the answer for Clara that at last she might have found the man she would marry.

"Is it about that boy, Clara?" she said gently.

It was a long time before Clara answered her. She sat and waited in the silence knowing Clara would tell her about it all. She could see the hurt on her daughter's face. It was a hurt that cut through her heart as well.

"Yes," Clara said softly, hating to even voice her fears. "You have always known what was wrong in the past, why should I be surprised that you are able to guess why I am so out of sorts now."

"Because maybe I know what you are going through? Maybe I have had an experience like yours in some way, Clara." Her voice was soft as she cast her mind back to her years before she was married.

Clara sighed deeply before saying what she figured her mother already knew. "He promised to write, and it has been weeks." The corner of her mouth pulled into a tearful frown. She fought the need to cry.

Her mother smiled compassionately. She had been right about what was bothering her daughter. It saddened her too. She remembered what it was like to wait for a letter from someone special. Every day was like an eternity. Every day that there was no letter in the post was a devastating disappointment.

"You know, dear, that men are never as good about writing as we women are." She nodded as Clara looked at her, searching her mother's face for the answer and maybe some shred of hope.

"They're not?" She raised her eyebrows.

"I'm sure he will write when he has time," Bertha Lindgren tried to reassure her.

"It's been more than a month since he said he would write." Her expression revealed her pain and fear of being forgotten.

"Remember he is a college man, and that takes a great deal of time, study and concentration. You want him to do well, don't you?"

Clara sighed deeply and nodded to her mother. She hoped that he was just busy with his studies and had not forgotten her.

They sat for a little while longer in the automobile before her mother prompted her. "How about that trip to Beno's now?"

"Sure," Clara tried to smile at her. Her mother only wanted her to feel better. She didn't want to distress her any longer. Clara forced herself to smile and was rewarded with a smile and a hug.

* * *

Clara trudged up the stairs and went to her room, weary from the day of shopping. She had helped her mother bring in the provisions and put them away in the pantry. Then she carried the fabric her mother had purchased for her at Beno's up to her room. Her mother bought it for her hoping to cheer her up.

Clara sighed.

She was tired of sighing. But she wasn't ready to laugh, not with this ache that had settled over her heart. Sometimes she could find some relief in playing sad music on the piano. There was a new song by Irving Berlin that she played until her brothers had told her to quit. She hummed the tune and half spoke some of the words, as she knew her singing voice was less than stellar.

"What'll I do when you are far away and I am blue, what'll I do? When I'm alone with only dreams of you that won't come true what'll I do?"

She really didn't want to cry anymore either.

She had been feeling so depressed since no letter had come from Erdman. She had tried to push the memories of him away, and packed up her hopes once again. She didn't feel like she could ever be cheerful again. She knew that in time her pain would fade away and she would go back to just living her life, alone.

She placed the fabric on the bed, thinking of what she might want to make with it. Her mother had paid too much for the cloth, so she didn't want to waste it. She knew it was her mother's way of trying to get her to feel better. Material things were no replacement for someone caring for her.

She sighed, correcting herself for thinking that someone had cared for her. She turned to look at herself in the mirror of her dressing table.

She saw an envelope lying on the table. She hurried across the room.

She snatched it up.

It was addressed to her.

The postmark was from Ames, Iowa.

She closed her eyes, afraid to hope too much.

"Could it be?" She whispered softly, but there was no one to hear the words she spoke. There wasn't even a creak or pop from the old house to make reply. She knew her mother was in the yard now, tending to the chickens. Her sister was at school still, and her father and brothers had said they were going to spend some time in the shop that day, tending and repairing the equipment. She was all alone in the house.

Dare she hope?

She wasn't ready to open her eyes.

"A letter at last from Erdman?" Her voice was the only sound in the room, she was afraid to move for fear she would waken and find it was all a dream and there was no letter in her hand. Yet, she could feel its weight, the texture of the paper, where the stamp was affixed, and even where the pen had cut into the paper ever so slightly as someone wrote her name and address.

"Oh, God, please let it be from him. I doubt I could bear any more disappointment," she whispered, a catch in her throat made her voice sound strained.

She opened her eyes and studied the envelope for a moment more before taking the letter opener and slitting open the top. Her father liked to tear off the side of the envelope, but she was afraid she would tear the contents, and didn't want to take that chance.

She pulled out a sheet of heavy, creamy white bond that had a short note written on it in purple ink. She saw the signature was Erdman's.

She clutched it to her heart.

Her heart was beating rapidly.

Joy.

A tear was welling in her eye.

She wiped it away. She didn't want to take the chance that it would spill onto the letter and smear the ink.

Purple ink.

Erdman's ink.

She read the brief message he had written.

Clara,
Thinking of you. Very busy here. Will be home next week.
Write soon, let me know if you want to get together.
If I hear 'yes' from you I will be by Friday night, six o'clock.
I'll honk once.

Hope you are still interested.
Erd

Clara caressed his signature lightly with her fingertip. She felt that strange tingle rush through her body again as she remembered the soft brush of his lips on the back of her hand.

She smiled at the letter.

"Of course I am still interested, silly boy. What did you think? That I could forget you so easily?" She chided the written page as if she was answering him directly. She was so pleased that he wanted to see her again. Though disappointed that he hadn't written more, at least he had finally written.

Erdman had written to her.

She trembled in excitement again.

He still cared.

"I will write to him immediately." She took in a deep breath and sighed happily. A happiness that had faded from her soul the longer she had waited to hear from him. Now she was filled with joy once again.

She took her letter with her downstairs to the writing desk, and began to write her reply. She couldn't afford to waste a minute, he would be home soon, and she wanted to be sure he would receive her letter before heading home.

She didn't want him to think she no longer cared for him.

* * *

That night at supper her father asked her if she had found the letter that had come for her today. He had put it on her dresser when he had come in for lunch and collected the morning post.

Her brothers said nothing.

Her mother had smiled at her, and her sister Ingmar began to giggle. They were all happy around the table for the first time in a month, since her gloomy mood had not cast a dark pall over them all.

That night there was a light in Clara's eyes that brightened all their hearts.

CHAPTER 9

The days passed so slowly until Erdman said he was going to come by and honk for Clara. She wished that he would come to the door and call for her, but this was a different world than the one her parents had grown up in. At least they were not pestering her with endless questions about where she was planning to go and with whom was she going to spend the time.

She was no longer a child, and her parents treated her as an adult. They let her make her own decisions, and come and go as she pleased. Her father was a man of few words and her mother knew there was someone, but she had only said one thing since the letter had arrived: *That he may be worthy of you.* Clara had laughed; she was thinking that she wanted to be worthy of him. After all, she was older, and so much less experienced than Erdman. He *was* a college man.

Clara's brothers said nothing, as they knew nothing. She almost feared what they might say about her beaux. Brothers never seemed to see a sister as anyone, but the female who washed their clothes and made their meals. She loved them dearly, but wondered if they had ever once seen her as anything more than another pair of hands to help their mother.

It was with her sister that she shared some of her life and budding romantic involvement. Ingmar had teased Clara the night of the wedding, and had tried to keep her cheerful as she waited the long weeks until Erdman had written at last, and today Ingmar had helped her get ready. Clara had finally needed to send her from their room so she could get dressed in peace without Ingmar hovering about making her more nervous than she already was. With Ingmar out from underfoot she took her time.

Clara dressed carefully, doing her hair, buffing her nails to a fine glossy sheen, and even applying a little blush that she had dared to purchase in the store at Ingmar's insistence. She didn't think her mother had seen when she paid for the rouge; or think her mother would approve. In their household, face paint was definitely considered to be worn by fast women. Though Clara was anything but fast, she wanted to be stylish, and rouge and lipstick were what fashionable women were wearing nowadays. She didn't want to be considered a hick from the sticks.

She was ready a full hour before he was expected. She tried to settle herself down by reading a book. She read the same paragraph five times before putting the book aside. She didn't want to miss the single honk of the horn that would summon her from the house. Plus, she couldn't concentrate on the words.

At six o'clock on the dot, Clara was waiting in the front parlor for his car to pull up and carry her away to an evening with him. She looked at the clock, the minutes ticked by.

Six-ten and no Erdman.

Her mind began to race. Negative thoughts flooded about her.

Did she have the right night?

She ran back upstairs and took out his letter again. She had secreted it away under the carpet so no one would find it and snoop into her business. She read what he had written, yes, tonight was Friday, this was the date she was sure. She checked the little calendar on the table. Yes, it was the right date. She put the letter back in its hiding place and walked to the window.

She pulled back the lace curtain and peered out of the window at the darkness before her. A pale moon shone onto the snow-covered fields that stretched out to the distant horizon. Barren trees cast long shadows on the bluish light. Nothing stirred in the chill darkness of the night. There was no sign of him. She couldn't even see a hint of a headlight coming down the road.

"Oh God, was it all a game?" The tears began to well in her eyes. She fought them back. She didn't want to ruin her make-up. "You are such a fool, Clara," she chided herself, sitting on the bed. She wanted to crawl in and pull the covers over her head and not come out until spring.

The clock in the hall chimed six-thirty.

Clara sighed deeply.

He was just playing some game with her.

Her shoulders sagged, no longer anticipating an evening with Erdman. She went down the stairs again.

She might as well put her coat back into the closet.

She wasn't going anywhere.

"Are you going out, Clara?" Her mother asked her. She was sitting in her favorite chair in the parlor knitting a new sweater, the clack, clack, clack of the needles never pausing as her nimble fingers wrapped the yarn into intricate designs hardly looking to see her progress.

"I thought I was," Clara said in a hoarse whisper, her hand on the doorknob of the little closet. She didn't dare speak any louder for fear she would betray herself and begin to weep.

The sound of a horn blasted through the silence of the night.

Clara's head snapped to face the direction of the sound, her face broke into a smile. She headed quickly to the door and threw it open. There he was in a sporty-looking car that was definitely not a Model T Ford.

"I guess I am going after all," Clara said, leaving the house without waiting for her mother to answer.

Erdman was seated in the car; he had opened the passenger door from the inside, and waited for her to climb in. She settled herself into the front seat and closed the car door of the speedster. She didn't want to say anything about his being half an hour late.

"Good to see you," Erdman beamed a smile at her that made her forgive him on the spot. "Sorry about running late, the parents insisted that we have a chaperone, and the chaperone wasn't ready on time." He stepped on the gas and they lurched forward out of the drive and onto the road.

"A chaperone?" She was surprised. Not that she minded. She was just happy to be with Erdman. She was pleased to have an explanation as to his tardiness.

"Yeah, meet little brother, Bergin." He tossed his head in the direction of the back seat. "He's the chaperone. He is all of nineteen, so watch out." Erdman laughed as a hand came over the back seat to shake hands with Clara.

"How do you do? I'm Bergin Halverson," his voice was soft and resonant. He sounded a lot like his older brother.

"Clara Lindgren." She shook his hand. "Nice to meet you." She turned to look back at Bergin. He was also blonde haired and had blue eyes. He resembled his brother a great deal. She thought he looked familiar, but dismissed it telling herself that he resembled his brother, that was all. Yet, a blurred memory still persisted. She would think about it later, maybe even ask him if they had met before.

"How beautiful you look!" Bergin blurted out without thinking.

"Thank you," was her soft reply as she felt the color rise in her cheeks.

Clara turned back to face front as Erdman gave the roadster a gun of the engine, and tore off down the dirt road pushing thirty-five miles per hour. The rush of the wind on her face exhilarated her. She had never gone so fast in an automobile. The ride was not as smooth on the back road as she might have liked, as the car bounced over the rutted dirt road. She wondered what it would be like to go this fast on a smooth roadbed.

Was this what flying felt like? She asked herself as a smile played on her lips.

"Bergin, you should know by now that I am always in the company of beautiful women!" Erdman reached over to take Clara's gloved hand, and brought it up to his lips and kissed it as he drove to the main road to town.

Clara liked that she was included in a group of beautiful women, but she didn't like that he said there were others. What else could she expect; he was so handsome that of course he would be popular with the girls, just as her sister, Ingmar, was popular with all the boys. She should just be glad that he chose her to spend the evening with; even though he had to bring his little brother.

"Where are we going?" Clara asked.

"I thought we would head out to a little barn dance I heard about from some friends of mine. They asked that I make a special appearance." He flashed a smile at her that she couldn't help but respond to in a smile as well.

From the back seat came a soft groan as Bergin rolled his eyes.

* * *

Bergin had found out that Erdman had arranged a date with Clara. He had insisted that he go along though he hated the sort of places Erdman liked to go for his idea of fun. Erdman liked to go to wild parties with drinking, flappers and where the musicians played jazz, rags and blues. He didn't think a woman like Clara had ever been to such an assembly and was hoping his brother could see that, though he doubted it. Erdman never seemed to see anything, but what he wanted in the moment he wanted it.

Bergin had enlisted his father's help in getting to be the third party on the date and for once had even gotten his parents to support him. At least they understood about what was needed to be a neighbor and get along in the community.

"What can it harm if you take him along? You have taken him before, do it again tonight," his father had said. "I know how strict old man Lindgren can be about his girls. We don't want to take the chance of anyone starting any rumors like that bad business with the Stanton girl a while back, now do we?"

"I never could understand how they could be blaming you for something you didn't do," their mother had said as she patted Erdman's cheek like he was an innocent boy of ten.

Bergin had tried not to laugh. His mother was completely blind to Erdman's every fault. Erdman could wrap her around his little finger in a heartbeat. She simply refused to believe that her favorite child was a rake, a user, a drinker and general all-around cad. At least Bergin had finagled a chance to go along and keep an eye on his brother and possibly protect Clara.

Erdman was fit to be tied, but he wasn't going to argue with his father. He scowled at Bergin as he climbed into the car. Bergin paid him no mind. If he worried about how often his brother was angry with him he never would have been able to accomplish anything. As Bergin settled himself in the back seat, he noticed there were some cases of alcohol so he knew this would also be a business deal. Would Clara be Erdman's cover if they were caught by the cops for bootlegging?

He hated how his brother used everyone around him.

As they drove up the lane to the house, Erdman had warned Bergin to stay out of his business. He had made it patently clear that he would do him harm if he messed with his evening, because Erdman stated that he had definite plans and things he wanted to do with the girl that did not need a nosey Parker brother hanging about.

"Keep your mouth shut and your eyes open, and even you might just learn something," Erdman had then added in a low hiss.

He watched as Clara bounded out of the house and down the steps to the car, a wide smile on her face. She looked so happy. It was the sort of happiness that is partner to pain and disappointment. He wondered if she had been hurt by how late Erdman was in coming for her tonight. He was sure that she had no idea that Erdman moved about the world on his own time, and didn't care or notice real time by the clock. So he was habitually late for everything.

Bergin had forgotten how very pretty Clara was, and had made a fool of himself when he saw her again in the car. He didn't think that she had remembered him from the dance. In a way he was relieved, yet in a way he wanted her to remember so he could ask about her sister.

He sat back and remained quiet for the rest of the journey to the party Erdman said they were going to attend that night. Clara and Erdman had little conversation on the way to the dance, and he noticed how often she would sneak a look at Erdman, that look of painful joy mixed with insecurity on her face.

* * *

Erdman drove them to the barn dance just outside of Council Bluffs. The night was dark, the moon had slid behind the cover of some clouds, and a chill wind blew across the open fields. It smelled of snow.

He pulled up close to the barn and backed into a parking place.

Erdman got out of the car, and began to walk to the barn door. "Well, come on! What are you waiting for?" He turned and motioned for Clara and Bergin to follow. "The party is this way!"

"He doesn't believe in holding doors for girls," Bergin said softly to Clara.

She nodded and stepped out of the car. Bergin tumbled out of the back seat after her. He slammed the door shut and caught up with his brother and his date. The ground was still frozen and a little slippery underfoot. Pools of ice had filled in the ruts.

Erdman opened the door to the barn and warm light spilled out into the darkness where Clara stood. The smell of hay and warm bodies wafted about her as she entered the barn. The floor had been cleared and swept so that people could dance and not get straw all over themselves. A small band of a fiddle, bass, and a piano were set up at one end of the room on a makeshift platform of boards. Refreshments were at the other end, and people were dancing under Japanese lanterns strung from the rafters with electric lights illuminating them.

Clara was in awe to see electric lights out in the country. They still used kerosene lamps at home, and the electric light was only a faraway dream on their farm. Clara had never seen anything so magical.

She smiled happily and looked to Erdman.

He did not see the look of delight in her eyes. He was busy greeting some fellows who had crowded around him asking him if he brought *the stuff*.

Clara had no idea what *stuff* they meant.

Bergin smiled at her, noticing the joy in her face.

She smiled back at him shyly.

"Hey, Erdie, got the hooch, baby?" A woman came up to Erdman and placed a proprietary hand on his chest. Her lips close to his mouth, she spoke softly to him in a hoarse whisper. She gave Clara a quick and disdainful once over and then turned her full attention back to Erdman. "Who'd you bring this time?" The woman was dressed in a pale, yellow chiffon print, the layers of her frock fluttered when she walked. Her curly, blonde hair was bobbed and she wore a circlet of paste diamonds across her forehead. Red lipstick colored her heavy lips, and thick mascara clung to her lashes.

Clara could only stare at the woman before her. She looked more like a circus clown in all her paint than a woman at a dance. Her face was round and her eyes didn't quite look in the same direction. Clara noticed to her surprise that the woman was smoking. She was shocked that Erdman could possibly know a woman like this at all.

"I see your stiff, little, boring brother is here again." The woman looked over at Bergin, an expression of disgust was displayed plainly on her face.

"Hi Laura Jean, nice to see you again, too." Bergin shook his head at the creature and he too watched as she began to search through Erdman's pockets looking for something.

"Stop it, Laura Jean." Erdman pushed her hands away.

She pouted for a moment before casting a look at Clara.

"So, who is the frowsy creature you hauled in here with you?" Again she looked Clara up and down like she was some sort of infestation. "Was'sa matter, forget to close the car door before you drove through the barnyard?" She spoke in a babyish tone then flashed an ugly smile at Clara.

Erdman threw his head back and laughed.

"Why don't you walk west until your hat floats?" Bergin said back to Laura Jean with a snarl.

"In case you couldn't tell, little boy, I am not wearing a hat." She let loose a vicious cackle, tossing back her head as she laughed. Then she took a deep drag and exhaled smoke in Bergin's face.

He coughed and stepped away.

"Erdie?" Laura Jean cooed at Erdman, looking up at him through her mascaraed lashes. "Did you bring it? Lil' ol' me is thirsty," she reverted to baby-talk again as she ran her hand up and down his lapel.

"Yes, Laura Jean, it's in the car. If you can keep your panties on for a minute, Fritz and Pauley will be hauling it in." He gave Fritz and Pauley a nod of his head and touched the side of his nose. "In the back, guys, haul it in."

"Right!" Fritz grinned as he turned to hurry out the barn door, Pauley right behind him.

"But I wants a taste from your private stock," Laura Jean whined, her hands were all over his jacket, feeling for something. She pulled a flask from his pocket and before she could open it, Erdman had snatched it back from her and tucked it back in his pocket. He cast a quick glance to see if Clara was looking.

Clara couldn't help but wear the expression of a stunned animal, eyes wide and her mouth agape. She hoped she didn't look too ridiculous or shocked.

Erdman stepped closer to Clara and mumbled softly to her that he would have to make sure to give her other memories of their night together.

Clara simply blushed.

"Erdie, what about me?" Laura Jean whined, pulling at his sleeve.

He turned his attention back to her with an angry look on his face.

"Not tonight. Now, get lost." He shoved her away from him. "You are being a real brat tonight. Just go off and get drunk and soon you'll forget I even exist."

She stumbled back a few steps. Her seductive expression flashed over to rage.

"You'll be sorry for that!" She barked back in a shrill voice. "No one pushes me around. No one."

"Oh yeah? Then why do you let Frankie use you for a punching bag?" He snapped back at her.

"Don't say mean things about Frankie." She scowled at him, her face screwing up into a tight, angry expression.

"Frankie is an abusive brute who likes to talk with his fists and you should dump him," he spat back at her.

"Frankie loves me," she retorted, her displeasure was plainly evident from the livid expression on her face. "He's worth ten of you! How dare you say anything against him?" She tried to take a swipe at Erdman with her fingernails, but he caught her wrist in his hand, and forced her to her knees.

"Keep your hands to yourself," he growled at her in a low voice barely audible but full of menace.

Laura Jean paled as she looked up at him.

"This isn't fun anymore. Let me go," she cried.

He let her go; tossing her hand to the side with enough force that it caused her to fall over. She pulled herself up and brushed herself off, giving him an icy look.

Erdman had already turned away.

As he walked away he motioned for Clara and Bergin to follow him. Fritz and Pauley came back in carrying some bottles that looked like alcohol.

"We got the remuneration for you at the table," Pauley winked.

Erdman nodded.

"Be right back." He cradled Clara's chin gently in his hand. "Wait for me?" He flashed a smile at her and all she could do was nod.

A group of men clustered around Erdman as he headed to the end of the room where Fritz and Pauley were carrying some more bottles.

Clara could hear them laughing as they greeted him.

"Good old Erd, we knew you wouldn't let us down," one of them said, slapping Erdman on the back. He was a toothy fellow with scraggly brown hair that resisted the attempted control of the brilliantine he spread on it.

"Erd, the man who we can always count on to liven up any party," another spoke up, smiling at him with perfect teeth, and

Nordic good looks. "I hope this is as good as the last stuff you got for us." He chafed his hands together in anticipation of something wonderful.

"He always supplies the lightening for the punch," Bergin said quietly, standing beside Clara.

"You mean alcohol?" She turned to face him, her eyes wide with disbelief. She had never tasted alcohol. Her father said no one needed to have it. That it was the drink that could make a fool of anyone great and small, young or old and reduce them all into pitiful, blubbering idiots. Her father often boasted that he had never taken a drink of it in his life.

Clara didn't really have any curiosity about the stuff. She had smelled it once, and it had reminded her of gasoline. It was not a smell she liked one little bit. She couldn't imagine anyone wanting to drink anything that smelled that bad.

"The very same." Bergin and Clara watched as someone handed Erdman a thick envelope with a laugh and pat on the back. Erdman tossed his head back in a guffaw of laughter as he stuffed the packet into his pocket. "It's how he earns his spending money."

Clara and Bergin stood in silence watching everyone make a fuss over Erdman.

Clara wondered why he had brought her to this dance. She felt so out of place. She didn't wear lots of makeup, she surely didn't smoke, and she had never taken a drink in her life and her clothes were so conservative if not dull in comparison to the flashes of color, beadwork and feathers on the other ladies' gowns.

She looked at the rest of the girls in the room. Their clothes were so revealing; she knew it was the style, but she still couldn't bring herself to go sleeveless or even to reveal that much leg or bear so much of her chest. They were all so relaxed about the booze, the smoking and then the music that had started up again.

She listened intently as the band began to play again.

"Bergin, what is that music they are playing?" she asked with a faint smile.

"Ragtime. Pretty hot stuff," he replied, looking over at the band.

"I've never heard anything like it." She stood very still, allowing the sound of the piano music to flood over her. The sound was strange, the rhythms were just a little off from what she was used to. It was a sound that drew her in, and made her want to move her feet. She was fascinated. "Who wrote it?"

"I hear that some colored man named Scott Joplin wrote some of these." Bergin looked at Clara, impressed that she was so accepting of the music. Most people on first hearing act like they had been insulted.

"A colored musician?" she said, her eyes wide in amazement. She lived such a sheltered life, had she never met Erdman and come out with him tonight, she never would have learned about this new music. She wondered what her family would make of it. She didn't think they would like it at all.

"Pretty radical stuff, isn't it," Bergin smiled. "There has been some amazing music coming out of New Orleans, Chicago and St. Louis from the Negro people. They really know how to put their heart and soul into their music."

"I can feel the pain, longing and suffering in the notes as it struggles to be cheerful. It is so sad and so beautiful. That is all mixed up, so that at other times, I feel the need to enjoy life, to kick up your heels and take what one can from life." The music touched her soul, it spoke of all her emotions, joy, love, pain, loneliness all wrapped up in the melody that filled the air. She allowed the music to embrace her, and filter down into the marrow of her bones.

"Clara, you surprise me," Bergin smiled at her.

"Me? Why?" She looked at him, eyebrows raised in astonishment.

"I would not have pegged you as a woman to be so open to this sort of music, that's all." Bergin blushed a little as he looked away, unable to meet her gaze anymore. He turned back to look at her as she watched the musicians play.

"Hey, Bergie, you been taking care of my girl for me, little brother?" Erdman's hand clamped onto Bergin's shoulder like a vice.

"We were listening to the music. Clara said she liked it," Bergin replied softly.

"Oh, Erdman, the music, it is so wonderful." Clara turned to look up at Erdman.

"Great to cut a rug to, hey?" He wrapped an arm about her waist, pulling her body against his, as he danced a few steps.

"Erdman, what are you doing?" She tried to push him away from her.

"Dancing with you." He grinned at her. "Did you miss me while I was taking care of business?"

"Business?" She wondered if he meant the alcohol.

"Yes, baby, business. Nothing for you to worry your pretty little head about." He patted his pocket and flashed her another disarming smile. "Come on, let's do some dancing; that's why we came here, to dance."

"Erdman—" she started to say, but he cut her off before she could finish.

"Come on, baby, I want to hold you in my arms and nuzzle in your neck." He drew her closer to him again, gently kissing her neck. "You're wearing that perfume again. I just can't help myself."

She felt herself melt into him, unable to resist.

* * *

Bergin watched as his brother wrapped an arm around Clara. He wondered if Erdman had any idea what an incredible treasure he had in someone like Clara. He seemed to treat all women like they were his playthings. Erdman never called them by their names, it was always baby or sweetheart or something. Maybe because that way he wouldn't have to worry if he called one by another girl's name; or maybe it was because they didn't really mean anything to him at all.

Bergin watched his brother at work. Sometimes he wished he could be half as smooth as Erdman, then again, he was happy he was not such a callow fellow. He shook his head slightly and asked himself: *what had made Erd even take a second look at Clara?* Had it been because he thought he could do one better and show up his little brother? That Erdman could best him by getting Clara to dance with him at the wedding back in December, when he himself had not been able to entice her to the dance floor. It was true, he really wanted to dance with Ingmar, not Clara, and maybe Clara had seen that and was smart enough to turn him down. He smiled as he looked over at Clara clasped in his brothers arms.

She was nothing like his usual following of floozies.

She was different; she was special. He even wondered if he was forming a silly, schoolboy crush on her. He would have to be careful not to let it show, especially around Erdman. He didn't want to be too obvious. He smiled and shook his head, chiding himself. He liked Clara; he liked her frankness, her gentleness and the simplicity of her.

Usually his big brother dated easy women with vapid brains who were all so hardened by life already; they smoked, drank and even cussed. Bergin doubted Clara had ever heard a cuss word.

Bergin felt that Clara was more his type, as was her little sister. He smiled inwardly as he thought of Ingmar and wondered what she might be doing that night. He wondered if there was any chance he might get to see her sometime soon.

A lot of what he would do about seeing Ingmar depended upon what happened between Clara and Erdman.

He watched his brother nuzzle at Clara's ear, and wondered what he was saying to her that made her blush. He looked away, saddened by the thoughts that were coming to his mind.

CHAPTER 10

Clara tumbled in the door shortly before dawn. She was drunk on giddiness. Erdman had kissed her. He had held her in his arms and kissed her. She shivered again with the chilling pleasure of remembrance. Of how he had held her on the dance floor, whirling her about in the fast steps of the new dance, nuzzling close to her.

She gently touched her lips remembering the feel of his lips on hers: tender and hesitant, warm and inviting.

She crept up the stairs as quietly as she could. No one was stirring yet. Her sister was fast asleep as she closed the bedroom door and slipped out of her frock. She crawled into the bed, and nestled down deep into the soft linens already warmed by her sister's body. She closed her eyes and saw the evening again in her memory. She wanted to seal it there so she would never forget.

In the depths of her reminiscences, she slipped quietly into a deep sleep.

* * *

She hadn't really intended to fall asleep, just lie back and remember until it was time to get up and help her mother in the kitchen. She must have made some noise giving away the fact that she was awake, for Ingmar was suddenly hovering over her with a big smile on her face.

"Well, how was your big night out?" Ingmar's eyes were wide with curiosity as she climbed back into the bed with Clara.

Clara stretched and smiled. As she remembered, once again her body tingled with the memory of his caress and his kisses.

"Clara!" Ingmar chided, unable to bear the suspense. She wanted so much for her sister to be loved and appreciated. She also wanted to know what had happened so she too could gauge her own conduct by her sister's.

Clara stirred again under the covers, and sighed. She looked at her sister's eager face and she smiled at her, touching her cheek softly, much as Erdman had done to hers.

"It was wonderful, little sister." She took a deep breath as if she was breathing in again all the memories of the night, and held it for a moment as if to fix her recollections, and then slowly let it go. She smiled recalling all the little things that made up the evening, things that had never happened to her before. Things she hoped would happen again and again. "Wonderful."

"So, did he kiss you?" Ingmar asked eagerly anticipating the answer.

Clara laughed and a tinge of color rose in her cheeks.

"He did! I can tell, you're blushing. Clara!" Ingmar giggled. "Oh! I'm so happy for you. Will you see him again soon?"

"I hope so." Clara blushed even a deeper shade of crimson. "We didn't make any definite plans other than he said he would see me the next time he was back from school." She hoped he would be back very soon. She was anxious to see him again.

"Oh, tell me everything, please," Ingmar could hardly contain her excitement.

Clara sighed, remembering again the sweetness of his caresses. She nodded and sat up in bed; she could not help but smile so that her face tingled. Slowly, as if reliving what now seemed to be a dream, she began to tell her sister about the dance they had gone to. Clara left out what had happened when they first arrived, for she had put all that from her mind. Erdman had wrapped her in his magic spell and cast those memories from her recollections almost completely.

"I began to learn that new dance that is all the rage now, the Charleston," Clara giggled with her sister. "I'm not very good at it yet."

"Can you teach me?"

"I can try; it is a little tricky in parts. It is so fast, so silly, so much fun."

"My big sister dancing the Charleston. Oh, Clara!" She hugged her sister. "Be careful or you'll turn into a flapper," she warned her.

"I hardly think I could be like one of them." Clara remembered the girl who had come up to Erdman when they first arrived. How sad she was really. She didn't seem happy to Clara. Laura Jean tried to chase happiness from what Clara had seen. That happiness was ever elusive for the poor girl.

"Why?" Ingmar asked, noticing the shift in Clara's countenance.

"They're so free and easy, like there wasn't a care in the world for any of them." She smiled as she remembered some of the other girls she had seen at the dance. "But so many of them seem to be running away. Running away as if their lives depended on it."

"Running away?" She furrowed her brow. "From what?"

"Life, reality, responsibility? I don't really know. I don't think even they know what they are running from," Clara said, thinking about them again. Wondering what it was that had given her that impression. "Running from something or maybe they are simply chasing something that is not attainable."

"What could be unattainable?" She sat back and studied her sister's face.

"Happiness, maybe?" Clara shrugged a shoulder.

"You don't need to worry about that anymore." Ingmar hugged her sister again. "I can see, you are happy! So very happy."

Clara embraced her in return, afraid to let go for fear that her own joy might be as elusive as the happiness those girls at the dances were seeking.

* * *

The pale light of dawn was cresting over the fields, and Bergin was awakened by the sounds of his mother in the kitchen. He wanted to roll over again and go back to sleep, but the smell of bacon frying pulled him from under the covers. That and the chores he knew needed to be done around the farm before breakfast was ready. He knew his brother was not going to get up and do them.

He broke through the thin but frozen layer of ice, and poured some water from the pitcher into the bowl on the washstand and splashed some on his face. He had not been able to speak much to Clara during the evening as Erdman had really paid her close attention. He was puzzled; maybe Erdman really did like Clara, and was finally smart enough to see what a wonderful woman she was. He remembered an old saying that said something about young men sowing wild oats, and then coming home to the nice girl next door when it came time to find a wife. He would be pleased if his brother really did fall for Clara and choose her as a wife. She was the sort men married as opposed to those floozies who Erdman usually kept company with.

He dressed and headed down to help his father with the morning chores. As he passed Erdman's room, he could hear him snoring. Just as he thought, his brother could sleep in since nothing was ever expected of him. Maybe that was why he never seemed to amount to very much.

His mother greeted him with the sharp edge of her tongue as he passed through the kitchen. "About time you got yourself out of bed. Your father has had to do all the morning chores alone. Hurry on out there and get to work, lazybones."

Bergin shot an angry look at his mother as he opened the back door. He knew it would do no good to remind her that she had another son and he was upstairs sleeping off a hangover instead of helping around the farm.

"I saw that scowl too, Bergin Halverson." She waved a knife in his direction. "Wipe it off your face if you expect to get any breakfast in this house today."

Her harsh words followed him out the door.

He tried once again to shrug it off.

One day she and his father may push him too far, then there would be hell to pay.

What did that really mean?

He didn't really know what he would do. The darkness of his rage that had been building for years now frightened him more than he wanted to admit.

CHAPTER 11

Spring seemed sweeter this year as Clara looked out across the barnyard area watching her father getting ready for planting. She loved the dry scent of the wheat berries as she ran her hand through them in the storage bin where they were waiting to be transferred to the seeder.

She felt as if her senses had been heightened because of the feelings that were breaking loose within her. She smiled as she wondered if this was what love felt like. It seemed as if the colors, smells, tastes, and sounds of spring were more intense this year.

She loved the fragrance of the warming, sweet scent of the earth as winter's white mantle of snow drew back and melted into the fields darkening the rich, black loam. The days were growing longer, the light strengthening in the sky.

The trees were beginning to bud, new leaves coming slowly awake on the branches like a fine, pale green halo of light around the ends of branches. Grass was beginning to awaken from the long slumber of winter and even the flowers were budding in the garden.

She laughed at herself thinking about her heart, like a flower was opening with the spring and the time she had spent with Erdman.

School had kept him busy so Erdman hadn't made it home as often as she would have liked, but she, like the earth, was awakening to things she didn't know were possible; feelings began to blossom and grow in her heart, and she pondered them all, treasuring each moment she had spent with him.

He wrote when he could, which was not all that often. Not as often as she wrote to him. She would write so much in her letters to him, and his letters were usually a page, maybe two, always brief and not too full of news. She reminded herself that he has his studies, papers and tests to take; he couldn't spend all his time writing to her. She fantasized that he would sit in class and daydream about her at times and maybe even get in trouble with the professor as he was called back to the classroom and his lessons.

She spent a great deal of time daydreaming about him, what they would do, what they had done already; of his kisses and caresses. Each time she recalled their intimate moments she would shiver with delight. Sometimes her mother would catch her daydreaming and would only smile with a gentle shake of her head.

Clara had taken down her copy of Romeo and Juliet and read the play again, feeling so much like Juliet, and the new love that promised so much. "This bud of love by summer's ripening breath may prove a beauteous flower when next we meet," Clara said one day as she walked the edge of the field, looking at the sprouts of new life pushing up through the rich, nurturing soil.

She hoped that she would be able to say another line from the play that resonated with her whole being. "Trust me gentleman, for I shall prove more true than those who have more cunning to be strange," she giggled at young Juliet's words, knowing that she too should have been more strange, not so eager.

She could not help herself.

Clara adored Erdman Halverson, and so wanted to be his one and only love, the woman he would ask to be his wife and spend the rest of his life with. She wished that she could say those things to him. She wished she could be the one to choose, for she would choose him, Erdman Halverson. She was still a bit old fashioned, and Clara would wait for him to ask her the question she so longed to hear.

She knew she was being sappy, but she was enjoying every moment of it. So was Ingmar as she listened to Clara tell her about all about what they had done, the dresses the other girls had worn and the music the bands were playing. Especially the music, for it stirred a deep longing within Clara that she had never noticed before.

Clara had gotten some of the sheet music from the C. E. Laustrup Piano Company at 340 W. Broadway in Council Bluffs on a recent visit. The clerk had known her for years and made a comment, wondering if this sort of music was appropriate for a young lady such as herself. She smiled and laughed at him and let him know she was buying it for a friend. She wasn't really lying; she had purchased it so she could play for Erdman and Bergin one day. She didn't really know if Erdman liked the music that they had danced to. It was Bergin who had let her know he had some favorites.

The sheet music that she had purchased was some Ragtime music by Scott Joplin, May Aufderheide and Mary Watson. Pleased with herself, she brought it home and placed it on the music stand of their upright piano in the parlor. Putting away her hat, coat and gloves, she settled herself on the piano stool and had tried playing one of her selections.

She was trying to get the timing right, and it was a struggle. It was not like any other music she had played. The left hand she had no problem with, it was a regulated march beat, but the ragged, disjointed timing of the right hand was what gave the music its special feeling. She kept practicing and soon the unsteady rhythms of the right hand began to feel right to her.

Her father wanted to know what was wrong with her playing, and she had laughed and told him it was written like that. He scratched his head, sat in the chair, and asked her to play it again for him. He had listened, then walked away shaking his head; he said, "well, you keep playing it; maybe it will grow on me." Then he added that he liked the old Goethe poem in music: *None but the Lonely Heart* that Tchaikovsky had set to music that she used to play so often. As a treat for him, she played it and he rewarded her with a smile and a soft kiss on the top of her head.

While in town, she and her mother had also looked at new fabrics for Clara to make some dresses that were a little more fashionable. She was still more conservative than the other women she saw at the parties, but at least she didn't look so out of place in the simple frock she had made since attending that first dance with Erdman.

She was changing; she could feel it.

Her life suddenly seemed to have meaning now. Erdman was changing her, changing her forever. She would never be the same girl she was when she first met him. It seemed that the bloom of love in her heart had even improved the roses in her cheeks.

She hoped that he would ask her to marry him, to spend the rest of her life loving him, caring for him, sharing every day with him. She would sigh at the thought of being his wife.

Soon the spring would warm into summer; soon Erdman would be home for that sweet season, her favorite of all.

At least, for now, he came home for the parties, and Clara went with him to every one he asked her to attend.

CHAPTER 12

Clara had gotten up early; the sun was cresting on the horizon, and tentatively began to caress the land. It was a special time of day for her as she witnessed the whole earth stirring to the rhythms of the new day. Birds chattered in their nests, waking their young; the earth seemed to sigh, releasing the chill of the night's embrace where it had slumbered. Dew clung to the new leaves, flowers and grasses perfuming the morning with the sweet scent of life stirring awake.

She could hear her parents waking in their room down the hall. Ingmar slept on undisturbed by Clara's hushed, cat-like movements of first light. She dressed in the semi-darkness, not needing to light the lamp. She knew the room by touch, and her clothes were laid over the back of the chair where she had set them out the night before.

She looked at her face in the mirror as she brushed her hair; though she was but a shadow in the dimness, she knew she was smiling.

She had dreamed of Erdman.

She crept down the stairs and out into the barnyard. She slipped into the henhouse and began to collect eggs. She would converse with them in soft tones as if her conversation would hurry the light into full glory of the morning sunlight. She did not want to rush the day.

Not yet.

This time was special. She could still be half dreaming and imagine the world as she would like it to be.

After finishing her chores, she decided to take a walk around the farm. The morning air was still cool and full of dampness from the night. The twitter of early morning bird chatter called from tree to tree in the orchard behind the house. They were preparing their young for their lives away from the nest. Clara sighed and hoped it would be the same for her too, that she would be able to spread her wings and fly off to a new life, married to Erdman.

She was pleased with the attention he was paying to her. She had even come to terms with the crowd of adoring females that always pressed about him when he first arrived anywhere. She was pleased to be with such a popular fellow. She smiled to herself as she watched a Robin bring some food to the nest.

"You have been stepping out a good deal with this boy, haven't you, Clara?" Ingmar smiled at her big sister. Teasing her was one of her favorite things to do now.

Clara jumped, surprised by her sister's voice. She hadn't seen her approaching. She laughed at herself for being so lost in her thoughts of romance.

"Yes, we have been seeing a good deal of one another." She blushed. The early morning sunlight was warm on her face. She loved the feel of the early morning air, tinged with the soft dews of the night and the warming sun as it rose above the treetops before it could warm the day. "He has taken me to a few dances each time he is able to get away from school."

"Are the dances fun?" Ingmar looked up at Clara.

"Fun?" Clara smiled and nodded, recalling her experiences. "Yes, they have been quite enjoyable really." Clara's cheeks colored slightly as she thought about dancing with Erdman, his body pressed so close against hers.

"Are there no adults there to keep an eye on things?" Ingmar asked.

"No, not really."

"Oh, my," Ingmar said, her mouth gaping open. Their parents had always been pretty conservative. "All alone with that good-looking man. Oh, Clara!" Smiling, she teased her sister.

"Erdman's little brother, Bergin, comes with us as chaperone."

"His brother? Bergin?" Ingmar raised her eyebrows in surprise.

"Yes, he is nineteen, and we often chat while we are waiting for Erd to take care of things at the dance. You would like Bergin, he is a nice boy." Clara brushed a leaf from her sister's hair.

"I know who he is from school," Ingmar nodded, a faint smile played at her lips.

"He is a nice boy, and is almost as good looking as his brother. Don't you remember him from the wedding back in December?" She smiled at Ingmar.

"I do remember him," Ingmar replied, turning away from Clara so her sister would not notice the color rising in her cheeks. She liked him better than any of the other boys in the area.

"Maybe you should get to know him better? We see them at church once in a while." On occasion, their families attended the same worship service, but usually her family went to the earlier service, and the Halverson family went to a later one.

"I would like to get to know him better, but rarely see him," Ingmar sighed, unsure if she wanted to say too much about liking him. "I wonder if he remembers that I am alive."

"I doubt there is a man in the county who doesn't know you are alive. You are so pretty and vivacious how could they not know." Clara rubbed noses with her little sister like they used to do when they were little. They both giggled.

"Does your Erdman drive a fast car?" Ingmar asked, changing the subject. "I thought I saw a pretty fancy one when you went out." She was full of questions.

"He is the proud owner of a Hudson Speedster. He told me that his folks had gotten him some old Ford for school, however, with the money he has made in delivering, uh, party goods, he says he was able to purchase this fancy car for only six hundred dollars instead of buying a new automobile for fourteen hundred dollars," Clara boasted. She hadn't any clue about things such as automobiles. She had paid attention when Bergin had told her about this new car of Erdman's. She was able to remember most of what he had told her and she thought she sounded informed at the least. She also had not told her sister that the "party goods" were really bootlegged liquor.

"That is an awful lot of money," Ingmar whistled, then clapped her hand over her mouth. Their parents had scolded her for such unladylike behavior before.

Clara could only laugh. It was the very same reaction she had experienced when Bergin had told her.

"What on earth is he doing to get that sort of money?" Ingmar wondered.

"Just between you and me I think he is delivering alcohol to some people at those dances we go to," Clara whispered, as if it were a secret conspiracy. She really couldn't keep anything from Ingmar.

"Alcohol?" Ingmar responded also in a whisper. "Isn't it illegal?"

"Yes," Clara nodded with a slight frown pulling at her mouth. She didn't want to think of Erdman in any way that was negative at all. If she had to find a fault with him, it may as well be that he sold liquor to people.

"Have you ever had any?" she asked, her eyes wide with wonder.

"No, I am not interested in the stuff. It smells terrible." She made a face.

"What does it smell like?" Ingmar cantered her head to the side, curious.

"Gasoline or worse." Clara wrinkled her nose as she remembered the smell.

"Gasoline?" She opened her eyes wide again in disbelief. "Who would want to drink something that tasted like that?"

"I don't know." Clara walked under a branch of an apple tree, pulling at a leaf. "I have seen what it can to do people. Poppa is right. It makes them into fools." She played with the leaf that had come loose in her hand. "I would rather be giddy on what joys life can bring rather than have some distilled liquor do it artificially," Clara said with determined pride. She had been horrified by some of the women and how they had acted after they had gleefully guzzled down some of that terrible smelling liquid Erdman had supplied. It was the one thing that really bothered her about him, his association with the demon alcohol. It was illegal, and she knew he could get into trouble.

He laughed at her when she expressed her concern for his safety.

He had told her about a night when he was delivering some booze to a party, and the cops had somehow gotten word and had come after him. He laughed, tossing his head back, showing his perfect teeth as he told her about how fine his car was with its powerful six-cylinder engine, and how he had been able to easily outrun the cops in their slow and meagerly powered, four cylinder vehicles, leaving them to eat his dust.

There had been one incident that had bothered Clara. Some strange, older man with a fancy diamond ring that flashed in the light, had arrived and made Erdman come with him off into the darkness of the night. She could have sworn Erdman was a little afraid of the man. When he returned, she could see he was visibly shaken, and his hand was trembling. When she asked what had happened, he shook off her concern, and though he tried to act like it was nothing, still looked over his shoulder too often for her to believe he was unconcerned.

That was not something she wanted to tell Ingmar. Nor did she want to think about it too much. She had not seen the man again, so the matter must be resolved now, whatever it was.

"Women drink the stuff?" Ingmar said, bringing Clara back from her reverie. "Do they get drunk?"

"They do. It's disgusting really." She shook her head, and let go of the leaf in her hand. She watched it spiral down to the ground.

"You are not tempted in the least to try it?" Ingmar queried.

"Not at all," Clara replied. "I have witnessed how it makes people do stupid and silly things. There are some stories I've heard about the stuff that have put me off the idea of even trying it at all." She shuddered with a revulsion that shook her slender frame.

"What stories?" Ingmar pressed her for more information.

"They say some people have gone blind from drinking this so-called bathtub gin," Clara answered, her eyes wide with imagination of such a thing happening.

"Why do they call it bathtub gin?" She asked her sister.

"I think it is because they brew it in the bathtub," Clara shrugged her shoulders.

"Maybe one day I can go to a party and see all those things you talk about," Ingmar stated. "I hear your stories and I am so curious about what all goes on there."

"I'm sure you will sometime. However, it is not the party that is where the fun is. The fun comes from being with someone you enjoy." The color rose in her cheeks and her sister smiled at her.

"Are you going to go off and marry him, leaving me all alone?"

"I don't know." Clara looked at the ground. She could feel the color in her cheeks intensify.

"You would like it if he asked?" Ingmar bent over to look up into her sister's face with a grin.

"Yes," Clara laughed and turned away, patting her cheek with the back of her fingers to temper the rush of warmth.

"And you would say yes, wouldn't you?" Ingmar danced around Clara to face her once again.

"I think so." Clara looked into her sister's eyes.

"Then I hope he will ask you." She held her sister's steady gaze and nodded.

Clara hugged her sister and kissed her hair.

"You are so sweet. Thank you, Ingmar."

CHAPTER 13

The party had already begun; Erdman always came late to a party and made a grand entrance. It made Clara smile to watch him strut into a room expecting everyone to stop what they were doing and give him their full attention. He always got it, too. She had become accustomed to her role, stand quietly with his younger brother, Bergin, and wait until he was finished accepting the accolades the crowd threw upon him. Then he would reappear, and make her feel special.

He was special to so many, but she was special to him?

It was enough, she told herself.

"Don't you ever get sick of it?" Bergin said softly; almost like he had been reading her mind.

"Sick of what?" She didn't want to say much. She had spent almost as much time with Bergin as she had with Erdman and felt she knew him well. She liked the idea of getting him together with her little sister. She would amuse herself that they as sisters would marry brothers and be doubly related.

"Sick of following around behind the big man, Mister Party, the man who just can't come into a room quietly. Why does he have to be the center of attention all the time?" Bergin said in an impatient tone of voice.

"Because they all adore him." She smiled enigmatically as she watched Erdman float through the throng of his admirers. She was surprised at the undercurrent of anger in Bergin's tone. Clara wondered what had caused it.

She looked at him.

"They don't adore him really." Bergin looked back at her. "He may think so, but what they really adore is what he brings, and for a price." Bergin made a face as he turned back to watch his older brother still lapping up the accolades of his adoring public.

"Bergin, you can't mean—" she didn't finish her thought.

"Can't mean what?" He turned back and studied her face. "You don't even know what you mean," he snorted a bitter laugh.

"Bergin, what is it?" She searched his face. He seemed so at odds with everything tonight. Usually he was so easy to be with.

"He likes to blame it on me, say I'm the one that isn't ready in time. It's not true. He sits about waiting until he thinks he has gotten it right so as to make the most of the timing. You know what I mean? His grand entrance. We always have to be late so he can swan into the room and be fawned over, and you are left at the side to wait for him to come back and throw a few crumbs of affection and attention your way," Bergin's voice had a hard edge to it.

"I don't mind," she lied to Bergin. Clara had been lying to herself about the same thing for a long time now. She had never given it voice. She looked down at her hands writhing against one another in agitation of hearing her concerns spoken so plainly. She grasped them together tightly in order to still them. She didn't want Bergin to notice.

"But you should," he replied quietly. Neither of them spoke for a moment. Bergin nodded once before he spoke again. "Why can't he come into all that attention with you on his arm?"

"I don't think I would like that much attention," she said quickly, blushing as she looked at Bergin and away again, unable to meet his eyes. "You see, we're different in that he needs the attention, and I don't. All I want is his attention, not theirs."

"You only get his attention when he is good and ready to give you some. He doles it out like a stingy miser, buying what he needs in the moment. When he senses that you are slipping away and losing interest in him he turns on the charm and reels you back into his web," Bergin spat out his words angrily. "Clara, you are too good for him."

Clara looked at him in astonishment. He had said exactly what she had been feeling creep into her conscious mind little by little. It unnerved her that he could see it so clearly. Not that she was too good for him, rather, that he could always pull her back into his sphere of attention whenever her doubts seemed to plague her mind. She shivered with the realization.

She turned and looked at Erdman, and all the people fawning over him, even the girls brazenly pawing and even kissing him.

She did mind.

She resented the fact that they would come in the room, and he would direct her off to some corner with his brother to wait until he had lapped up enough praise from the fawning crowds. She hated it that she was always in the shadows. She hadn't really wanted to admit it, but she felt like his little secret, a clandestine little affair not the woman he was proud to be with.

She buried her face in her hands for a moment. She was ashamed of her thoughts. They had fought deep inside her trying to be heard. Now, at last, she had heard her deepest fears spoken aloud by Bergin whom she regarded now as a good friend. It made her heart ache.

If Erdman really was proud of her, Bergin was right, she would be right there with him, in the center of the room. She could still stand quietly beside him and allow him to be fawned over, they would all know that she was also someone; that she was important to him and maybe even someone might fawn a little over her as well.

It was not something she thought she could admit, and especially not to Bergin, no matter how on the mark he was.

"You and I are different too, Bergin. I just don't need all that attention," she said, but didn't dare look at him for she knew he would see that she was lying. He struck a nerve.

"I just feel that you deserve better, Clara," his voice was soft with no trace of bitterness. "You are a wonderful person; I wish he could really see how wonderful you are." He didn't meet her gaze, but instead he stared off in Erdman's direction.

Clara could feel the color rise in her cheeks. No one, not even Erdman had ever said something so nice to her. Bergin thought she was wonderful. It almost made her want to cry. Words she wanted to hear so much from Erdman were spoken by his younger brother.

"Thank you, Bergin. You are so kind to say that," she said in a whisper, she dared not speak any louder, not trusting the steadiness of her voice.

"It's not kindness. It's the truth; it is how I feel," he said in a voice that was barely audible. He wasn't sure if she heard him, but he had to say it.

They sat together in the intimacy of the silence that embraced them.

It was a good hour or more that she waited for Erdman to come back to her. Bergin hadn't said another word. They both sat quietly and watched the revelers like they were watching a play. In that time she had been thinking about what Bergin had said, and the feelings she had tried to keep from herself. She was confused by Bergin, his words, his actions and even the look in his eyes when she would notice him looking at her. She pondered his words, too.

Try as she may, the question came into her mind and would not be pushed aside.

What did Erdman really feel for her?

Why was she with him and why was he with her?

Did Erdman really care for her? Or was she just a convenience to use and toss aside when someone more fashionable and younger came his way. She had heard about the girls he had at college. She rubbed the pain over her heart as if it would go away, but it was there, and had been there for some time, growing like a cancer.

She didn't really fit into this world in which Erdman seemed so comfortable.

She sat back and took a good look at what was going on about her. What was it that made her feel so much on the edge of this world, these people were her peers after all? But they were so different than she was. As one at the sidelines, she could see things in a different light than those who stood in the spotlight reveling on the dance floor. She wondered what things would look like from the spotlight for a change.

She had felt it before in the midst of these people; a frantic need to escape, to forget all the realities and pains of the life they were living. She had felt a certain amount of pain in her life; it let her know she was alive. She was not willing to numb away the sensations of pain, for then she would also deaden the feelings of her joy that were so fleeting, yet were so exquisite.

Maybe it was the Great War they all wanted to forget. She had been reasonably sheltered from its happening, living out on the farm, attending to the everyday life of crops and beasts. A few of the boys she had gone to school with went off to the war, so many never returned. Jimmy, they said, was shell-shocked, and was in a hospital somewhere. She never saw him again.

So many lives were lost, so many men that would have or should have been home to take wives and maybe even the man she might have married, he would have been in their number; a nameless, faceless man who never got to come home and find her.

No, she never knew him.

He died over there, before she could meet him, know him, touch him or smell the scent of him. Men's foolishness of war had cost the lives of too many young men, and left too many women standing on the sidelines wondering why they had never met that certain someone.

She looked over at Erdman again. He was standing in the center of a circle of his friends, laughing, enjoying himself without her.

Without her.

It hurt to think of that.

She asked the question that would no longer keep silent in her heart: *Is Erdman the right man for me?*

Just as silently as the question was posed the answer came back, cutting her to the quick. *No.*

She sighed and walked away from the forced gaiety before her, out into the soft night as the tears welled in her eyes and fell down her cheeks.

Bergin watched her, but made no move to follow.

* * *

Bergin and Erdman had fought earlier that evening. Bergin had asked his brother if his intentions were honorable toward Clara, did he intend to marry her. Erdman had cut him to the quick by the maliciousness of his laugh and his cruel quip that even if she were the last woman on earth he would be loathe to marry her.

Yet Erdman was still seeing Clara. What did he want from her now? Maybe Erdman suspected how much he had come to regard Clara; maybe it was to torment him that Erdman continued to see Clara. There were times when Erdman would be nuzzling Clara's neck and he would look about and lock eyes with him, a mean smirk spreading across his face until Bergin would look away.

That was his mood tonight, when he waited with Clara at the sidelines of Erdman's latest gathering of adoring fans. Bergin had allowed his disdain and anger to show. He was sorry for it, and had seen how it affected Clara. He knew she was having doubts about Erdman. She fought so hard to conceal them. Erdman knew he was losing her as well. That was when he would crank up the old charm, and whisper in her ear all the things she longed to hear, drawing her back into his maze of deceit.

Bergin knew he couldn't just say that Erdman was all wrong for

Clara. He knew that she would not want to hear it. Those words would only force her deeper into his web of whatever he was spinning about her.

After his outburst, they had simply sat together in an uncomfortable and what seemed to be an endless silence, waiting for Erdman to remember they were there. He had said nothing to her when she walked out into the night. He thought he had seen a tear well in her eye, caught in the reflection of the party lights about them.

CHAPTER 14

Clara sat with her mother preparing the supper for that evening's meal. Her thoughts had been haunting her from the dance the other night. She didn't know what to do with her questions. She didn't want to say too much.

"Momma, how do you know when you are in love?" Clara asked at last.

"Such a question, Clara." Her mother looked up at her with her eyebrows raised.

"I mean it," Clara had trouble saying the words. "How do you know?"

"Well, you just know." Her mother looked at her as if she was trying to figure out what Clara was really meaning. She sliced through the potato Clara had finished peeling and dropped it into the pot for boiling. "I don't know how to explain it. You just know."

"How did you know with poppa?" Clara insisted.

Her mother put down the knife for a moment to give her daughter her undivided attention. Clara likewise stopped peeling the potato in her hand.

"Well, we were keeping company together; he was seeing a lady on Thursday night, and me on the Monday night. I asked him if he was serious about dating me, and he replied that yes, he was. So, I said that if he was, then he needed to see me on Thursday night and not the other girl," she explained. "See, Thursday night was the night of the week when the gentleman would take out the girl that he was most serious about."

"Did he?" Her tone held so much hope for her own predicament.

"Yes, he did." Bertha Lindgren smiled as she remembered. "But he also asked me to stop seeing the other boys that I had been keeping company with," she giggled softly like she was that girl again.

"Other boys? Momma?" Clara smiled in surprise. She had never thought of her mother as a young girl with so many of the same hopes and fears as she too had in her own heart. For her, it was as if her parents had always been together and never had to deal with the struggles that plagued Clara's heart.

"Don't look so surprised, I was very popular with the boys when I was a girl." A touch of color rose to her cheeks, and it wasn't from the warmth in the kitchen. "So, I asked him, why should I stop seeing other boys? He replied right back to me that he was in love with me. And that was that. We got engaged after that night." Her mother picked up the knife again and sliced another potato.

"But how did you *know?*" Clare pressed the question as if there was a secret that could be imparted from one woman to another. A secret knowing that was handed down from mother to daughter through the generations all the way back to Eve since creation.

"It just felt right when he said he loved me and wanted to spend the rest of his life with me." She shrugged her shoulders. "I don't know what else I can tell you, sweet girl." Gently she took Clara's chin in her hand and cradled it.

"I guess then I will have to wait for when I know," she said sadly.

"Do you think you love this boy you are seeing?"

"That's just the problem." She looked up at her mother, a pleading look in her eyes. "I don't know."

"Then, I would venture to guess that you are not in love with him. Not the kind of love you are asking about." Her eyes held a sadness for Clara. She wished the girl could find someone to love her the way she deserved to be loved.

Clara sighed. It was not what she had wanted to hear. For so many years she had waited for something like this to come to her, and if it was not right, then what? How long would it be before she would meet another man who would pay her any attention that she would bother with seeing?

"Will it ever come to me?" she said in a voice that was little more than a whisper.

"I am sure it will. You are a wonderful and beautiful girl. Any man would be a fool to pass you by." Her mother looked at her with a loving smile on her lips.

"Then there are a lot of fools in the county." She picked up the potato and began to peel again.

"Oh, Clara, you need to be patient. You will find the right man. Sometimes it just takes a little longer," her mother assured her.

Her mother's face looked worried.

Clara wondered if she would ever really find the right man, and questioned whether or not she would *know* when it was right. There were so many things about Erdman that she adored, and, yes, loved. But that little seed of doubt that crept into her mind at the dance the other night.

That doubt deflated her totally.

She had asked herself if he was the one, and she had gotten a *no* in reply so quickly, it was as if she had been slapped in the face.

It had upset her and she had gone off for a good cry before returning to the dance. Bergin had left her alone, thank goodness. Erdman hadn't even noticed that she had been gone. He had been too busy being the center of attention.

She shook her head to expel her thoughts.

Erdman was the man she would marry, if only he would ask her. He may be her last chance to get married. She knew that had to be their fate, to be together. She kept repeating that to herself over and over as she finished peeling the potatoes.

CHAPTER 15

The evening was warm; the spring flowers were fading to the robust blooms that would come with the warm days of June. The air was thickly scented with the fragrances of their blossoms, blending into an embrace of scent enhanced by the warm velvet touch of the night air.

Clara, Erdman, and Bergin had arrived at a party in the Village of Trainer outside of Council Bluffs. Erdman parked the car and jumped out without looking back to see if Clara and Bergin were right behind him. Clara opened her car door and stepped slowly from the car. She paused, inhaling the sweetness of the air, wrapping her arms about herself as she allowed the sensation to enfold her, taking her into the realm of her fondest daydreams. She smiled to herself, and sighed, enjoying a private pleasure she didn't think anyone else would understand.

She was pulled back to the present by the sounds of laughter and music carried across the soft air. Someone called Erdman's name, and there was an increase of the sounds of chatter on the air. Warm light spilled out, and she stood a little longer in the seclusion that the night allowed her, reluctant to leave the floral scented air.

Bergin noticed that Clara was quieter than usual. He watched her hesitate before she stepped into the path of light that led to the party sounds. She stood looking into the festivities as if reluctant to enter. He could see her eyes followed his brother as he made his way through the crowd that pressed in about him.

She seemed so changed.

He wondered what was different tonight.

He looked at Clara and instantly he knew that she was not in love with his brother. He couldn't put his finger on how he seemed to know this; there was something in her posture, in the angle of her head and the intensity of her gaze as she watched Erdman. It was as if she was studying him now, not looking at Erdman with a smitten look of adoration.

In a way, he was pleased that the infatuation was wearing off.

Maybe she would escape with as little hurt as possible. Maybe she could go away and forget Erdman.

Erdman had made his usual entrance and had been the center of attention once again. When he seemed to tire of the accolades, he strolled over to Clara, took her into his arms, leading her to a more secret secluded corner and kissed her. Her body didn't seem to yield to him as it had always done in the past.

If Bergin had to guess, he would say that Clara was bored. He wanted to ask her what she was thinking, but Erdman never gave him a chance to speak to her unless he was off gathering attention from the crowds, pretending like they didn't exist.

He knew how Erdman hated to be rejected, and hoped that tonight she would tell him to jump off a bridge or something.

* * *

Clara was distracted tonight. The things she and Bergin had discussed the last time they were all out at another party came back to her mind as she watched Erdman move through the crowd. She tried to push the thoughts away. She wondered why he never took her in his arms and kissed her when the others could see?

Was she his dirty, little secret?

It was not what she wanted, and it was not what she was going to tolerate anymore. If she was special to him, then he better start showing it.

She wanted to ask, but she was afraid of what he might say in reply.

She watched as Erdman made his way over to where he had left her standing with Bergin. Erdman walked with his head down as he crossed the room. Why didn't he look up at her? What was the matter?

Even Bergin was unusually silent tonight.

Was it them or was she the one who had set the mood of silence among them all? She didn't believe she was that powerful, that she could affect them all that way.

Erdman looked up, and reached out to take her by the hand and lead her away from the others into a quiet place outside, beneath some flowering trees. Many of the petals had fallen, giving way to the bright green of new leaves. The ground was covered in fragrant pink and white petals. He sat down and pulled her to the ground next to him. He nuzzled at her neck a little before seeking her lips, but she wasn't inclined to respond as she usually did. Too much nagged at her mind.

"Hey, baby, I feel as if I am losing you. You seem so distant tonight. What is it? What have I done?" Erdman looked up into her eyes from his recumbent pose.

She sat on the petal covered ground next to him, but felt a million miles away. She wondered if she should say anything to him, let him know what was on her mind. He seemed so open and caring at the moment as if he sensed her pulling away from him.

She thought about what she really should ask him.

He stroked her hand.

She took a deep breath and let it out slowly before she spoke.

"Erdman, why do you chase after pleasures so?" She looked into his eyes as he lay on the ground. "Why are you always working so hard to be the life of the party? Sweet boy, you know it can't last."

"I know it can't," he replied abruptly. He looked away into the distance before he spoke again. The words seemed hard for him to say. "It's, well, I . . . I just don't talk about it."

"You can tell me." She wanted to wrap him up in an embrace and ease the pain that she felt had suddenly welled from his heart.

He propped himself up on an elbow so he could look into her eyes intently, cupping her face in his other hand. Searching for the trust he wanted so desperately to find. "Yes, maybe I can tell you." He kissed her forehead softly and turned away again. "You see, I had an uncle, my mom's youngest brother, he was everything I wanted to be. I was just a silly child when he went off to fight in the Great War."

"Yes, the war to end all wars," she said softly. This was a side to Erdman that she had never seen before. It was the sort of man she had been longing for, not the party boy, but a sensitive man who cared about the world and others.

"Oh, God I hope so," he sighed falling silent.

"Tell me about him?" She wanted to know more.

"He was dashing and handsome, everybody loved him, and he was worthy of their adoration for he was a kind and generous soul," Erdman said, as if he could see him right in front of him. "Until that war," his tone was now bitter and angry.

"It altered many a life, I know," she agreed.

"Innocent babe in the woods that you are, it did a lot more than alter them." He looked at her, fighting not to look too burdened by sadness. "It rent the fabric of our world and shredded the remnants of what was left into tatters that can never be repaired."

Clara said nothing; she simply gazed into his eyes. His words were passionate, and even poetic. Again, something she had never experienced from him. A seriousness in him that was so different. An earnestness that was so much more appealing to her.

"My uncle heard about the war, America was not yet engaged in the fighting, so, fool that he was, he hopped a ship bound for England and the dupe enlisted."

"Erdman," she whispered. She fought the urge to bundle him up in her arms and rock him like a small child. He seemed so close in one way, yet so distant in another. She dared not touch him.

"See, he went to this place in Belgium called Flanders Field where so many were slaughtered. He saw his friends' heads blown off by sniper fire; others were cut to shreds by shrapnel. Once he was resting in his bunk to get away from the cold and damp of the trenches, see, they dug out barracks in the earth, and one of the guys came in after a round of shelling and he sat for a moment, then a mist began to rise from his clothing, the mustard gas was inert in the cold, but in the warmth of the barracks it began to diffuse into the air. A greenish-yellow mist rose from the man's clothing. They all ran outside, but the poor guy, by that night his eyes were running with sickly mucus, and he lost his sight," his voice was tense and broke as she spoke.

Clara listened intently. She had heard some of the nightmare stories from others who had been in the war.

"He came home after being gassed. He was one of the lucky ones he said. He told us about what happened when you got gassed. That there were blisters about the size of your palm all in the tender warm places of their bodies, under arms, between the legs and all over the face and neck, even the back. Their eyes all steaming and hurting in a way that sin never hurts, he said," Erdman's voice broke, and he fought back tears.

Clara reached over to wipe them away, but he pulled away from her.

He went on, telling her more of the horror, "I learned that the mustard gas usually took a person about five painful weeks to die from it at its worst. Most were strapped to their beds as they tortuously died. Mucous colored blisters filled with a sickly, yellow ooze, everything all stuck together, they spoke in hoarse whispers, their throats closing, fighting for every breath. It killed over 4,000 men alone and maimed nearly 17,000 of them for life," he sighed deeply, his pain evident.

He looked over at her. She gave a slight nod of her head for him to go on, and tell more of the gruesome story.

"One of them was my best uncle. I remember what it was that he said to me shortly before he died. He said that the strain was very great, shelling seemed endless, and his nerves were all awry. He watched some of the others; men who were gassed clawing at the air. He told me about the dying men all around him reeking with mud and the foul stench of green, stained bandages, shrieking and crying, writhing in pain, of blood gurgling in froth-corrupted lungs and of dead men with fixed empty eyes and shiny yellow faces," his voice was little more than a whisper.

Erdman tried not to weep, but his emotion and tenderness touched Clara's heart. She couldn't help herself. She wrapped him up in her arms and rocked him gently. He stayed close against her heart, fighting the tears that burgeoned in his eyes. Soon his breathing evened as the near sobs subsided.

"Don't leave me," his voice was barely a whisper.

"I won't. I'm here, right here," she replied, still holding him fast.

"You know I care for you," he said softly into her ear.

He began to stir, his lips kissing her neck, his hands pressing her back against the soft earth. She wanted to stop him, but she felt things stirring in her being that had never done so before. This was the Erdman she loved, so much more than the man who sought to be the center of attention. This was the man she wanted to be with, now and always.

"I want you to love me," he said, and then covered her mouth in a kiss so she could make no reply.

His hands touched her; her body reacted in ways she hadn't ever felt before. She didn't know how to stop it, she felt as if she was drowning, yet she was able to breathe under water. Confusion assaulted her, her senses overloaded; she didn't know how to stop, or if she wanted to stop.

She could hardly feel her body any more, but she felt him, he was touching her there, down there, where no one had ever touched her, he shouldn't. Waves of sensations over took her physical being and she didn't know what to do. She knew she should stop him, yet her body shivered in delight.

"Oh, baby, I want you so much, I need you," he whispered into her ear. "Comfort me, hold me close. Seal us closer than ever before." His breath was warm on her face, his hands seemed to be everywhere and nowhere, his words were imploring her, caressing her, pulling her senses someplace she had never been before. His lips seeking hers, taking kisses from her as if she could restore him to life.

There was a frightening desperation in his neediness.

And she responded.

Sensations shook her being; he was inside of her, and she gasped. Pain and pleasure all mixed together as she writhed in the sensation of what was happening. He moved rhythmically, and sought her mouth again. She moaned as her body betrayed her, giving way to feelings she never knew existed. Their bodies moved together in a dance of primal instincts that she didn't know she possessed. Then he arched back and cried out, jerking spasmodically, then becoming very still before collapsing on her. Then he rolled away.

She reached out to touch him; he turned and nuzzled at her neck.

"I love you, baby. That was incredible," he said in a soft voice as he let go a deep sigh of pleasure.

He began to kiss her neck again, as his hands touched her legs and thighs, creeping up ever closer. This time she stopped him. She wasn't ready to repeat again what had just happened to her. She needed to be alone, to think, and to see if she had changed, if she looked different at all. She was afraid it would show on her face and everyone would know what she had done.

She wanted to go home; she didn't think she could face anyone, not now. She couldn't face them all now. Not now, not after . . .

He protested.

He wasn't ready to go; the party was still in full swing.

He was a little angry with her for ending the evening so soon. But he did as she asked, and drove quickly to the farm, and dropped her off without so much as a goodnight kiss.

The car sped out of the lane and he was gone.

She knew he was displeased at her for wanting to leave so soon. She knew she had changed; she didn't want the others at the party to see her like this. Bergin hadn't said a word on the way back. She sensed that he could tell the difference in her demeanor. Erdman was sullen like a spoiled child that hadn't gotten his way, and she was afraid to speak to him for fear of what she would hear.

Quietly she opened the door of the house and climbed up the stairs softly, hoping no one would hear her. She didn't want to see anyone. Not now, not until she had a chance to see how much she had changed.

Surely, something like this would show on her face.

It had to.

She had the lamp wick turned down low, not wanting to wake her sister.

She sat before the mirror, searching her face, where did it show? Would it be in her eyes then, since nothing was obviously different on her face? She touched her cheek and leaned in closer to the mirror.

Would someone who had known such pleasures be able to see it?

Would others be able to tell?

Could they see it on her face?

Could they see that she had . . . that she was no longer a . . . she knew that somehow, in some way it had to show.

* * *

Bergin had watched as Erdman had taken Clara off to a secluded part of the grounds around the barn where the dance was going on. He had started in on her with his *I think I'm losing you* line. Clara had not fallen for it as Erdman had expected. His expression gave that away when instead she asked him why he chased pleasure and good times so hard. It was something Bergin, himself, had wondered, and had never been able to get a straight answer out of his brother.

He didn't think his brother was capable of giving anyone the truth; just a pack of lies that kept people guessing or dancing to his tune. Something in Clara's words or voice had elicited a response from Erdman that was honest, painful and for a change the truth. Erdman spoke about their uncle and the Great War. He remembered their uncle, and the news had just come to their mother that he had killed himself. She had left the letter lying on the table, and Erdman, not one to pass up an opportunity to nose into someone else's business, had read that letter.

It was the first time he had seen his brother shed a tear.

Typical of Erdman, he had manipulated Clara's trust and concern for him into a chance to take advantage of her. Bergin had walked away in disgust. Later he only looked at her once, wondering what was going through her mind. She had averted her eyes quickly. He thought she was somewhat ashamed. She had not said anything on the ride home. Not that Erdman had given her the chance; he allowed his anger to show. Selfish once again, he had wanted to stay and party some more, not caring what he had done to her, or how she might be feeling.

After they had dropped her off and she seemed to scamper into her house like she was afraid of something.

"How could you?" Bergin confronted Erdman.

"How could I what, little brother?" Was his smug reply.

"How could you take advantage of Clara like that?"

"Take advantage of her? Whatever are you talking about?" He shot him a nervous look and plastered an insincere smile on his lips.

"You seduced that poor girl," he shot back, trying to break down Erdman's complacency. "What if she finds herself with child? What then?"

"Well, first off, I don't appreciate your spying on me. What we do is our business, not yours," he started to say, but Bergin interrupted him.

"It is my business; she happens to be our neighbor and a friend of mine, not just some slut you are using until you tire of her and toss her aside as you have with so many other woman who have crossed your path."

"Still have a schoolboy crush on her?" He clacked his tongue at Bergin in mock sympathy. "Maybe I was right about her, that she did reject you, and you are just jealous that she likes me better than she likes you," he laughed. "So, I'll tell you what, if she does manage to get herself in a family way, well then, you can marry her since you seem to care so much about her."

"You are despicable," Bergin said, clenching his fists so he didn't pommel his brother. It was the last he spoke to Erdman for days.

* * *

No one said a word to Clara about the great transformation of her being. No one noticed she was different.

No one except her.

She knew she had changed. Forever.

CHAPTER 16

Clara was amazed that no one had noticed the great change she had felt in herself. She had searched the mirror again over the next few days, and saw nothing that would give it away. She looked at the faces of others and wondered how they felt about what she had allowed Erdman to do to her.

No.

More like what she had allowed him to take from her.

Erdman had taken her to another dance a week later. This time he had not brought Bergin along with him. It had been a little uncomfortable, just the two of them. He hadn't really had much conversation, and she wasn't sure what to talk about.

It had been awkward all evening.

It had been harder to endure sitting at the sidelines while he lapped up the praises of the others. He had been nipping into the bootlegged booze he had brought with him. He had drained the contents of his flask, and had helped himself to some of the spiked punch as well.

Then he had wanted to do it again.

She wasn't too sure she wanted to do it again. She was still wrestling with the idea of what they had done.

He had pressured her, saying that if she loved him she would let him take her again. His voice was so soft, his kisses so insistent, and his full attention had been on her. At last, worn down by his incessant pleading and nudging she had acquiesced. She wasn't really sure she liked it, but it had kept him close to her. He'd said he loved her every time before they had come together, and sometimes after as well.

The words had been ones she had longed to hear. That he loved her. . . could she trust those words?

Could she really trust him?

He said he loved her and hinted at the life they could share together.

It was that expectation she hung her hopes upon. It was why she had allowed him to take her again.

Soon he began to expect it from her every time they were together over the summer. She didn't want to lose him, so she gave in to his demands. She was confused and needed to talk to someone. Bergin hadn't been with his brother since that first time she and Erdman had . . . she couldn't even finish the thought.

She was surprised that she missed Bergin's company.

She was sure Bergin knew what had happened. Maybe he didn't want to see her anymore. She didn't want him to think ill of her, and it was one of many things that were bothering her.

Clara was worried about something else now. She had missed her monthly cycle.

She knew what it might mean.

No one had said anything to her because she had taken on the household chore of washing the heavy diaper-like, cotton padding they wore each month to catch the flow of blood. Her mother no longer had to endure the flow, but she and her sister did.

Clara knew that what she and Erdman had been doing could create new life in her womb. She had seen what happens often enough on the farm among the livestock. She wasn't ready to say anything to her family. She hoped that maybe it would soon pass on its own. She had taken some herbs she had heard about, so far they had not changed her condition.

Her belly began to swell a little. She hoped that no one would notice.

Her mother was heading into town. Clara had expressed a wish to accompany her, making the excuse of wanting to do some shopping too. Her mother had smiled and said she would be glad to have Clara's company.

Clara's mother dropped her off at Beno's Department Store while she went on to pick up some other things. Clara had told her mother that she wanted to get some nice fabric to make some new things. She was aware that she would need to adjust the clothes just enough to hide her condition. She was glad the fashions were rather shapeless dresses that hung from the shoulders and did not accentuate the waistline.

Her fingers ran along the bolts of fabric, loving the tactile sensation of how the woolen, cotton, crisp linen and silk fabrics felt on her fingers. It was her mother who had taught her to shop with her fingers. She inhaled the fragrance of the fabrics and the dyes. These were scents she had always loved.

She noticed two young women standing by the table displaying the new arrivals in the fabric department. Something one of them said made her come close enough to overhear their conversation.

"Erdman is so amazing," the girl with the brown, Marceled hair peeking out from the brim of her cloche hat, gushed to her blonde friend. "I can't believe that he and I are actually going to the big dance in Omaha in two weeks." She picked up a bolt of salmon colored fabric, unfurling it and holding it up to her face. "What do you think?"

"I heard he had a girlfriend already." The blonde wrinkled her brow and shook her head, dismissing the choice of fabric with a wave of her gloved hand. "Why isn't he taking her?"

"What about this one?" She picked up another bolt and held it up much as she did with the other one.

"I wouldn't be caught dead in that color, Maggie." She waved that choice away as well. She studied the selection for a moment before pointing at a spring green and pink floral pattern. "This one should do."

"Very nice." Maggie dropped the other bolt on the table and snatched up the one her friend indicated. "This will catch his eye."

"So what about the other girl this Erdman has been seeing?" Her friend asked.

"Oh yeah, he told me he had been seeing some hick from the sticks, a peach right off the farm who was ripe for the taking, and that he had already gotten what he wanted from her, and he was moving on." She shrugged a shoulder as she looked at the fabric her friend had chosen for her.

"That does not sound like much of a recommendation. You sure you want to be with him?" She looked at the fabric selection on the rack by the next counter. "Come look at these, they are terribly smart you know."

"He is a bit of a bad egg. But that's what makes him fun to be with." She took one of the items from the rack. "Isn't this interesting?"

"They are all the rage right now and so simple to make as well." She lifted another off the rack and held it up for a look. "All the beadwork is already done for you. All you have to do is sew the

French seams and presto, you have a couturier gown," she giggled. "Almost."

"They are a little spendy, but I guess they are worth it." She looked at the price tag that was pinned to the hem of the fabric dress goods.

"Be careful that you don't get hurt by him now," her friend warned, giving her a concerned look as she replaced the dress pieces on the rack.

"Erdman, hurt me? I don't think so. I can take care of myself." She selected a dark blue dress length of the fabric with iridescent blue beading.

"Famous last words," her friend laughed again. "So, he's left the farmer's daughter behind? The old girlfriend? You know that for sure?" She cantered her head and blinked at Maggie.

"He sure has, and he said that he couldn't escape fast enough." Her laughter was shrill. "Come on; let's go see if we can find some shoes to go with this new dress I am going to have to sew." She left the bolts of fabric on the counter, and took the beaded selection with her.

The girls laughed and walked away.

Clara felt as if someone had punched her hard right in the stomach. She clutched her swelling belly, wondering if she had been a fool.

"He said he loved me," Clara whispered for no one in particular to hear.

CHAPTER 17

The summer was almost gone, and the crops in the fields were ripening quickly. The fragrance of the corn, wheat and beans was carried on the soft breeze. The fruit trees in the orchard also perfumed the air with the ripening of the apples and peaches that were weighing down the branches.

Clara's body too was ripening; the child growing within her womb. No one had seemed to notice that she had filled out a little. She had made adjustments in her clothes that had so far been able to hide her secret. She had tried on occasion to tell her folks, but something had always interfered just as she was about to speak. So she left it alone and said nothing to them.

Erdman had not been around as much as she hoped. With summer she wanted to see more of him. He'd said that he was working on the farm. Too soon school would begin again. She knew she had to tell him about her condition, but she was also a little afraid to mention it.

She was still hurting from the conversation she had overheard at Beno's the week before. She tried to tell herself that it was some other fellow named Erdman that the two women had been talking about, not her Erdman. It couldn't be her Erdman. She had told herself that over and over again.

Erdman had not been around for a month. She decided to go see if she couldn't find him and see what was going on. She needed to know for certain whether or not he had dumped her, or if he was going to a dance in Omaha with that woman from the store.

She decided to go seek him out and see for herself what was happening and why she had not seen him. She rode one of the horses out to the fields of their farm where Bergin told her Erdman was working that day. Her heart skipped a beat as she saw him working as she rode up to him.

"Erdman, I haven't seen you for a while. Where have you been?" She dismounted and came over to where he was standing.

"Been working the farm. Not much time for pleasure." He ran

his fingers along her arm, making her shudder with delight. He smiled at her.

That smile melted her resolve. The way he was acting didn't seem to her as if she had been dumped. He had smiled when he saw her ride up to him. That was a good sign she told herself as she smiled back at him. It felt good to be in his company again. She had missed him more than she wanted to admit.

"I heard there was supposed to be a dance in Omaha this weekend," she said tentatively. She was afraid to look at him directly, so she looked up through her lashes.

His head snapped her direction. "Omaha?" He tried to smile, but his lips only twitched. "What makes you say that?"

"I heard some girls in town talking about it, that's all," her voice was barely above a whisper. His tone had intimidated her. He had never spoken harshly to her before.

"Oh. Well, I hadn't heard about it at all." He shrugged his shoulders. "Want me to see if we can go? See if I can find out where it is?"

Clara let go her breath, she didn't realize she had been holding it. "No, don't bother." She dug her toe into the soil. She wanted to ask him what they might be doing that weekend. It had been a while since they had seen one another, and she needed to tell him what had happened. "Can we do something this weekend?"

"Better not. Got a lot to do here on the farm." He made a sweeping gesture to the crops growing about him. "Harvest is upon us just about, and there is so much to do. You should know that. I'm sure your father and brothers are in the fields from dawn to dusk." He looked at her.

"Yes, that's true, they are," Clara nodded in agreement, chiding herself for being selfish and missing the obvious.

Silence hung between them as he stood looking at her, and she was reluctant to tell him what she knew she must. She gave him a tight, little smile before she forced herself to speak.

"There is something I would like to discuss with you." She couldn't look him in the eye, but she heard him let go a sigh.

"Well, we can talk later. I better get to work if I am ever to finish in time to get back to college." He reached for her.

She took a step back.

He gave her a funny look.

"Oh, yes, when will you go back to school?" She replied.

"Couple of weeks, and then I am back at my studies." He looked at her, stepped closer and wrapped his arm about her, and kissed her. "You want to make me happy?"

"Don't I make you happy?" She said a little hurt at his words.

"Baby, you have the secret to making me happy, you know that." His breath was soft on her cheek as he closed her tighter in his arms. He smelled of sweat and dust from his labors. "You know that little garden of pleasure you have, that I like to visit whenever you'll let me." He kissed her, arching her back, wanting her to lie back on the ground "Come on baby. I haven't seen you in so long. You know how I love you," his breath was shallow, his voice pleading. He began to run his hand up her skirt.

"Right here? In the fields?" She fought not to react to his hands; he always knew just where to touch her.

"Why not?" He said, nuzzling at her neck.

"I better get back," she blurted out pulling away from him. She had almost given in to him again.

"If that's how you want things to be," he didn't really finish his sentence.

He let her go; she thought he looked a little angry; he said nothing more. She mounted her horse and headed back to her home. *At least he was not going to a dance in Omaha with the woman in the store. It must have been another Erdman that they were talking about. And he did want to. . . well, do that again, so he must still care.*

She was so confused by him.

* * *

Bergin waved at her as she rode back along the lane. He had missed seeing her when Erdman had taken her to the last few dances without him tagging along. After what he had seen his brother do, he didn't want to be a part of it anymore. Erdman had gotten what he wanted from Clara, and Bergin hadn't been able to protect her. He was ashamed of himself for not being able to keep her from harm.

"Did you find him, Clara?" He called to her. She looked prettier than he had ever seen her. Her skin seemed to glow. She was different, but he couldn't say how. It was more than the relations she was having with Erdman.

"Yes, Bergin, I did." She smiled back at him and reigned in her horse to a stop. "Thank you."

"Is he anywhere near finished?" He made a semi-helpless gesture. He knew that his brother was lazy, and he was only in the fields because their father had insisted that they both work today.

"It looked like he still had a few more rows of beans to walk." She looked back to where Erdman was working on the other side of the little hill.

"I hope he gets them finished and doesn't expect me to pick up his slack." Bergin took off his straw hat, and mopped his brow with his kerchief. "He says he has to get to Omaha for some big deal Friday night."

"Omaha?" Clara stammered as her heart skipped a beat. "Friday night?"

"Some dance or something he says he is going to." Bergin looked up, and saw the pained expression on Clara's face. "Clara, oh, I am so sorry, he's not taking you?"

All she could do was shake her head now as the tears welled in her eyes.

"That cad," Bergin scowled. He reached up and placed his hand on hers. "Please, I am so sorry. Can I do anything?" He wasn't too sure what it was he had said, but he had hurt her. Was it that he was not taking her to that dance? Had Erdman finally cast her aside? Was it over between them? If it was, then maybe Clara could put her life back in order and forget the rotten brother he had. Erdman wasn't half good enough for Clara.

"I best be going." She looked down at Bergin's hand on hers. "Good bye, Bergin. It was nice to see you." A tear slipped down her cheek.

"Bye, Clara." He stepped back.

He watched her ride off; he could tell she was crying from how her shoulders trembled. He wanted to kick himself for being so stupid. Since he had not been going along with Erdman anymore, he didn't really know when the last time he had taken Clara to one of his parties.

He looked back at where Erdman was supposed to be working, fighting the urge to go beat him senseless for his selfish cruelty to Clara.

* * *

Clara gave the horse a gentle kick and trotted off in the direction of her home. *Why couldn't Bergin be Erdman, and Erdman be Bergin. Bergin always seemed to care so much about her, her feelings and her ideas.* When she was far enough away to be sure Bergin could not overhear her words she blinked back her tears.

"He lied to me." She said out loud through the sobs that racked her body. "Erdman lied to me, and then told me he loved me. Why? I don't understand."

CHAPTER 18

The summer was coming to a close and fields were ripe; harvest was about to begin. Clara was in the orchard picking some of the ripe fruit weighing down the branches of the trees. She too was coming closer to her time as well. Clara lightly touched her growing belly.

Still, no one had noticed as yet. For that she was glad.

She had not seen Erdman since she had spoken to him in the field that day.

Clara wasn't sure she even wanted to see him. She was still hurting from the discovery that he had lied to her. She knew she had to do something. Erdman was the father of her child. She needed to let him know so he could do the right thing. She was sure he would marry her as he must, he wouldn't turn her away. When he found out, he would come to her and make everything all right again.

He had to.

How should she let him know about his child? She didn't want to try to catch him again at work on his farm. Every time they were together, he wanted to have his way with her. She just could not do it again, not until she was a married woman.

She thought that she should write to him and let him know.

How to put it in writing?

For days now, she had wrestled with the words in her head.

She knew she must ask the one important question. Will he marry her as he should? And when?

Then another nagging thought crept into her consciousness. Will he even answer her? In all the time she had known him, he never was very good at taking responsibility for his actions.

She decided if she did not hear from him she would have to write to his parents. They might be able to have him face up to his responsibilities and take care of his new family, as he should.

She seated herself at the writing desk when she was alone in the house. She really didn't want anyone to come in and read over her shoulder. She dipped the pen into the ink, and for a moment, the pen hovered over the writing paper before she began to write. She could always try more than one draft if it didn't come out right. She would put her rejected drafts into the fire so no one would inadvertently find them.

She dipped the pen into the ink again, she wanted to make sure she had a steady flow, and that the letter be done in her best handwriting. After all, this was a letter to the father of her child, and hopefully, one day soon, her husband.

Erdman,

Since I did not have the chance to see you in the few weeks since we met out in the field, I have to resort to sending you my news in this letter. As you recall, we have been intimate a number of times in the past few months. You know that you have been my first and the only man I have ever been with. As a consequence of our passions, there is a new little life that has taken hold, and is growing in my body.

You have said that you love me, and I am hoping that you will do the right thing. Please, let me know as soon as you can, so we can make the proper plans and be married for the sake of the child. Your child.

As ever,

Your Loving Clara

She sat back and reread what she had written.

It will do.

She wasn't sure how else to put it. She took out an envelope and addressed it to Erdman at his parent's farm and slid the letter inside. She licked the envelope and sealed it shut. Within it were so many of her hopes and dreams.

She took out a stamp from the drawer and affixed it to the envelope.

She looked at the clock, and knew that she could get the letter into the post right away. The postman was just coming up the lane.

* * *

Erdman had received letters from Clara, but had tossed them aside, just as he had done to her. She no longer held any interest for him, nor was there any challenge anymore. She was not so compliant anymore either. He had gotten what he wanted. He had claimed her most prized possession, her virginity. After that, besides a few more tumbles in the hay, there was nothing more to hold his interest. He had always found her dull and uncultured. Though he hated to admit it, without his little brother in tow, Clara was a complete bore.

He had moved on, and wished that Clara would move on as well. He was looking forward to going back to school so he could get away from the farm and the ever-present shadow of Clara trying to entwine him into a tangled mess of a relationship. She was a clinging vine, and he hated that in a woman.

Only a few more days and he would be back at school. Only a few more days, he thought to himself as he looked at the calendar on the wall of the kitchen.

* * *

Bergin had tried not to interfere with what was happening, or for that matter what was not happening between Clara and his brother. He still felt guilty that he had said something to Clara about that dance. The look on her face cut him to the quick. He found out that Erdman had asked someone else.

He felt like such a prize fool for opening his mouth and ruining things for Clara.

Maybe it was better in the long run. Clara was able at last to see Erdman for the cad he was. She was so innocent and trusting, and Erdman was completely rotten. Maybe now Clara was at last free to find someone worthy of her.

It was late in the day when Bergin came into the house to wash up before dinner. He picked off the dried leaves that had clung to his shirt, and went to toss them in the trash bin. In the bin he found two discarded letters from Clara addressed to Erdman. She had written her name and return address on at least one of the letters. He picked them out of the waste papers and looked them over.

They were both unopened.

"What on earth?" He said aloud. "Maybe Erdman didn't mean to toss them out." He tucked them into his back pocket and went to look for Erdman and give them to him.

Erdman was resting under a tree in the orchard, a bottle of beer in his hand, and a few empties scattered about him. His eyelids were drooping as if half asleep.

Bergin guessed his brother was a little inebriated.

"Oh! Gads, what the hell do you want?" Erdman's tone was surly.

"Did you know that you had some letters from Clara Lindgren?" He asked, ignoring his brother's rude tone of voice. He was about to reach into his back pocket for the letters when he paused, surprised by Erdman's answer.

"Don't want them. Don't care," he said, slurring his words. "Can't wait to get away from here and away from that clinging vine of a girl. Ugh." He motioned vaguely with the beer bottle, then as if seeing it for the first time in his hand, tipped back his head and poured the beer into his mouth with a satisfied moan.

"You don't want your letters then?" Bergin asked.

"Nope. Threw them out so they will be burned with the rest of the trash." He polished off the rest of his beer. "Don't give a darn what the lying creature has to say. It is over, ended, no more. If you want her, by all means, little brother, she is all yours." He tossed the empty bottle away.

Bergin sighed, knowing that Erdman had done the same to Clara. He was sorry he could do nothing about it. He did wonder why Erdman had said she was a liar though.

Disgusted with his brother's callousness and state of inebriation he walked away.

He touched the letters in his pocket and thought about what to do with them. He was not a snoop. He didn't want to pry into her business. But something told him not to toss them away. So Bergin decided to keep Clara's letters to his brother. He was not sure just what to do about them. He didn't really want to read them, but he couldn't let them be burned unopened.

He tucked them away in a drawer in his nightstand. He would ponder the options, and see what happened in the next few days.

CHAPTER 19

Clara was getting anxious. She had not heard back from Erdman after writing the letter with her news of the baby. She wondered what she would do next. Write to him again in case the letter had been misdirected? Go see if she could find him and confront him? No, she couldn't do that. She would give him another chance. She decided she better write to him again and tell him that she might have to write to his parents if he didn't respond.

Clara did not hear from Erdman even after she wrote to him again, saying she would have to go see his parents, hoping they would make him do the right thing in marrying her. She hoped that she would hear from him.

Again, the days passed and no letter came for her.

Ingmar would give her a worried look and ask her what was wrong, but Clara would only shake her head and say nothing was wrong.

"Clara, I know something is wrong," she insisted.

"What could you possibly know?" Clara asked her little sister, afraid she might have guessed about the little stranger growing in her womb.

"I know that your young man has not been by to take you out lately. Did you two have a row of some kind?" She looked up into her sister's face, hoping for a reply.

"I don't know what's the matter." Clara burst into tears and ran out into the orchard to be alone with her grief.

Ingmar followed her sister.

"Where has he been then?" Ingmar touched her sister's arm lightly. "Everything was going so well for you both."

Clara could not hold back the flood of her emotions any longer. She looked at her sister's concerned expression and something in her broke away, and she began to let it all go, flooding over her, washing her away.

"I am afraid he has grown tired of me. I have written him, and he is mute. He makes no reply at all, and I'm not able to do anything about it. I can't just go over there and make him talk to me. What would his family say?" She spat out the words mixed with anger, pain, fear and frustration.

"I wish I could do something to help."

"So do I, but there is nothing anyone can do if he will not write to me or even come by to see me." She wiped away the tears that fell from her eyes with her fingers. "Women have to be content to sit and wait for the man to make the first move. I fear he has forgotten me."

"But he cared so much, didn't he?" Ingmar asked, fiddling with her braided hair.

"I don't know anymore. Maybe he grew bored with me. Maybe he found someone more his own age. Maybe he just does not want to be with me anymore." She looked up at the sky as if asking God why. Clara's voice was ragged from crying. "I just know that he is not around anymore, and I am powerless to do anything that will make him come to me as he should."

"You should go over there and make him tell you what's wrong." She furrowed her brow.

"Silly, foolish, innocent child. It's just not that easy," Clara replied, recalling the conversation again she overheard at Beno's, and of the news she had told him. Maybe he had just used her and when the child got to growing he dumped her, as so many men have done to women for centuries. He had used her and tossed her aside. She hated the thought that she had been so foolish, so compliant and so easily taken in by him.

It angered her that she had fallen for his lies. Bergin had tried to warn her, but she thought it was different for herself and Erdman. What a fool she had been.

She walked away from her sister without looking back.

This time Ingmar did not follow her sister.

* * *

Clara knew that she now had no other choice.

Erdman's silence conveyed to her that he was not going to respond to her letters. That he was not going to do the right thing without some prodding. She had to write to Erdman's folks. Surely they would make him take up his responsibilities for her and the child. Wouldn't they? If they were decent folk they would make him do the right thing.

Her hand trembled as she dipped the pen into the ink and began to write.

It was a difficult letter to pen, but after a few tries she managed to get it completed. She threw the rejected attempts into the kitchen stove, burning them, so no one would find them.

She left her letter to Erdman's parents in the post box for the postman to collect.

Clara knew they would get her letter early the next morning.

She wondered what their reaction would be.

CHAPTER 20

Clara did not hear from his folks either. But there was a letter waiting for her by the afternoon post. Erdman had written to her, at last.

Ingmar happened upon her as she was sitting on the floor of their room in a puddle of sunlight. Clara was crying. In her hands she held a letter. It was many pages thick, and was written in purple ink on cream paper. Scattered about her were a number of other letters, again all written in that purple ink on the creamy bond paper.

Clara looked up at Ingmar and held out the letter in her hand.

"Erdman has written to me, at last," her voice was ragged.

"Clara, what did he have to say? Why are you crying?" She scrambled onto the floor next to her sister.

"I was sitting here re-reading all the letters he has written to me. See, I've kept them all," Clara didn't answer her sister's question. Instead she picked up some of the letters that lay in her lap.

"Clara, what did he say in his letter?" Ingmar looked at her sister with a worried expression. "Can you tell me?" She implored.

"He begins, *Dear Friend*." Clara took a deep breath to calm herself and read from the letter.

"Dear friend? What is that supposed to mean?" Ingmar said in an impatient tone. "After all the time you have spent together, he writes *dear friend*?"

Clara could hardly look at her sister. She continued reading.

"I suppose you must think me awfully neglectful of you, but I haven't been at all." She swallowed hard before reading some more. "I've been to the hospital for a while where I had a couple of operations." Clara broke into another fit of crying, dropping her hand that held the letter to her lap.

"That's still not a good enough excuse for him not to have not been around or even written to you." A look of anger creased Ingmar's young face. "If he had been ill, why didn't he let you know? Or at least, why didn't his brother get word to you?" Ingmar scowled.

Clara started to laugh at her sister's expression. That only confused Ingmar more, and she made another face that sent Clara into more peals of laughter.

"Clara, what are you laughing at?" She demanded to know. "What is suddenly so funny?"

"You are, Ingmar. Your expression was just so incongruent with your demeanor that I couldn't help but laugh. Anger is not an expression you wear gracefully." Clara wiped her tears, glad of the relief her sister had brought, even though she hadn't planned it that way.

"Well, what does he want then?" Ingmar gestured to the letter.

"He wants me to meet him." Clara looked down at the letter in her hand.

"Well, that is a good thing. Isn't it?"

"I suppose," Clara said thinking a moment before she spoke again. "You have to keep mum about this though."

"Okay. I'll do my best." Ingmar nodded her eyes wide with curiosity.

"He wants me to meet him, so we can elope," Clara whispered with her head down, not meeting her sister's gaze.

"Elope?" Ingmar squealed with delight. "You mean it? He wants to marry you then?" She beamed a big smile at her sister.

Clara immediately hushed her, telling her to keep her voice down. She needed to make up her mind if this was what she wanted to do. If it was, if she was going to meet him, then she wanted to surprise her parents when she came home a bride.

"Of course you'll come home his bride!" Ingmar said. "Isn't that what you've been wishing for all these many months?"

"I never said my wishes out loud." Clara stiffened a little, her eyes traveling to the dried bouquet of flowers on her dresser. The ones she had caught at the wedding nearly nine months ago. Even though they were brown and shriveled, they still held a promise of hope that one day she would be the one to toss her flowers to another hopeful young woman.

"I could tell. I knew that was what you wanted. You deserve to be married and happy, Clara." Ingmar wrapped her arms about her sister, kissing her on the cheek. Then sitting back, she looked at her sister as another thought strayed into her mind. "So why were you crying?"

"He gave instructions that I was to burn all these letters." She looked about at the letters around her on the floor.

"Why?" Ingmar cantered her head a little, searching Clara's face.

"I don't know," Clara replied, frowning as she looked at the litter of letters scattered about her.

"Will you?" Ingmar asked as she picked up one of the letters still tucked neatly in its envelope.

"Yes. I think I must, so, if he asks me I cannot lie to him." She picked up a letter and slipped the note from the envelope. "I thought I might read them all again, just one last time," she sighed.

"I'll be right here with you if you want." She reached out to touch Clara's hand.

"Yes, that would be sweet of you. I don't think I could do it alone." Clara took her sister's hand in hers and gave it a squeeze before letting it go.

Tears began falling down her cheeks again.

She assured Ingmar that they were tears of joy mixed with tears of sadness. Each envelope she picked up, caressed the letter, and reread the words written that had been her lifeline for nearly the past year. She gave them up one by one to the small fire in the grate, but she clung to the envelopes. She couldn't destroy every trace of him. Ingmar watched silently as Clara tucked the envelopes back under the rug where she had been keeping the letters.

"He said to burn this one too. But I can't. Not yet. Maybe I will after we have gotten married. I just can't let this one go up in flames as yet." She clutched that letter to her heart.

"When will he come for you?" She asked softly.

"At midnight." She looked into Ingmar's eyes for a moment before looking away again. "That is, if I decide to go."

"Why wouldn't you?" Ingmar questioned her sister. "You love him, don't you?"

"I'm not really sure." She gave a wan smile to Ingmar. "That is something I'll need to sort out in the next few hours."

"Well, I will leave you to it then." Ingmar stood up, and kissed the top of her sister's head. "No matter what you choose to do, know that I love you very much."

"I love you, too, Ingmar," Clara smiled at her.

Ingmar turned and left the room. Clara carefully secreted the remaining letter away where only she knew where it was and pondered her decision while she waited until it was midnight.

CHAPTER 21

Clara had wrestled with the idea of eloping. She knew that if nothing else, for the sake of her unborn child, she would need to get married. She could figure out her own feelings later. There were times when she loved Erdman so very dearly, and at other times, she didn't know what she felt for him.

She dressed carefully in her new undergarments, shoes and stockings she had been keeping in her hope chest for the day when she would finally need them. She had chosen to wear her favorite coat dress in the pretty fall colors that she had made for a dance they had attended a few months ago. It had been more temperate then, so she knew she would need her warmer coat.

She was ready.

She looked about the room for what she hoped would be a last time as an unmarried woman. She saw her vial of perfume on her dressing table and decided to take it with her. She dabbed a little behind her ears and dropped it into her purse. This was the perfume she wore the night they met. He had said it confused him.

She smiled at the memory.

As an afterthought she opened the small box where she kept her jewelry. She had a few necklaces and a pin her mother had given her. She decided upon the pearls. Simple, elegant, and understated. She slipped them about her neck and closed the lid of the box. She could collect the other things later on when she returned.

She knew what she was to do. Erdman had given her instructions. It was time now to go. She didn't dare miss their appointed rendezvous. The house was quiet, her sister was breathing quietly in the bed, held gently in slumber. Clara had heard her brothers settle down at last, and listened as her mother put away her clothes and climbed into bed. She had not heard her father come upstairs yet.

She couldn't wait anymore. Her heart thumped loudly in her chest, she felt sure everyone would waken to so much noise.

She crept down the stairs trying to avoid the treads that

squeaked.

Her father was sitting in the parlor reading, it was late. She slipped past him silently and thought she heard him ask if she was going out.

"Yes, Papa, I'm just going out for a quick breath of fresh air and to take care of what is necessary," Clara said softly as she opened the front door. She hated that she had to lie to him. She had never lied to him before. She had left a note upstairs on her dressing table. They would read it in the morning and know she was gone. She would tell them everything when she came home with her husband. Then her father would understand why she hadn't told him, or really said goodbye.

She thought she heard him trudge up the stairs as she slipped out the door. She looked back once and the house was quiet.

And she was gone.

She saw the headlamps come up the roadway, then watched as he doused their brightness. She heard the car pull up, only a soft muffled crunch of the gravel in the soft soil under the tires. The car idled in a muddy patch of the drive. As she walked out to greet him, she worried about the soft mud ruining her new shoes.

She opened the door and climbed into the car, and they were away.

BOOK TWO

CHAPTER 22

Christian Lindgren had fallen asleep in his chair in the parlor. The newspaper that he had been reading had fallen to his lap and some to the floor. The kerosene lamp was low. Something had awakened him. He saw his daughter standing in the doorway. She looked so pretty.

"Clara, are you all right?" He asked her in a soft voice, still not sure if he was awake or dreaming. He had such vivid dreams at times. He looked over at the clock. It was five minutes to midnight.

"Yes, Papa, I'm just going out for a quick breath of fresh air and to take care of what is necessary." She said as she opened the front door and pushed open the screen door.

"Good night, then." He stood up, blew out the lamp and headed for the stairs. The screen door slammed shut behind her. Clara was heading down the front steps when he noticed some automobile headlamps in the distance. *Who would be out at this time of night?* The lights disappeared, but he thought he saw the automobile turn at the end of their lane. He couldn't make out that anyone was in the vehicle, though it looked familiar. He closed the door, and trudged up the stairs to bed.

He slipped easily into sleep, but his dreams were restless.

After what had seemed to be just a little while, he woke feeling a great tightness and weight of despair press down on him. He woke his wife and asked her if she had heard Clara come to bed.

"I think she did," she mumbled half asleep.

He slipped back into sleep himself and began to dream.

He got up out of bed, pale light was filtering in through the windows, the dawn was coming. He heard the sound of the rooster crowing in the barnyard. He walked past his daughter's room and looked in. Ingmar was sleeping, but there was no Clara. He became frightened and fought to tear away the delicate mesh of sleep that held him fast.

He sat up in bed, waking his wife again. He heard the clock strike the hour of four. He had gotten only a few hours of sleep.

"What's the matter?" She asked, rolling over to face him.

"Bertha, would you go see if Clara is in her room?" He asked in a hushed voice. He was afraid to voice his fears too audibly. "I have the most terrible feeling that she is gone. Forever," he trembled as he spoke the last word.

Bertha Lindgren put on her robe and slippers and headed down the hall to look in their daughter's room. She saw Ingmar sleeping peacefully, but she was alone in the bed. Clara was not there.

She hurried back down the hallway to her bedroom, closing the door softly behind her. Her heart pounding.

"Christian, she is not there," Bertha said to him, climbing back under the warm covers. "Clara is not in her room."

"Bertha, I have a feeling that we shall never see her again." He buried his face in his hands and wanted to weep.

"Oh, no. Please, not our Clara." She reached for him to comfort him in her arms as much as to be comforted herself. "Maybe she is outside; we better go have a look."

He nodded in agreement, but somehow he knew it would be an exercise in futility. He lit a lantern and they took a look about the house and then around the barn and yard, and even in the privy.

There was no sign of Clara anywhere.

A rooster crowed as a pale glow of light began to color the distant horizon.

CHAPTER 23

Mrs. Halverson was kneading the bread on the oak kitchen table. Bergin carried in another load of firewood for the stove so she could fix breakfast. He saw a letter on the counter.

"What's this, Mother?"

"What's what?" She replied, her words punctuated by her fists pounding the bread into a workable mass.

"This letter?" He thought he recognized the handwriting.

"It come the other day. Nothing for you to worry about. It's just trash," she said without looking over to where he was pointing. "I will put it to the flame."

"What do you mean, trash?" He was puzzled. He picked up the letter and slipped it from the envelope. He glanced quickly at the signature. It was from Clara. "Why is Clara Lindgren writing to you, Mother?"

"You know who she is?" She paused in her work to look at him with a sour expression. "You know this trash? Disgusting." She looked him up and down as if he was some sort of infestation. Then turned back to her work.

"Yes, she is a girl Erdman has been seeing for a while now." He held the letter out a little distance almost pointing to her with it.

"What's that? You say your brother knows her?" She placed her fists on her hips in a defiant pose, her eyes scrutinizing Bergin. She was frowning.

"Yes." He looked back at his mother, surprised by her hostility.

"Pfh," she made a sound of disgust and turned back to the bread, working it aggressively with her strong hands. "Little bit of baggage thinks she can entrap our Erdman into a marriage with some story of a child. Claims it's his. As if your brother could do something like that."

"Like what?" Bergin narrowed his eyes at his mother. He knew a lot more about his brother's activities than his mother did. She still thought he was an innocent boy. Nothing could be further from the truth. He had not been innocent since the supposed accident in the barn with the other little boy. His brother was nothing like the image his mother held of him, and she would hear nothing of the truth either.

"Erdman could not get some tramp in a family way." She punched the dough. "Probably just wants to get her hands on his money, knows he will inherit some day."

"She's not that sort of girl." He rubbed a place by his heart; it seemed to ache deep inside. He thought of Clara. She was anything but a gold digger, and she had been the innocent one in this scenario, not Erdman.

"What makes you suddenly an expert, young man?" She paused again and looked up to scowl at him. "Just who is this piece of trash who wants to trap your brother? Someone we never heard of. He never mentioned her, he never brought her around, so who is she? No one, nothing." She made like she wanted to spit, and puffed the air out her lips. She turned back to the bread, giving it one last fold and kneed before dropping it back into the bowl; she covered it with the damp towel and set it on the counter near the stove to rise again.

Bergin read the letter as his mother finished preparing the bread for the second rise. A tightness grabbed at his heart as he read her words.

Dear Mr. and Mrs. Halverson,

I am sure you folks will be surprised to hear from me, and what I have to say. Know that I am a good friend of your son Erdman, and am sorry to say that we are in a pinch and have to get married, if God is willing, and you folks are willing to help us.

I wrote Erdman a letter some time ago and told him I wanted to see him, but have not seen him come down. I saw him with you folks at the church on Sunday, but did not have a chance to speak with him. Please ask him to come down one day or night this week so I can talk to him.

Also let me hear a few words from you.

I do not like to get Erdman in trouble so I hope you folks will help us before my folks find out what's coming. Please, be good to Erdman. I know he never meant to leave me in this way. It is only four months left now until I will be delivering so I hope Erdman and I can get married this month and make our life worthwhile.

Will close with love and God's blessings.

Clara Lindgren.

P. S. Excuse the writing as I am in haste and am hoping to hear from you and see Erdman soon.

Bergin folded the letter carefully and put it back into the envelope as his brother Erdman strolled into the kitchen. He noticed the letter in Bergin's hand and looked away quickly.

"What do you have to say about this, brother?" Bergin waved the letter under Erdman's nose.

"I never seen the girl." Erdman batted it out of the way as if he was afraid it could infect him with a dread disease. "Don't know anything about her." He crossed the room and stood so that their mother was between them.

"Erdman!" Bergin said a little louder than he planned.

"Bergin, watch the tone you use talking to your brother. He done nothing to you." She waggled a finger in his face.

"Erdman, it is Clara, you know you are the only man she has been with," Bergin protested, tempering his tone for his mother. He did not want to feel the back of her hand.

"So you do know her?" Their mother raised her eyebrows as she looked at her eldest boy.

"Well, yeah, I met her a few times."

"A few times? It was much more than that." Bergin was not going to let his brother get away with lying to his mother if he could help it. "You seduced her under the tree at the dance at Trainer."

Erdman scowled at his brother but said nothing.

Their mother eyed the two of them for a moment before speaking. "If this really is yours, get her to come see us, we can have a doctor look her over."

"It's not mine. She got her dates mixed." He lifted the cover on the bread bowl; his mother swatted his hand away. "Can't be anything to do with me." Erdman began to twist a fancy diamond ring on his finger, around and around.

Bergin noticed the ring. Erdman glared at him as a warning to keep his mouth shut. Bergin rolled his eyes. Bergin knew that his parents did not know about the bootlegging and the amount of cash Erdman always seemed to have. He had earned in a month, more money than their father had made in any good year. He knew the ring was a reward Erdman had given himself, a gambler's ring. He liked to sparkle, and the ring said it more than anything else.

Mrs. Halverson reached up and patted Erdman's cheek affectionately.

"Erdman is little more than a boy; he's not even fully grown yet. I'm sure it is all a mistake." She stood on tiptoe and planted a kiss on Erdman's cheek. "There'll be plenty of time for girls and marriage in the future." Then she turned and glowered at Bergin before going to work at the stove preparing their breakfast.

Bergin shot an angry look at his brother before leaving the room. One day all his brother's many indiscretions would catch up with him and he wondered how his mother would react. He stood in the hall and realized the letter was still in his hand. He looked at it again. He was not about to let it go up in flames.

Something was going on, and he meant to get to the bottom of it. Clara was a good person, and Erdman was a selfish prig. He would keep the letter for now, keep it with the others Erdman had tossed in the trash unopened.

He felt a sudden chill rack his being. Were they still where he had left them?

He headed up to his room to see if the letters were still where he had secreted them. Clara's letters to Erdman. Probably telling him about the child and asking him to be an honorable man.

He sighed. His brother was anything but honorable.

He came into this room and closed the door. He didn't want anyone to know he still had Clara's correspondences.

He reached into the place he had hidden them away.

The letters were just as he had left them. He touched them gently. He still could not bring himself to open the letters. Not yet.

He had a feeling that before long, he would have to.

He knew that his mother would wonder later where that letter had gone, and so might Erdman. He had to let them think he burned it. He took a piece of writing paper from his desk and an envelope. He went back down stairs to the kitchen. Erdman was sitting at the table drinking coffee, and their mother was cooking some eggs.

Bergin opened one of the covers on the wood burning stove at the back, and tossed the letter into the flames, trying not to smile at his duplicity. He had never done anything so dishonest, but in the long run it might prove to be the better thing to do.

"Sorry, I forgot to put this in the flame. Get rid of it, like you wanted." He replaced the iron cover, and looked at his mother with a blank expression.

"Good boy," she nodded at him. "You know we got to take care of our Erdman." She turned to look at Erdman, who smiled back at his mother, but made no eye contact with Bergin.

CHAPTER 24

The morning was cloudy; a chilly wind blew in from the north, scented with a hint of the cold that would soon follow as winter approached.

"Have you seen our Clara?" Mr. Lindgren asked of his children as they assembled around the breakfast table. "I not see her this morning."

The boys shook their heads no, but Ingmar pulled a note from her pocket and placed it on the table next to her father's plate.

"I found this on her dressing table when I dressed this morning." She slid into her chair. She had read the note. She had read some of the letter Erdman had sent Clara the day before. She was with her sister as she burned his letters, keeping only the envelopes, secreting them away under a corner of the carpeting in their room. Ingmar did not feel that this was the time to tell all of this to her father.

She felt her father's eyes on her and reluctantly she looked up into his pale, blue eyes. He nodded slowly, then he touched the folded sheet of paper gently.

"You know, I had a dream last night. About Clara," Christian Lindgren said with a touch of sadness to his voice. He still spoke in a thick accent of his native Sweden where he had been born.

"Did it come true yet?"

"Yah. It happened in the night. Your mother knows." He looked over at her as she placed a platter of food before him and took her seat across the table from him. Bertha simply nodded and took her napkin from the silver napkin ring and placed it in her lap. He picked up the note to read it. Christian's hands trembled as he read the words his daughter had written.

I didn't know I was going until late this afternoon, but couldn't make up my mind until now. Please don't take it seriously, as it will mean nothing, only a little surprise. I am taken good care of and will be back soon.

Lovingly,

Your Clara.

"Did she go off with him?" Bertha Lindgren asked as she passed the platter of sausages to Ingmar after taking some herself. "This boy she was seeing?"

"Yes," Ingmar blinked back tears.

"Tell me what happened." Her father patted her hand gently. He was not angry with her.

"Yesterday, Clara got a letter from Erdman," Ingmar managed to say without breaking into tears. Soon they betrayed her and began to fill her eyes and fall down her cheeks. Before she could continue, her brother looked up, surprised.

"Erdman? You mean Erdman Halverson?" Her brother, Peter asked in an annoyed tone of voice as he skewered a sausage with his fork and wrapped it in a piece of warm bread.

"Yes, Erdman Halverson," Ingmar replied. Her brother's tone set her on edge.

"I heard of him," Hal said with a shake of his head. "That guy always was bad news." He sliced a piece off his sausage and put it in his mouth, chewing slowly as he remembered Erdman Halverson. His displeasure showed on his face.

"He always thought he was better then the rest of us in school," Peter said, taking a bite of his sausage.

"Yeah, used to brag that he was going to go to college and get the heck away from the farm," Hal added with his mouth half full.

"He was always on the edge of trouble, too." Peter waved his bread-wrapped sausage at his brother across the table.

"His parents always bailed him out of whatever mess he got himself into." Hal took a sip of coffee to wash down his breakfast.

"Remember the supposed accident in their barn with the Stenns boy?" Peter said, before taking another bite of his food.

"What accident?" Ingmar asked, looking back and forth between her brothers. She had never heard any of the news about Erdman. She had thought he was a nice man because Clara had chosen to date him. Suddenly, she was worried about Clara.

"Yes, what accident are you talking about?" Christian Lindgren asked his son. He had heard something about an accidental death of a child many years ago, and something about the Halverson boy being involved. But he had not known which of their sons had been involved.

"He shot the boy while they were supposedly playing in the barn," Hal replied, placing his cup on the table with a decided thump for emphasis. "Claimed he didn't know it was a loaded gun."

"Sometimes little ones don't always know about guns," Mr. Lindgren said in defense of the child.

"Come on, the kid won all the marksman contests at the fair every year. He knew guns well enough to know it was loaded." Hal shook his head. "Remember how none of us could ever compete? He was a crack shot."

"The sheriff ruled it an accident, if you remember," Christian spoke up, waving a hand to signal the boys to slow down their speculative conversation.

"Only after Erdman's father pressured the sheriff to drop any charges." Peter ignored his father's caution.

"We don't know that for sure," Christian Lindgren remembered it all too well.

"No, we don't, but I recall Erdman bragging about how his dad told the sheriff what to do." He gave his father a knowing look. "We were all in school together, and Erdman's big mouth was not something one could avoid hearing when he was flapping his jaws."

"It was a terrible thing that happened. It tore apart the community as the Stenns family mourned the loss of their only son. They sold their farm and moved west; to Washington State, I believe it was," Bertha Lindgren said in a quiet voice.

"You say our sister was stepping out with that Halverson guy?" Peter narrowed his eyes at Ingmar as he aggressively bit off another hunk of his sausage.

"She had been seeing him for a while," her tone was hushed.

"So, a letter from him came yesterday?" Bertha asked her daughter.

"Yes, he sent her a letter yesterday; it arrived about two in the afternoon." Ingmar pushed the eggs around her plate with a piece of bread. Her appetite was gone.

"Tell me what happened, daughter." Christian looked into her eyes; a little smile of encouragement crinkled the skin around his eyes.

Ingmar nodded slowly before she began to relate the events of the day before.

"Clara began to cry as she read the letter from Erdmann. This time he had written her a long letter. Usually his letters were pretty brief. She always wanted him to have written more, but she was happy to have heard from him at all," her words poured out of her in a torrent that she was unable to stem.

"What did this letter look like?" Her father asked.

"It was a cream paper and was written in purple ink. He always wrote all his letters to her in that color ink." She smiled a little as she recalled the many letters of purple ink that had so pleased her sister. "I guess he must have said something about burning his old letters, because I sat and watched as she burned them in the grate. But she couldn't burn the envelopes, nor that last letter."

"What did she do with the envelopes and letter?" Bertha asked, knowing how sentimental Clara could be about things like letters and mementos.

"We secreted the envelopes away under the carpeting in our room. The letter, well, she tucked that in her dress, close to her heart." She mimed the action of placing the letter in her bodice and patting her heart. "She didn't say much for the rest of the day. She was trying to decide just what to do, so she said."

"She was pretty quiet when she helped with the evening milking," her father commented. "She didn't say much at supper either."

"I asked her if she was all right, I remember, and she said she was fine, just trying to make up her mind about something," her mother recalled.

"She was trying to make up her mind about going off with him," Ingmar said in a hushed voice. She knew she shouldn't be telling them so much. Clara wanted her to keep it all quiet, but seeing her parent's faces she couldn't keep mum any longer.

"Then, I saw her go out of the house last night about midnight." He scratched his scraggly, white beard. "I do think I saw automobile headlights come up near the lane. Then it was suddenly dark, like the lights were put out and I couldn't tell for sure."

"We should go see if we can locate tire tracks or something. The ground has been pretty soft from the rains," her brother spoke up.

"Yes, that might tell us if there was an automobile." Christian Lindgren rose and walked to the door in trancelike movements.

He still could not believe his favorite child was gone.

* * *

"It was about here that I think that I saw the car," he said pointing to the lane.

"Here, look, here. Don't those look like shoe prints?" His son Peter asked.

"Yah, yah they do. About Clara's size too," Christian Lindgren replied looking closely at the impressions in the soft ground. He touched the imprint gently.

"Here, look, tire treads." Hal knelt by a rut newly made in the mud. "Hey, does that look like the tire might have been patched at all?"

"It does," Peter nodded in agreement.

"How about we go see what's up at Halverson's place. See if this Erdman is home; see if Clara is there and if his car has a patched tire," Peter said, hands on his hips, and an angry scowl on his face.

* * *

Bergin was walking across the barnyard when two men drove up the lane of the Halverson farm. He raised a hand in greeting as they parked the car.

"You Erdman Halverson?" The tall one called to him, getting out of the car.

"No. I'm his brother Bergin Halverson. What can I do for you?" He looked the two men over as they climbed out of their car. He sensed that they were angry about something, and guessed that his brother must owe them money or something.

"We're Clara's brothers." He pointed to himself and the other fellow. "Peter and Hal," he said it as if Bergin should be intimidated.

"Good to meet you. I'm very fond of Clara. She is an exceptional woman." Bergin extended his hand and each of the brothers hesitantly shook his hand. They looked a little confused by his greeting.

"Yah, we think so, too." Peter folded his arms across his chest.

"Were you looking for my brother then?" Bergin asked raising his eyebrows. He wondered what these two could want. The thought crossed his mind that they also knew about Clara's condition and had come to get the father to make him marry their sister with a shotgun as best man.

"Your brother anywhere about?" Peter asked.

"Yeah, I saw him go in the barn. Why?" Bergin stopped to look at who had come, shielding his eyes from the angle of the sun.

"We wanted to speak to him about something," Hal said

"About our sister Clara," Peter said uncrossing his arms. It was like they spoke in tandem completing one another's sentences.

"Is your sister all right?" Bergin's tone conveyed his concern.

"That's what we come to inquire about," Peter replied looking Bergin over.

"I don't understand," Bergin furrowed his brow and looked back and forth between the brothers. "Why would you come here to ask about her?"

Erdman came out of the barn and looked over at his brother and the men standing by the car. He made no move to come over to where they stood.

"Erd, these are Clara's brothers, Peter and Hal," Bergin introduced them and watched his brother's face. Bergin wondered what was going on, first that letter from her to their mother and now her brothers had come to ask about her. He wondered where Clara was. He waited for Erdman to answer.

"Oh? What can I do for you?" Erdman said, casually looking them over, but not moving from where he stood.

"Have you seen our sister?" Peter asked his voice was gruff.

"No," Erdman said with a laugh.

"She is not at home this morning," Hal said. "So, we come here to look for her."

"Why would you think she would be here?" Bergin asked. This was all too baffling for him. Clara would not have come here with Erdman, especially after what he had said about not knowing her well.

"You're wasting your time. She's not here." Erdman turned to walk away.

"We know all about it, Halverson," Hal chimed in. "She was supposed to meet you last night."

"Me?" Erdman turned to face them again and pointed to his chest and raised an eyebrow. "Last night?" He shook his head and mouthed a silent *no*. He reached down and broke off a long stalk of grass and put it in his mouth.

"We also want to see your car. The mud on our drive captured a pretty clear imprint of a tire tread," Peter demanded. He was not someone people argued with.

"It had a very distinct patch on one of the tires. We wanted to see if it was yours," Hal added. They both stood hands on their hips waiting for Erdman to reply.

"Be my guest," Erdman shrugged and motioned in the direction of his car parked along side the house. He followed behind the boys as they looked the car over and checked his tires.

Bergin thought he had seen a momentary shadow cross his brother's countenance. It had been fleeting, so he couldn't be sure. Erdman seemed unruffled by their visit; and maybe a little too cool and unconcerned. Bergin tried to remember what had happened last night. Did he hear his brother go out or not? If Erdman did go out late, when had he returned?

He joined the Lindgren brothers as they inspected the Hudson's tires.

"Hey, these are all brand new," Peter said in an angry tone.

"When did you get new tires?" Hal demanded.

"What difference does it make?" Erdman gestured, palms up and open to the sky.

"To us, it makes plenty a difference," Peter's reply was tart.

"Oh, I guess a few days, maybe." Erdman scratched his chin in thought.

Bergin looked closer at the tires. He tried to recall if his brother had been working on the car lately.

"They don't look like they have been used at all." Hal took a step closer to Erdman who stepped back a little.

"Brand new and I would bet they were changed in the last few hours, not days." Peter also took a step closer to Erdman, his hands balled into fists. "They don't got no dirt on them all around. Like no one drove on them, if you see what I mean."

"Think what you like," Erdman said with a little nervous tremolo to his voice. "I replaced them a few days ago. I just have not had to drive anywhere since then." He flashed a look at his brother and back again at the Lindgren boys.

Bergin did not miss the look his brother shot him. It was as if he should know something. But what? He couldn't remember right now.

"We know she was to meet you last night," Hal said.

"Sorry, couldn't have been me," Erdman smirked back at them as he chewed on the stalk of grass. He turned and walked back into the barn.

"We're not done with you, Halverson," Peter stated, not trying to hide the menace he was feeling toward Erdman Halverson.

"We will be watching you," Hal said.

"We will find out what happened to our sister, one way or another." Peter waved his fist at Erdman. "If we find you had anything to do with any harm coming to her, your life won't be worth a plug nickel. Do you understand me?"

"I don't take kindly to threats made by oversized oafs." Erdman backed away from Peter who was breathing heavily, his anger palpable.

"Just so you know, Halverson, this is not a threat, it is a promise." He flashed Erdman a nasty smile.

Erdman ducked into the barn like a scolded child. No one made a move to follow him. They turned their attention to Bergin.

"Bergin, you let us know if you see her?" Hal asked with a nod of his head.

"Yes, I will." He nodded as well. "Please let me know when you find her, and where she has gone." He had a cold feeling that was growing in his gut. He was worried for Clara. She was not the type to go off without letting someone know, or for that matter, she probably would not have gone off alone.

The boys climbed back in their car and drove out the drive.

Bergin stood silently, watching as their car disappeared down the lane, a cloud of dust kicking up behind them, obscuring them from his vision.

Erdman walked back out of the barn once he heard they had gone and plopped himself down on the running-board and ran his fingers through his hair.

Bergin looked over at his brother with a worried expression.

"Erdman, what have you done?" Bergin almost whispered, afraid of what he was thinking his brother was capable of doing.

"Me? Done? Nothing, Bergin. Nothing at all." He got up and walked away from his brother without so much as a glance back over his shoulder.

Bergin looked again at the automobile and the new tires. They did look like they had never seen a revolution in the dusty barnyard, let alone the muddy roads. He walked about the car, and saw in the ground what looked like the impression of the car jack.

"What is going on?" He whispered to himself out loud. "Where is Clara?"

Bergin's mind turned to the letters his brother had so carelessly tossed aside. Maybe he should read them now.

CHAPTER 25

The day was hot. The humidity hung thick in the air. A haze seemed to encapsulate the land and everything seemed to shimmer as if a mirage. It was too late in the year for it to be so warm. This was what people called Indian summer. A final last burst of warmth before the cold gained mastery.

"This is the sort of day Clara would have loved," Christian Lindgren said in a sad tone as he sat in the shade on the porch next to his wife. "I hope wherever she is, she is able to enjoy the warmth of this day," he said it almost as a prayer.

"What are we going to do, Christian?" Bertha looked at her husband.

"I don't know," he shook his head. He was weary from sleepless nights worrying about where Clara was. He would pace for hours, and still be too restless to sleep when he did go to bed. He stood up and walked to the railing of the porch, looking out at the fields nearing harvest time. "I think we should go see the sheriff. Maybe he can help us find where she has gone."

"You want I should go with you?" She asked, coming to stand by him, patting his rough, calloused hand.

"Is good. You come, keep me from losing my temper if he is no help." He smiled at her, and kissed her cheek. "You know why I love our Clara so much more than the others?" He looked into her eyes.

"No." She shook her head.

"Because she is the one most like you, her momma." He caressed her soft cheek. "She is always so smart, so sweet and so good in the heart. Just like you, and I love her, and I love you." He touched her cheek and brushed a few stray hairs from her face.

"I love you too, Christian." She gently wiped his tears as they fell down his cheeks. "I never regret one day I have spent being married to you."

He did something bold then, he took her into his arms and kissed her. He had always been a reticent man, and was never very demonstrative with his affections. They held onto one another in an embrace for a moment before he spoke again, his voice revealed his darkest thoughts.

"I don't know what I would do if anything happened to either of you." He stepped back and looked at her again. He blinked back tears that flooded to his eyes. He was afraid to express his worst fears.

They stood in silence, looking out together at the panorama before them. Each remembering the years they had spent together, the joys and the sorrows that had been their lives. It had been a good life with little turmoil and little trouble, until now.

"Well, let's go see if the Sheriff can help us at all," he said patting her hand.

* * *

Frank De Boer had been sheriff for the last four years. It was a job that he had found hadn't been too terribly taxing. The biggest crime spree he'd had to deal with was the theft of two horses, and five head of cattle and it had been an easy crime to solve. He didn't, however, have much experience with missing persons. Christian and Bertha Lindgren sat across the desk from him telling him about their daughter, who had gone off in the night and had not been seen or heard from again in over a week.

"I don't know what to tell you folks. She probably went off, and will come back home soon." He tried to think why a shy young woman would go off and not return. "Maybe she went off to meet someone?"

"No, sir. The boy she had been seeing was still home the next morning. My boys go see for themselves," he argued.

"There really isn't too much we can do, officially, you understand."

"Can't you go look for her?" Bertha Lindgren spoke for the first time.

"We just don't have the manpower, or the resources to do anything for you." He shrugged, wishing he could help, or at least offer some hope for them. "Maybe you should hire a private investigator. He could dedicate himself to the task and maybe get some answers for you."

"You know where we can find one of these men?" Lindgren asked.

"Sure, I can give you the name of some operatives in Omaha from the Burns agency and the Pinkerton agency as well. Both are reputable companies with good men working for them." He searched in his drawer where he kept the names of private investigators, and wrote their addresses and numbers on a piece of paper. "I wish we could do more for you. Maybe one of these men can." He offered the paper to Mr. Lindgren.

"Well, we have to do something." Lindgren frowned. "Now, maybe we learn a little more when we do this thing you suggest, hire an investigator," he sighed as he accepted the paper De Boer handed him.

CHAPTER 26

Christian Lindgren sat at the table in the kitchen with his wife. He was still not sleeping well. He was worried more and more about Clara.

"It has been two weeks, Bertha, since our Clara left us," he sighed.

"Only two weeks? It seems so much longer." She shook her head, rose from her seat and walked to the stove. She took a clean cup from the drain board and filled it with coffee.

"Every day I think we are going to hear from her." He looked back at her, the tears filling his eyes. "And every day, nothing."

"Should we take the sheriff's advice and hire the man to look for her?"

"I don't know. I don't know what to do," he groaned. "Maybe I write to them today, see if they can help."

"I think that is a good idea, Christian," Bertha said, nodding her head slowly. "Then maybe we can get some news of her."

"I keep holding onto the hope we will hear from her. All I can do is worry."

"I too am worried about her. It's not like her to go away and not tell us." Bertha brought him a cup of coffee and sat at the table, wrapping her hands about her own warm cup. "Something must have been wrong for her to act like this."

"I am afraid of what I am thinking," He said peering into the coffee cup as if he would be able to scry the answer in the steam that rose from the dark-colored liquid.

"No, Christian, no. Please, don't even think that." She reached out and put her hand on his.

"If Clara was alive, she would have written to me. She is not afraid of me. No matter what was wrong, my Clara would have been able to tell me." He took his wife's hand in his as a tear plashed onto their coupled hands.

"Maybe I should go see this Erdman Halverson, see what he knows about my Clara," he said, taking a deep breath and letting it out slowly.

"Yah, I think is good idea. You go speak to him yourself. Maybe he knows where she is and why she is afraid to come home," she nodded in agreement.

* * *

Peter drove his father up to the college so they could confront Erdman and ask if he knew where Clara was. They found Erdman lounging on the grass with some friends smoking and laughing about some dance at the school a few days ago.

When Erdman saw Mr. Lindgren and his son Peter approaching across the lawn he shooed his friends away. He affected as causal an air as he could especially when confronted with Peter's anger and Mr. Lindgren's pitiable weariness.

"Halverson, what you done with my daughter Clara?" Mr. Lindgren said before they had finished walking up to Erdman Halverson.

"I don't know what you mean," Erdman tried to shrug off the question as unimportant. "*Don*e with her?" He asked back in a surly tone.

"That night, you were to meet her," the older man persisted.

"I didn't see her," Erdman shook his head, unable to look at them. "I was going to but changed my mind and I never went."

"I don't believe you," Mr. Lindgren's tone was harsh.

"I really don't care what you believe or don't believe," Erdman got up off the ground. He wanted to be ready to walk away from this conversation at his pleasure, not theirs.

"I can prove what I say," Christian Lindgren said, not willing to let it go so easily.

"You can't prove anything on me, old man." Erdman turned and began to walk away from them.

"You gave her instructions to burn your letters," Mr. Lindgren said in a hoarse whisper that carried across the grass.

Erdman froze in place and then began to turn slowly to face them. His face was pale, and his mouth taut. This was not the news he had expected to hear from them.

"Did you see this letter?" His voice was constrained.

"No, I did not, but her sister Ingmar did. She was with Clara when she put them to the flame." He walked closer and put his hand on Erdman's shoulder. "Erdman, I just want to talk with you a few minutes."

"Okay," Erdman sighed heavily, thrusting his hands in his pockets.

"You told her in your letter that you would meet her at the door at midnight, didn't you?" Lindgren asked in a soft voice.

"I did," Erdman's reply was barely a whisper.

"Did you send somebody else in your place to take her?" Peter asked.

"No," Erdman shook his head.

"You called her out to the road. I see the car. I see her go out to you," Mr. Lindgren related. "Where did you go?"

Erdmann stared at the ground for a while before answering, his voice barely audible. "I took her over to Red Oak."

"I don't believe you," Peter retorted, his body tense with anger. "I saw the tire tracks the next morning. They went in the direction of Council Bluffs; they did not go in the direction of Red Oak."

"Oh, well, then, we went to Council Bluffs." He shrugged a shoulder like he was trying to cast off his guilt. "So what?"

"Then what did you do?" Mr. Lindgren queried.

Erdman didn't answer. He stood looking at the ground.

"Please, this is my daughter, my Clara. I just want to know she is all right," Mr. Lindgren pleaded with Halverson.

"I gave her fifty dollars. She got on the train to Chicago," Erdman said, still looking at the ground as if there was something to see there. He did not want to look into the faces of his interrogators.

"I see. Well, we don't have any strings on her, she is an adult after all, free to go where she likes." Mr. Lindgren looked off into the distance as he spoke. "But if you could do us a favor we'd appreciate it."

"What do you want?" Erdman finally looked up at the older man for a second, wondering what he could possibly want him to do.

"Ask her to at least write to her father and mother, it need not be a lot, just a few lines so we can see that she is alive and all right," Lindgren said, trying to force a smile.

"Yeah, I can do that," Erdman nodded his head, but still wouldn't look directly at either of them.

"You got to go bring her back so we all can see that she is still alive." Lindgren patted Erdman's shoulder.

"Sure," he replied like he was somewhere else.

"Erdman, if there is anything between you and Clara that we don't know about, just bring her back. I will help you all I can." Lindgren made Erdman face him. "The two of you can go ahead and get married. We have plenty of room I can give you some land, I have plenty."

Erdman didn't answer for a while. He was trying to think up what to say in return. This was not what he wanted.

"If you can give me a little time, I can bring her back," he said at last.

"You got until Thursday," Mr. Lindgren replied his voice was stern.

"Thursday?" Erdman sputtered. "What if I can't find her right away?"

"If Clara don't show up by Thursday night, I will get the sheriff after you." Mr. Lindgren took a step back, indicating that the conversation was ending, and he had said what he needed to say.

Erdman simply blinked at them in disbelief as they turned and walked back across the college lawn to their automobile.

* * *

In the quiet of the night, Erdman couldn't muffle the sobs that came from his fears. The terrors circled close around him and all had the voice of one woman, Clara. He remembered the last time he had seen her, and buried his face deeper into the pillow muffling the cry that welled from his gut. He didn't want to think about it. He didn't want to think about her, but she tormented his waking hours and had now invaded sleep as well.

Why had he ever gone up to her at that wedding and asked her to dance. He never should have spoken to her. He blamed her for what had happened. If she hadn't come to the dance none of this would ever have happened. He cursed her in the darkness that held him fast.

Fearful sobs wracked his frame.

He hated being like this.

He hoped his roommate had already gone to sleep so he couldn't overhear his weeping. Erdman was scared. He didn't like it that Mr.

Lindgren had laid down the law so precisely. The man demanded he bring Clara back to him by Thursday.

"What if I can't bring her back by then?" He said to his pillow.

Erdman Halverson tossed and turned that night trying to decide what to do. He had never been in a jam that he hadn't been able to get out of, or that his folks couldn't dispel for him.

He was in it deep this time, and he didn't know what to do.

For a short moment he contemplated taking his own life, but knew he didn't have the guts to end it like that. He began to run through his options as the moonlight poured in the window, making patterns on the floor. The pattern of moonlight had moved and changed a great deal before he finally decided what he would do.

Quietly he rose from his bed and went to the desk. He had two letters to write before doing what he knew he had to do.

There was no other choice for him.

CHAPTER 27

Christian Lindgren and his sons decided it was time to give the sheriff another visit. It had been more than three weeks since Clara had disappeared into the night, and her father was worried sick. He was not eating nor was he sleeping too well. It was late October and the harvest work on the farm was not getting done in a timely manner. Peter and Hal were worried about their father and wanted their sister to come home.

Hal even had to restrain his brother to keep him from hunting down Erdman Halverson and making the little coward face the business end of his rifle and tell him what had happened to their sister, Clara.

Nerves were on edge and tempers were wearing thin in the Lindgren household. It was suggested that maybe a conversation with the sheriff might help ease the tensions that threatened to tear the family apart.

Sheriff Frank De Boer received the Lindgren men cordially the fall afternoon that they came to his office.

"What can I do for you gentlemen today?" He asked motioning them to take the seats in his office.

"You know my Clara is still missing," Christian Lindgren informed him.

"Since I saw you last time I did hear some rumors about her having gone away, but nothing concrete enough to follow up at all." The sheriff steepled his fingers, he slowly tapped his index fingers to his lower lip. "You have heard nothing from your daughter, Clara, since that time?"

"Not a word," Christian Lindgren said. He was weary with worry.

"This time we want some answers, Sheriff," Peter said, leaning forward in a menacing attitude.

"We know who done this to her," Hal added with a frown and the same anger present in his voice.

"Boys, I can appreciate your concern for your sister, but

threatening me won't do any good. Do I make myself clear?" De Boer was not a man to take guff from anyone.

"All right, but we don't want to go out of here without some sort of answers," Peter backed down somewhat.

"Did you hire any of those private investigators?" De Boer addressed Mr. Lindgren.

"Yah, I speak to them. And I talk to a lawyer. They all tell me that she is dead," his voice broke. He took a moment to recover his composure. "I just can't accept that. My Clara can't be dead. Oh God! She can't be dead." A tear welled in his eye and spilled down his cheek. He wiped it away.

"I hope she is alive, Mr. Lindgren. For your sake, I hope she will come home soon. But I have to say, the more time that passes, the slimmer the chances are of her being found alive and well." De Boer studied Christian Lindgren. "Okay, tell me everything again, from the beginning."

"About three weeks ago now, about midnight, my girl slips from the house, said she was going to take care of the necessary and get some air. She never come back inside again," Christian Lindgren explained, telling the story again. "Then I see what I think may be headlamps from a car come along the road. Then nothing but darkness." He rubbed a calloused hand over his forehead then through his unruly, thick, white hair.

"Do you have any ideas who she may have gone off with?" He asked, even though he had heard the rumors about who she had been running around with. He couldn't go on rumor. He needed facts if he was to do his job.

"She had been keeping company with that Erdman Halverson," Peter said, his face dark with anger.

"Erdman Halverson, you say?" De Boer leaned forward in his chair, interested. Enough time had gone by to allow stories to circulate through the county. The rumors were true then that he had heard about him taking up with a nice girl from the country. "Have you spoken to the boy?" De Boer had not been out to the farm to speak with the Halverson family, he hadn't enough of a reason to follow up on the scant information he had learned about Clara. Rumors were not enough to motivate him into action.

"Yah. I just wanted you to know that we went up to see this Erdman Halverson, let him know that we know she had heard from him. Then we give him until Thursday to bring Clara back to me, or at least get her to write and let us know where she is, and that she is all right," Christian said, looking the sheriff in the eye.

"When did she hear from him last?" De Boer asked, needing more information.

"The day before she go away. He send a letter telling her to meet him," Mr. Lindgren replied.

"Did she meet him?" De Boer wrinkled his forehead.

"He says she did not. What I want to know is, who was it then that come for her that night. According to Ingmar, her sister, the Halverson boy was the only one she had been keeping company with."

"What do you want me to do about it, Mr. Lindgren?" The sheriff sat back in his chair not sure what he could do about the missing girl.

"I want you should go speak to the boy, tell him to let us know where she is." Christian slapped his fist into his open palm.

"I can, but what will he tell me that he won't tell you?" The sheriff was shaking his head. "I bet she ran off with her young man, and has not written as yet, maybe she is afraid you may be upset with her for eloping. Hopefully, she will soon come home married," the sheriff hesitated. "Or, well, what can I say?" He stammered, not sure what to say about it all.

"I never be upset with my Clara, she know that. Something is just not right with all this." Clara's brother pounded the desk with his fist. "He knows where she is, and is just not telling us the truth. He will tell you, he has to, you're the law!"

"Well, I'll look into it; see if I can't get anything out of the boy," De Boer promised. He wished more people had the same idea that Peter Lindgren did in regards to him being the law, so that they would tell all and tell the truth about things. From what he knew about this Halverson boy, he was not going to suddenly confess if he had done something wrong, just because the sheriff asked him. "You say he is up at the college in Ames?"

"Yah, we seen him there the other day. He didn't seem to be telling the truth from what I could tell." Christian Lindgren got up out of his seat and extended his hand to the sheriff. "Thank you for your patience and help."

"Don't thank me yet." He took Lindgren's rough, calloused

hand in his giving it a firm shake. "I'll see if I can't get some intelligence from Halverson on where your daughter, Clara, has gone."

He sighed to himself as he watched the Lindgren men walk out of his office. He hated missing person's cases, especially daughters who had been dating men with bad reputations. He figured she had gotten herself in trouble, the boy wasn't going to make an honest woman of her, and she took off to have the baby in secret. Then, after she had given the child up for adoption she would come home.

It didn't seem as if her family knew about any child, or he might have been investigating the murder of one Erdman Halverson.

CHAPTER 28

Erdman had packed a few things, and made sure his hoard of bootleg money was safely stowed in the secret compartment under the seat in his roadster. It was quite a lot of money, and he knew he could live off of it for a long time, if need be, or at least until he could get things straightened out.

As the sun was cresting in the sky, Erdman looked back at the college as he drove away. He knew he would never be able to return. On his way out of town, he dropped two letters in the post box knowing that he would have a few hours lead before they managed to get to their destinations.

He had a long drive ahead of him. He was headed off to South Dakota to lay low until the trouble could blow over. He had no intention of letting his involvement with Clara Lindgren ruin his whole life.

* * *

Christian Lindgren came in from the fields where they had been finishing the last field of the harvest. He was so weary and decided to call it quits for the day before he had an accident. His sons encouraged him to head home. They could work until the sun finally set that evening. It was only eight o'clock when Christian headed back to the house, but he felt as if it were midnight.

He was dirty and weary from work. He peeled off his coveralls, and left his boots on the back porch. He shook the dust out of his hair as best he could before coming into the kitchen where he worked the pump at the sink, so he could wash his hands and face. The dirt had mixed with his sweat and he was covered in a fine, brown paste.

When he felt he was sufficiently clean enough so his wife would not scold him for trailing in more dirt than was necessary, he shuffled to the front of the house. He plopped down in the wooden rocker in the parlor and began to read the paper that was sitting on the table. His wife always had it on the parlor table knowing he would like to sit and relax after being in the fields.

Bertha Lindgren came into the parlor with a cup of tea for her husband.

"I thought I heard you come in." She put the cup down on the table, and kissed his forehead. "Here is your tea."

"Thank you my dear." His smile was weak. "What would I do without you all these years?"

"A letter came today," she said, reaching into the pocket of her dress.

"From our Clara?" He said, looking up at her with a hopeful expression.

"No," she shook her head and handed him the letter. It was a cream envelope, the address was written in a purple ink. He remembered hearing that the Halverson boy had written to his daughter with this same color.

"It's from him?" Reluctantly he took the envelope from her hand and stared at it.

"I think so." She moved the kerosene lamp closer then took a seat on the loveseat across from him.

Lindgren tore the end of the envelope off and fished out the letter inside. His eyes scanned the short missive for the words he wanted to see. They were not there. He snorted in anger, his hand fell to his lap and his head fell to the back of the rocker. His anguish was clearly visible on his face.

"What does he say, Christian?" His wife prompted him, impatient for news.

"I read it to you." He wiped a tear from the corner of his eye and read the letter to his wife. "There is no salutation, nor is there a signature, but we know who it is from."

He took a deep breath before reading.

"Just a few quick lines to let you know that I will no longer be at college after tonight. I am going to make myself scarce enough so you can't find me or Clara. Just where she is—is my business at present. And after the bunch of lip that I got from you the other day I'm not caring a great deal either. I believe she is all right in health and such, but where she is I can not say. I am leaving because I don't like the idea of the sheriff coming up here if I couldn't find her.

I'll come back when she comes back."

"Oh, Christian." Bertha Lindgren rushed over and kneeling by his side she embraced her husband. They held one another in close embrace as they wept for their daughter. "Do you think he has done anything to her?"

"I think he has, or he would have brought her back by now. Or we would have heard from her." He smoothed the hair from her face, and kissed her brow. "She never fear what we would say. She knows we love her. Our Clara would have let us know where she had gone. I do not have a good feeling about this, my dear." A frown pulled at the corner of his mouth. Suddenly he felt bone weary and he wanted nothing more than to curl up and be blown across the fields like the fine dust of the Loess Hills that dotted the landscape.

She reached up and wiped the tear that had fallen to his cheek.

* * *

The other letter arrived at Erdman's parent's house.

They too held one another in close embrace seeking comfort that their favorite son should have been driven away from his friends and family by such a wicked female as was this Clara Lindgren.

Mr. Halverson read and re-read the letter a couple of times, his anger growing in his heart for this Clara.

I suppose you have heard a lot of things already. I know that I did. I had some visitors yesterday, and they were not real nice about some things. You can guess who they were, I am sure. They seemed to think that they have me where I can't wiggle my toes, which is where they are mistaken, very much so.

He, the old man, claims that he has absolute proof that I know where she is. I haven't the least idea of her location, but I cooked up a story that she was in Chicago and that I would have some time to get her back here.

I am leaving tonight for some place where no one knows. I shall not even tell you folks, though God knows how I feel. I have thought of finishing everything, but life is sweet and hard to part with, but I say this, that I would rather take death than captivity.

I am taking the most necessary articles of clothing in the suitcase and am sending back the rest. This may seem like mockery, but what else could I do with them? Give Bergin everything that he can use of my stuff. He is only one brother in a thousand, and, it brings me to tears to think of what he has before him in the future. Poor little boy.

Sometime I may write to you, but I can't say that you will ever see me again, unless it's maybe in a coffin. Perhaps you may never want to see me again. I would not blame you if you don't. I have no money, but got some checks that will do me for traveling expenses, until I get some work. I will never stay long in any one place, for that would be dangerous.

Mother, I suppose that your health will suffer tremendously from this, and it might wreck father, but don't let it do that.

Live for Bergin; he will repay you many, many, times for what you sacrifice for him. No child has ever had truer mettle in it than he has. Forget me and live for Bergin. Send him to school and he will make you proud.

These people cannot prove anything definite, although they will try. Do not let them try and pull anything over on you folks. Please try to bear this with bravery, and forget me, as I am not worthy of your memory. Shut me out of your thoughts entirely, as though I never existed.

Good-by and God bless you all. You have not failed as parents, but I have failed as a son.

Erdman

P. S. No one will ever know me by that name anymore. Now it will be a different one. I told everyone that I am going to a doctor for an operation. It is true that I will have another operation. Friends will write when I don't come back. Tell them what you please, it is immaterial to me.

"No! I will not stand for this," Mr. Halverson bellowed as he crumpled the letter in his large powerful hand and tossed it away. "My son sent into exile for some snip of a girl who thinks she can get her grasping hands on all that I have built over these many years?"

"He will have to come home eventually." Mrs. Halverson cowered a little in the backlash of her husband's anger. "Erdman is still so innocent of the ways of the world," she replied, clinging to her husband.

Bergin stood in the doorway watching them. The crumpled letter rolled across the floor and came to rest at his feet. He bent over to pick it up, his anger rising as he thought about the damage his brother had caused to them all.

There were answers to so many questions he needed to get. Somehow, he was going to find out what happened to Clara, no matter what it cost, even if the price was Erdman's life.

He watched his parents cling to one another, weeping for their son.

He turned to go, knowing that they still couldn't see that he was even in the room. It was all for Erdman, even after all his brother had done, the times he had been tossed out of college, the trouble he had gotten into over the years as they grew up, even the accident with the other boy in the barn.

It was still all about his sainted older brother.

CHAPTER 29

The first Sunday in early November was cold; a north wind blew across the plains, promising more cold and snow to come. The farmers were rushing to finish their harvest before the first deep frost killed the last of the crops in the fields. It was Sunday and each of them took the time to come to worship God and give thanks for the bounty of the land, for their freedom, and their families.

The white clapboard church was full that Sunday. Nearly five hundred people could fit in the sanctuary, and there were at least three hundred people that had come that Sunday. Christian Lindgren and many of his neighbors had helped to build the church in the early days when cash was short; skills and time were readily given to their church.

On his way out of church, someone pulled at Christian Lindgren's coat sleeve. He turned to see Erdman Halverson's father, Adolph, standing there with a scowl on his face. He motioned with his head to follow him outside. Wordlessly he turned and exited the church. He didn't want to have cross words under the roof of the sanctuary.

Standing with his back to the cold wind, he waited for Halverson to speak.

"I come to talk about my boy," Halverson said, pulling his coat tighter about him to keep the wind from chilling him to the bone.

"What about your son?" Christian Lindgren inquired.

"You made a big mistake going up to the college and going after my son." His hands were jammed deep into his pockets.

"How could I have made a mistake? I wanted some answers. I wanted to know where my daughter has gone," he hardened his expression against his adversary.

"You threatened him and you scared him out of school and all that was rightfully his." Halverson waved a stubby finger at Lindgren. "Between you and me, you better drop the whole thing," he said, his scowl deepening.

"I won't drop it." Lindgren jutted his chin out at the other man in a defiant gesture. “I’ll find that boy and make him tell me where is my daughter, Clara, no matter what it costs me.”

“You’ll regret this, Lindgren,” Halverson threatened.

“All I want to know is: where is my daughter?” He replied looking Halverson in the eye, not willing to be bullied by the man.

Halverson looked away, unable to maintain eye contact. “That I cannot tell you,” he said with a frown.

“All I want is my daughter,” Lindgren said in a whisper.

A gust of icy wind made Halverson shiver. Lindgren wondered if maybe it wasn’t something more than the wind that had caused the man to tremble.

Halverson turned and walked away.

Lindgren watched him go before heading to his automobile to join his wife before they drove home.

Before he could walk away a young man came up to him and spoke to him in a soft voice.

“Mr. Lindgren, I am so sorry that no one has heard from Clara. She was a friend of mine, and I am worried as to what happened to her.”

“May I ask your name, sir?”

“Bergin, Bergin Halverson.” He saw the look of surprise on the older man’s face. “I was very fond of Clara, she was a good person. I want you to know that I will do all I can to find out where she is.”

“You would do this for my Clara?” He said, stunned by the younger man’s declaration especially in light of the rest of the Halverson clan’s reactions. “Even if it meant trouble for your brother?”

“Yes, sir, I will. No matter the cost.” Bergin held his gaze without wavering in the least.

“Thank you.” Christian Lindgren extended his hand. Bergin took the offered hand firmly in his, and met the man’s gaze directly. “You let us know how we can help you, too. All I want to know, where is my Clara.”

“I know, sir. Me too.” He smiled at Lindgren. “I miss her.”

“Me too, young Bergin, me too,” Mr. Lindgren said, turning away and walking to his automobile.

* * *

Mr. Lindgren had gone back to the private detective after getting the letter from Erdman. He had something he wanted the man to do. If he couldn't get the man to search for his daughter he could at least see if he couldn't get the man to track down that no good Erdman Halverson. If he found where Clara was as a part of his investigation, then that would be a bonus.

The detective had been on the case for about a week when Lindgren met with him for an update.

The private detective said that Erdman was most probably staying with relations, a grandmother in North Dakota. The detective had managed to get the County Attorney to send telegrams to the police in the bigger cities around the area – Milwaukee, Chicago, Omaha, Minneapolis and St Louis and even on the off chance that he had skipped across the boarder they were sent to the Royal Canadian Mounted Police. They were all told to be on the lookout for Erdman, and possibly Clara who may be with him. They were considered to be on the run.

So far there was no intelligence on either of them.

His next chore was to speak to the sheriff.

Christian Lindgren let Sheriff De Boer know all that he had found out and had asked him if they could search the county for his daughter. De Boer had replied that he didn't have any idea where they could begin such a search. Manpower would be a problem. The county was quite large.

Hal Lindgren suggested that they could get some of the men from the American Legion Post to come help. He had already posed the question, and they were more than willing, just waiting for a time.

* * *

The sheriff was concerned. He had asked a few questions about Erdman Halverson, the young man Clara Lindgren had been seeing. The news was not good. The boy had been in trouble off and on over the years. He was thrown out of college more than once, but his father had always managed to get the boy readmitted. It was also talked of that Erdman was a rumrunner, who supplied illegal alcohol to dances and parties in the state.

De Boer also remembered the stories of an accident when

Erdman was nine. He was playing with his friend, when a shotgun went off accidentally. The boy was killed. At the time the sheriff, his predecessor, gave into a lot of pressure from Erdman's father to rule it an accident, or at least that was how the story went.

No one had seen or heard from Erdman since he left school.

No one had heard from Clara since she had stepped out into the night in late September.

What surprised him the most was the man who had come by to see him. It was not what he expected, but he was willing to take all the help he could get. He had heard from others that Erdman Halverson was his parents pride and joy, and that they treated his younger brother, Bergin, like an indentured servant. Yet, here, sitting across the desk from him was the younger Halverson boy.

"I am here to see if I can help locate Clara, Sheriff De Boer," Bergin said. "I will do whatever is necessary."

"Even if it means trouble for your brother?" he asked, not quite trusting the man's motives. Bergin had those fair, Nordic good looks and strong build to go with them. He also seemed to be an openly honest young man. De Boer had always been a good judge of character and it had been an advantage in solving the cases that had come his way over the years. He hoped he could trust Bergin Halverson, and in that moment decided he would at least give the man the benefit of the doubt.

"Sheriff, if my brother has harmed Clara in any way, then he needs to face the consequences. That is not something Erdman has ever had to do much of in his life. Face the consequences of his actions," Bergin explained with a laugh, but his laugh was brittle and hinted of anger and resentment that had built up over many years.

"Do you know where he is?" De Boer studied the man.

"No," he shook his head. "He didn't tell me."

"Any ideas?" De Boer hoped that if Bergin Halverson was going to help, that he would have some information for him.

"I suspect he is hiding out with some of our mother's family in the Dakotas," he said, looking down at his hands for a moment before looking back up and meeting the sheriff's eyes. "A farm outside of Pierre. It belongs to my mother's mother."

De Boer nodded and scribbled a note to himself. "You hear from him at all?"

"Not since the letter that said he was running away," Bergin paused and shifted in his chair before he spoke again. "Sheriff, I want you to know that I will be doing everything that I can to figure out what really happened. I have a few ideas that may or may not lead to anything conclusive, but I want to try."

"You think you can dig up some information that will help us find either of them?" He raised his eyebrows creating a nest of furrows in his forehead. He wondered what the man could know that he was not telling him.

"I don't really know. There are some people Erdman knew, and I want to see if they know anything. Would that be all right with you?" He gestured the question with palms open, facing up. "I know you don't have a lot of time to dedicate to this. It might not even be a high priority considering no real crime has been committed."

"I see you understand my predicament. It's not that I don't want to help out the Lindgren family, but as you say, there has not been any crime committed here. A girl has gone missing, and so too has a guy who got scared and ran away. There might be something he knows that might help us find the girl. They might even be holed up together somewhere, but until we can locate him we won't know anything for sure. As you say, we don't really have the manpower to hunt him down. So, you see where that leaves me."

"I do," Bergin nodded.

"I can't stop you from snooping around, you will have no authority, and you might even get hurt. This is a risk you are taking on your own. Do you understand this?"

"Yes, Sheriff." Bergin stood and offered his hand. The sheriff shook Bergin's hand, hoping that he had an ally in his search for the answers to Lindgren's questions as well as his own.

CHAPTER 30

Christian Lindgren was weary from the day, maybe he was getting too old for the hard work in the fields or maybe he was simply worn out with worry. He sponged his body with the cloth, washing away most of the dirt he had accumulated in the fields that day. The harvest was at last complete, and the last of the feed corn was safely stored in the barn. Soon the ground would be covered in snow, and he could rest.

He put on his night shirt and crawled under the crisp, cool sheets next to his wife who was already asleep.

Wearily he laid his head on the pillow, and said the prayer he said every night, asking God to please let his daughter, Clara, come home.

He sighed and quickly slipped below the surface of consciousness.

Soon he began to dream.

It was dark; he sat in the parlor reading the newspaper. The kerosene lamp burned dimly, the wick was turned back, low. Little light reached the corners of the room, but he was not afraid.

Footfalls came gently down the stairs with a familiar creak on the steps, a figure passed him, and he recognized the fragrance. His daughter always wore that scent when she was going out. He had watched as Clara walked past him. She told him: "I'm just going out for a quick breath of fresh air and to take care of what is necessary."

He was still sitting in the parlor; there was just a little light to see by. The lamp was not lit anymore.

He heard a knocking at the door.

"Papa?" A voice whispered. "Papa, come for me."

"Who's there?" His voice cracked. He sat up and looked about him and saw nothing stirring.

"Papa, I'm so cold, and so alone," the voice, like a cloud of fog wrapped itself around him as if it were a shroud. He shivered in its

vaporous grasp.

"Who are you?" A tightness grabbed at his heart and fear painted his words. He found himself standing outside in the chill mist of night.

"It's your Clara, papa," her voice was soft, the voice he had missed now for many months.

"Clara?" He reached through the mist, trying to take hold of her. Where was she? He heard her voice, it was all about him, but he couldn't see her.

"Papa, I will show you where I am. Come," her words formed as mist in the air for a moment then faded.

"Clara, come home, your mother and I miss you so. What ever you have done, we forgive you, even if you have gotten in trouble. We love you, Clara. Please, come home, my darling girl." He felt the tears falling down his cheeks; they froze to his face. He could not wipe them away, for he knew that they were Clara's tears.

"I can't come back anymore," her voice, like a fine mist, tangled in the broken branches of a tree and were swept away to the skies.

He was no longer in his parlor, but he was standing in a barren field, the wind whipping about him, the fog clearing. The chatter of dried leaves mocked him as the mist began to take form and shape. The ruins of an old house that had collapsed in on itself years ago huddled near a grove of old trees. He stood in the broken doorway and saw the fields before him shrouded in a thick haze. Everything was a grayish white. The chill of the fog seeped into the depths of his bones and he shivered.

From the misty veil stepped his Clara. He tried to reach for her, but he couldn't move. She walked up a hill closer to where another grove of trees stood, and she turned then to face him. He couldn't see her eyes, only dark shadows where they should be. She raised her arm, slowly beckoning for him to come to where she was. Mist like angry smoke curled about her, sometimes obscuring her.

Slowly he was able to come near her, but not too close. He could see her better now, the mist curling about her like spectral friends caressing her.

She was wearing her very best coat dress, the one that she had made shortly before disappearing. It was a heavy cotton in the dark colors of fall, browns, greens, russet, and dark yellow. He remembered that dress and how she looked in it. Over the dress was her best golden-brown, woolen coat. He remembered she had worn it that night when she had gone and never returned.

There were leaves in her hair, and dirt on her cheeks. As she stepped aside, the wind blew through her; she was gone on the harsh breath of the wind. There was a long narrow hole in the ground where she had been standing.

At first; he thought it was filled with the clutter of leaves and broken branches. He leaned in closer to see what was there.

It was a woman, face down in the shallow grave.

It was Clara.

He knew without having to touch her. She was dead.

"Come find me, papa," her voice whispered on the icy wind.

He opened his mouth to cry out her name. No sound came immediately. But the pain of his cry tore at his throat as it struggled to be heard.

"Clara!" He screamed aloud.

He opened his eyes; his body was stiff from the nightmare. He called her name again, quietly. "Clara."

"Christian, wake up, you were dreaming." His wife was shaking him. His body was not responsive to her touch. "Wake up." She watched as his eyes opened slowly, and his head turned to face her, the movement stiff like a hinge long unused. She stared at him waiting for him to speak of his dream.

"I know where our Clara is," he uttered the words in a hoarse whisper that didn't seem to be his voice at all. His throat was sore from the nightmare scream.

"Where? Where is our daughter?" She had lived with him long enough to know that he often had prophetic dreams. She had doubted them when they were first married, but as she heard his dreams and saw them proven to be true, she never doubted him any more. He always knew the difference between the prophetic dreams and the dreams of a restless mind winding its way through the memories of the day.

The hall clock chimed midnight as Christian Lindgren tried to draw the courage to tell his wife what he had dreamed, or at least what it meant. He counted the chimes and sighed deeply.

"Clara is dead." He stirred; the nightmare's paralyzing stiffness leaving his body now. He didn't really want to tell his wife what he had dreamed. She still hoped that their daughter had run off to the city and one day might come home again. He knew he had to shatter that hope. He knew his dream was true. “Her body lies in a shallow, narrow grave not far from here.”

“Oh, God. I feared it, but didn’t want to think it could be true.” She wrapped her arms about him and she cried in his gentle embrace. They wept together for the daughter who had disappeared nearly three months ago.

CHAPTER 31

Bergin knew that if he told his parents that he was taking care of something for Erdman they wouldn't question why he was heading out late at night. They would also expect him to be up and ready to do his chores at the usual time. He wouldn't get a sleep-in like his brother always received.

He drove the old Model T Ford; his father had given him his permission.

The frigid night had settled about him with a blackness that could not compare to the gentleness of a summer's evening sky. Maybe it was because the darkness had a better chance of taking hold in the winter without the light of day coming so early and staying so late. The air was scented with the smells of coming winter, of the land settling down into a restfulness of sleep that would in spring awaken again renewed and regenerated.

As he waited for time to pass until he could begin his work he thought about the seasons, the earth and even why God had put him on it. He thought about Erdman and wondered what had made him the way he was. His thoughts eventually came around to Clara Lindgren, he wondered where she'd gone and why no one had heard from her. Surely, she would have written to her family, even if she had gone off in secret to have Erdman's child.

So, he was back to Erdman again.

He wondered how many other lives Erdman had touched, and in that touch caused pain, harm, and grief. He had seen his brother spin his web about Clara and drag her down into the mud with him, until she was so ashamed or hurt that she had to pick up and leave everyone and everything behind.

Had his brother really taken her to the train and helped her run away?

It was something he needed to find out because when he really took a hard look at the whole thing he felt that he was culpable in everything that had happened to the girl. His brother never would have spoken to her in the first place if he hadn't been trying to show off and get the better of him. Poor Clara had been Erdman's means of revenge against Bergin.

He felt that he owed it to Clara to find her, to give some answers to her family if nothing else. His journey to discover the truth depended upon his delving into the shadier corners of Erdman's life. He had no idea what he would find, but he was committed to finding any of the answers that could help locate Clara.

He waited until he heard the clock chime midnight before he took the car and drove into town. He had no other choice about the time of day; simply because his brother's dissolute habits were practiced late in the night and into the wee hours of the morning.

"It is midnight, and all good people were asleep in their beds," he said to himself as he drove in the inky blackness of the night along the country road into town. The headlamps illuminated the road ahead of him, a solitary beam of light against the vastness of the night. He felt so alone. "I wish I were there as well, asleep in my bed."

Bergin had been chasing his brother's shadow for a while now, and had only come up with some sketchy details of that last night, but few people were sure of anything. His brother's habits had become clearer now, and Bergin planned to return to Erdman's favorite haunts in town.

In town he parked the car near the pool hall he knew that his brother frequented. Lights from the windows poured yellow brightness into the street. He peered into the window, wondering where to begin looking for someone who knew Erdman who might give him some information. Inside a few men circled about their pool tables angling for their best shot. Smoke hung thickly in the air diffusing the light that hung over each table. Some men and a few women sat at the bar chatting.

He didn't see anyone he recognized from his occasional running about with Erdman. He turned and walked up the street to the Ogden Hotel. A man with a woman on each arm came walking up the sidewalk. The women were scantily clad, even in the chilly air. They stumbled as if they had been drinking.

"Who wants to dance?" The man said to the women, slurring his words.

"Me, daddy, me do!" The one woman laughed, reaching up to kiss his cheek.

"Oh yes, me too!" Giggled the other one, snuggling in closer to the man, tightening her grasp on his arm.

Bergin doubted that the man was with his daughters, and watched as he guided them past him and up the way to the next doorway. The man opened the door and ushered the women through with a gesture for them to precede him. Bergin turned and followed them to the doorway and pushed open the door to enter. A wide stairway led to the second level, and music drifted into the cool night air. He remembered his brother liked to hang out at the dance hall. He climbed the stairs determined to find someone he remembered. Someone who would admit to knowing his brother.

The room was crowded and warm with the smells of sweat, perfume, smoke and illegal alcohol. The voices of people rose above the reverberation of the band in a jumbled cacophony of confused sounds, none really distinguishable from the others. The dance floor was crowded, and the tables all seemed occupied.

Above the din, he thought he heard someone call out, and he turned his attention in the direction of the sound.

"There's Erdie, come on Christine, let's go see if he remembers us." Soon a slight woman with straight black hair, cut in a pageboy, emerged from the crowd, dragging a woman who looked very much the same. They wore beaded dresses in pinks and purples that complimented one another. "Erdie! Where the hell have you been, man? We missed you," the woman said, slapping Bergin on the arm.

"Erdie, don't tell us you have forgotten us already?" The other woman came up behind her and smiled at him. "Christine and Marie, the sisters with the most?"

"Christine? Marie?" Bergin repeated their names. He had to shout to be heard over the din in the room. The women looked at one another, shrugged a shoulder then looked back at him. "You know Erdman Halverson?"

"We sure do, silly. Don't you remember partying with us towards the end of September? Some fun we three had." She looked up at him.

"You gotta remember us, cause we sure didn't forget you." She looked into his face, then frowned. "Say, wait a minute. You ain't Erdie." She took a step back.

"I'm his brother," Bergin replied, looking about for a quieter corner to ask them a few questions. They said they had been with

Erdman at the end of September. "Can I get you a drink, ladies?"

"Sure, why not. If you are half as much fun as your brother, then we are gonna have a swell time tonight." She nodded her head and reached for his hand, pulling him to the side of the room. "Come on over to the table we got."

Christine pulled him along to a table situated near the wall where the noise was not so deafening. She pushed him into a chair and plopped down in the one next to his, leaving Marie to take the chair on his other side.

"So, you say that you partied with my brother at the end of September?" He asked the two of them, looking from one to the other. "Do you remember the exact date?"

"I dunno. Is it important?" Marie shrugged a semi-naked shoulder and gave him a vapid expression that looked more like she couldn't remember her own name let alone a date in her recent history.

"Does it have something to do with why Erdie hasn't been around lately?"

"Christine, then you know?" He lowered his eyes and sighed as if he had been carrying a huge burden. He hated to have to be less than honest with them; he needed to elicit information any way he could. He was not about to tell them his chicken brother had turned tail and had run away. "Can you help me?" He looked up into her eyes; it was a practiced move he had seen Erdman use on women when he wanted to get his way. To his surprise, it seemed to be working.

"Yes," Christine nodded her head slowly and bit her lip. "Well, we *were* with him here, that last time we saw him, on September twenty-fifth. He seemed, well, I dunno, a little preoccupied, sort of." She looked over at her sister for conformation. "You remember, Marie, that Thursday night, the last time we was with Erdie, he seemed all discombobulated and all."

"Oh, yea. He was not quite right that night. We danced a bunch of times together, but his feet didn't seem to know the steps all of a sudden. Usually he holds you real close, nuzzles at your neck and whispers naughty things in your ear. But not that night. He never done that before. He just couldn't get the steps right," Marie nodded as well, recalling that evening together.

"That was so dumb because it was the Fox Trot. Now who can't manage to get a Fox Trot right?" Christine said, making a face. Marie nodded in agreement.

"You're sure it was the twenty-fifth of September?" He asked. The sisters again nodded, and he sighed, allowing the hint of a smile to spread across his face. "You may have saved the day, ladies." He placed a hand over his heart.

"Oh gee!" Christine batted her eyes like she was blinking back a tear. "I feel so honored that I could be of help to Erdie. He was always so good to us."

"You have been a great help." Bergin rewarded her with a genuine smile. He took her hand and brushed his lips against the back of her hand, a move he had seen in a movie a while ago and always wanted to have a reason to practice. Christine began to giggle and gave him a coy little look. He still needed a little more information. "Do you remember what he did after dancing with you? Where did he go?"

"Hummm." Christine rolled her eyes to the ceiling as if the answer was written up there. She tapped a finger against her rouged lips. "I think he left us here and headed out after telling us he had to meet someone."

"Yeah, he did say he had to meet someone, but he didn't tell us who it was, so we assumed it was another girl."

"Yeah, another girl I think. He always had any number of us willing to go with him anytime he showed up. We knew that we always had to share him with others. He was still sowing his wild oats he would tell us all. So if we wanted to party with him, we had to share. Generous of us, wasn't it?"

"Did he leave here alone?" Bergin pressed for more information.

"As far as we know," Marie shrugged again. It seemed to be an involuntary habit of hers whenever she was asked a question. "We didn't see him pick up anyone as he went out 'a here did we?"

"Naah. I would have remembered who she was and given her what for."

"About what time of night was that when he left? Can you remember at all?" He had the date, now he needed to nail down the time as best he could. If he could.

"Oh, it was early for him. I think he was outta here by ten or ten-thirty."

"That's right, cause we then joined up with Kenny Battle and his pals. I remember because he came in here and said it was way too dead for eleven o'clock on a Thursday night, and Erdie had already been gone for a little bit."

"Right, and he was there, ready to stir things up." She giggled. "He sure stirred things up all right." They giggled together like they were part of a secret conspiracy.

"I want to thank you ladies for all your help. It will mean so much to Erdman when I tell him how gracious you have been," Bergin said, standing up and turning to face them. He had been searching the room for any other familiar faces, but had seen none. He needed to go to another one of Erdman's haunts to see if he could get more information and piece together that night. At least he knew that Erdman had been here in town on that night Clara had disappeared. The sheriff had told him Christian Lindgren had found his daughter missing the morning of the twenty-sixth. "Shall I send a bottle of something to your table as a token of my appreciation?" He gave them a hint of a bow, and they broke into peals of laughter once again.

"I hate to say so, but you are so much more elegant than Erdie. You can come around anytime, and maybe we will even be able to show you our appreciation by treating you to what we do best." She broke into peels of laughter and was quickly joined by her sister who shared in her mirth.

Bergin was afraid to ask what it was that they might do best. On his way out, he stopped by the bar and had them send over a bottle of their choice to the table where Christine and Marie were still waving at him and were now blowing kisses.

He headed down the stairs and pushed through the door to the street, welcoming the cold, crisp air. It had been so stifling in that dance hall he was glad to be able to draw breath that was not tainted with smoke or sweaty perfume.

It was getting late; he needed to head home if he was going to get any rest at all. He felt that he had accomplished something, too. He knew that Erdman had been out that night, and he knew where he had been, at least up until about ten or ten-thirty. It was a start. He would come back into town again on another night; see what he could find out.

* * *

As much progress as he felt he had made on that night, the next few weeks proved fruitless. Bergin had finally tracked down one of Erdman's bootlegging buddies, Gin Rummy Fagan, and in order to get any information out of the man, he had insisted that Bergin take one of Erdman's booze runs.

"I'm short handed, here. That rat of a brother of yours run out on me, and don't got enough guys to get the runs done on time. And that costs me money if the hooch ain't where it's supposed to be on time," Fagan complained, as a greasy smile spread across his lips like butter melting in a skillet. "You knows what I mean here, one hand will wash the other. You help me, I will help you." Fagan choked out a grunt of a laugh as he twisted a diamond ring on his little finger, the facets of the stones glittering in the dim light.

Bergin had acquiesced and had taken the run. He worried about getting caught with the contraband, especially in his father's old car. It was not very fast and would not be able to outrun the cops if they happened to tail him. He felt that he had no other choice. He wanted information.

The man had directed him to a poker game across the river in Omaha where Erdman was known occasionally to hang out, as well as make a delivery. Fagan handed Bergin an envelope and slapped him on the back. He said he would be glad to have him work "permanent-like" anytime he wanted to take over Erdman's runs. They loaded the car and Bergin headed down Broadway to the bridge over the Missouri River to Omaha. He needed to make a stop before he got too far. He ducked into an all night drugstore, that, once inside, he noticed that it sold a lot more than drugs.

He bought a map of Omaha, as he had never driven over there and was not terribly familiar with any city that large. As he walked back to the car he heard a man call out to him.

"Erdman Halverson? Erdman, you old son of a gun, where have you been all this time?" The man strode up to Bergin with a grin on his face. But the grin faded as Bergin stepped into the light and the man took a closer look at him. "Oh, sorry, I thought you were someone else. My mistake." He started to back off.

"Wait," Bergin said to the man putting his hand on the man's arm. "You know Erdman Halverson?"

"Yeah, but you ain't him," the man laughed as he scrutinized Bergin's face, as if he thought he was being made a fool of or something. His body was tense with apprehension. "You sure favor him though, that was why I thought you were Erd."

"I'm his brother," Bergin smiled at the man.

"Oh, well, that explains it." He smiled in return relaxing now.

"Did you know Erdman very well?"

"Sure, he and me was good pals. We hung out together often."

"When was the last time you two hung out together?" Bergin asked. He noticed the man suddenly looked wary. He had to reassure the man he was not up to any sort of mischief. "I am helping my brother with something, you see, he got himself into a spot of trouble, and I am doing what I can to help him. That's why I even ask."

"Oh, okay." The man looked him over, and slowly a smile spread across his face. "You look on the level. Last time I saw your brother he was driving down this very street and called out to me, asked if I wanted a drink. Well, not being one to refuse a kindness like that I accepted."

"Do you remember when this was?" Bergin could feel his pulse quicken, hoping for another little bit of news about his brother's movements.

"Shoot, I dunno. Ah, well, um." The man tried to remain in control of the conversation by hemming and hawing for a bit as he tried to recall. Then he snapped his fingers as it came back to him. "It were the last Thursday in September. I remember because I was tapped out, and knew that the next day was pay day, Friday, end of the month." He grinned at his recollection.

"Can you remember what time it was when you saw him that night?"

"That's easy, sure. They always throw me out of Kelly's at eleven whether I'm drunk or not." He laughed at himself, his belly jiggling as he did so. "It's an old arrangement they had with my wife starting years ago."

"Eleven o'clock on that last Thursday night in September?" Bergin repeated back to the man, hoping he had gotten the information correct.

"Sure, it was, or at least within fifteen minutes of eleven."

"Was Erdman by himself?" He asked wondering if he had Clara

with him.

"Funny you should ask," his reply was tentative. He looked Bergin up and down again as if he didn't really trust him.

"It's important, for Erdman's sake," Bergin said in a soft whisper.

"Well, as I remember back to that night I can say that no, no he wasn't alone. Had some stranger with him. Didn't introduce him neither. But then your brother was never one for the little niceties like an introduction. Some of the people he knows can be a little rough, if you know what I mean. This guy didn't say nothing, so I don't even know if he could talk. The three of us passed about the bottle until we drained it dry."

"How long did that take?" Bergin asked.

"Think about it sonny, three thirsty men pulling on the same bottle, it wouldn't have lasted more than half hour. We didn't spend too much time chewing the fat, if you know what I mean. We was all quenching our powerful thirsts." The man licked his lips like he could use a drink right then.

"What happened after you finished the bottle?"

"Then Max Moore, manager of the Ogden Hotel down the street came over to say hello. The stranger climbed into Erdman's car, in the back, and waited while we went into the pool hall for a while. Seemed a little odd to me that the man didn't come in with us. He never said a word neither."

Bergin only nodded.

"We came out of the pool hall as it was closing in on midnight and were talking with Erdman. I got a look at the man, well, as best I could as it was dark, and the streetlamp was behind him, casting no light on his face. I don't have a clue who he was."

"Ever see him since that night?"

"Nope," he shook his head. "Max don't know him neither. He later asked me, Max did, if I knew who the stranger was. I told him, I says, I didn't have any ideas on that subject."

"Then they drove off together?"

"As far as I know they did."

Bergin thanked the man, got into his car and headed across the river. He had discovered a little more of what all his brother had been doing that night. Instead of getting questions answered, he came away with more things he needed to know. Most importantly he wanted to know, who was this stranger that sat in the car when Erdman and his friends went into the pool hall. Where they had gone, and how did it relate to Clara on that last night she had been seen? Was Erdman involved in her disappearance? It was a question he wanted desperately to prove, that it was not Erdman who had a hand in her seemingly vanishing off the face of the earth.

Could Erdman have harmed Clara?

Lindgren's dream came to mind. He had heard about the dream, as had anyone who would hold still long enough for Mr. Lindgren to tell his tale. *Oh, God, I hate to think that Erdman could do her any harm.* He silenced his thoughts, but they still nagged at him. He was afraid that Clara was dead. He shut his eyes and sighed as he fought against the chill feeling of unavoidable density that grabbed at his soul.

He didn't know if he could handle the idea of his brother as a killer. Erdman was a lot of things; he was lazy, selfish and thoughtless to name a few. But was he a killer? Somehow he could not see his brother as someone who could take another person's life.

It was the shred of hope that he clung to as he continued to dig into his brother's shady life.

* * *

He found the address in Omaha where he had been told to deliver the alcohol. He was greeted by a large man with a shaved head who seemed to recognize him and motioned him to come in while he sent two men out to collect their delivery. He never thought he had resembled his brother so much as to be taken for him so often. In a way, it was a little amusing. In another way, it was disconcerting.

He was directed to wait in a room while they made sure the delivery was genuine. He learned that some guy a week ago had tried to unload something that was not what they had ordered. The big man laughed and said that the little creep was now keeping the fish fed in the Missouri river.

Bergin tried to relax, but found it impossible. He had no idea what sort of booze he was delivering, and hoped it was all correct. He did not like the idea of becoming fish food one little bit.

He had heard that his brother had some sort of connection with organized crime, though he hadn't believed it. He thought it was another of his brother's empty boasts. Bergin wondered if this wasn't the place where Erdman had met such people. Most of the other booze runs had been small bars or private customers. These men were intimidating.

After a little while a tall, handsome man, dressed in an elegant suit, wearing spats, came into the room. He was smoking a fat cigar that gave off a rich flavor in its smoke. He wore a three stone, diamond ring on his little finger. The man reached into his suit coat pocket and pulled out a thick envelope. He must have noticed the look of fear on Bergin's face and began to laugh.

"Don't worry kid; I'm not going to shoot you," then he shrugged a shoulder, and said with a malicious grin. "Well, at least I'm not going to shoot you this time." He released a growl of a laugh as he offered Bergin the envelope. "It's just payment for the delivery. We are so pleased the order was correct this time. Then you weren't the guy who screwed it up. I happen to know that he won't be making any more deliveries to us. Ever." The man chewed on his cigar.

"Right, he's gone fishing," Bergin said before he could stop himself.

The man stared at him for a moment before he burst into a guffaw of laughter and slapped Bergin smartly on the back.

"I like the way you think, kid. You got a nice turn of phrase." He placed an arm about Bergin's shoulder and walked him to the door. "I like you, I think you got some smarts, and I like to have smart people around me."

"Thank you," he said, not knowing what else to say.

"You play poker?" The man inquired with a sideways glance.

"Some, I'm not too good at it though," Bergin shook his head dismissively.

"We are light one person tonight, how would you like to sit in on our game?" The man said it as if it was a command not a request. Bergin could only nod. He was half afraid to refuse the man. "Come with me and let's get to playing. I'm feeling lucky tonight. You got a good cash tip in your pocket that will see you into the game for a while." There was a gleam in the man's eyes as he chafed his hands together.

The game did not go as the man had expected. Nor had it gone as Bergin had anticipated. Bergin had set his limit at two hundred dollars, the money he had gotten from his booze run. He figured he would lose the cash and then be able to get out of there and go home. It was already past two in the morning, and he was tired.

Bergin had been winning. It seemed that he couldn't draw a bad hand. He tried to lose some, but raked in even more. At last, the handsome man leaned back in his chair and stretched.

"Gentlemen, I think it's time we called it a night." The man looked at Bergin with green eyes that he could not read. "Better collect your winnings and get back across the river, kid," he smiled sardonically.

The others agreed, and pushed back from the table, disgruntled at having lost to the new guy. Bergin collected the money and filled his pockets.

The man walked him to the door. As he opened it, he leaned in on Bergin as if to share a confidence. "Listen, kid, I expect you to come back here some night soon and give me a chance to win back some of the cash I lost to you. Understand?"

"I would be more than happy to oblige you, sir. Yes, I will have to come back and give you all that chance to win some money back," Bergin assured him. He flashed the man a tense smile. "I don't want to go fishing just yet."

"I like your sense of humor," the man laughed again, slapped him on the back. "Remember now, come back next week. Because if you don't, we will just have to track you down and then you will be taking a long walk off a short pier."

Bergin thanked the man and hurried away from there, noticing that the sun was cresting in the eastern horizon. His father would kill him if he knew how he had spent his evening. He decided to make a few stops on his way back to the farm, if he was going to get yelled at, he might as well be good and late, and take care of a few things that he wanted to do.

Once back across the river in Iowa, he stopped to get some breakfast at an all night diner and thought about what to do with all that money. He had never had much to speak of. His father had never seen the need to give him hardly any spending money. He decided he was going to blow some of the cash on himself.

After he finished his breakfast, it was late enough that the shops were opening for the day. Bergin stopped into the men's furnishings store and had himself measured for a suit. He couldn't decide on which fabric he liked the best, so he ordered three of them. He could afford it after all. They let him know that the suits would be ready in a few days. He paid for them and arranged to have them delivered.

Next Bergin decided he needed some silent protection as he wandered the denizens of his brother's world. He bought a set of brass knuckles since he wasn't about to purchase a gun.

The last item on his list was an automobile. He stopped into the dealership where his father had always purchased all their vehicles and paid cash for a new motor car. He didn't want anything as fancy as his brother's Hudson. He didn't need to show off like that. A new Chevrolet would suit him. Then his father couldn't refuse to let him have the car for any reason.

That next week, as requested, Bergin returned to the house with a delivery. He was again invited to the poker game and he had the good sense to lose better than $300.00 to his host. He even folded a winning hand or two in order to lose. The man, suspecting something, slapped a weapon across the cards and insisted on looking at Bergin's cards. Bergin obliged him, and turned them over. When the man saw that he was holding a winning hand, and had tossed it aside, he gave him a wry smile.

"Ok, kid. You can go now," he said with a toss of his head. "And do yourself a favor, don't come back here and play at my table again. Got it?"

"Yes, sir," Bergin tipped his hat and walked away. He promised himself that it would be the last time he ever played poker.

He had learned that through some of these illicit connections, Erdman had indeed made contact with a man who was considered to be an unsavory character, even by the mob. This information was confirmed by the man Erdman did his booze runs for as well.

He was getting closer. Yet he still had so far to go.

He still did not know the man's name or how to contact him.

Bergin stopped in Council Bluffs for a bite to eat at the all-night diner. He sipped the strong coffee that had sat on the warmer too long as he contemplated where his search had taken him. His brother kept company with a dangerous crowd, and Bergin was not too sure he wanted to venture further into the shadowy life his brother kept hidden from his parents.

The waitress, a tired woman in her fifties slid his dinner plate onto the table in front of him. The fragrance of the food revived him a little.

"Someone asked me to give you this." She snapped her gum as she fished into the pocket of her uniform and pulled out a note.

"Someone? Who?" Bergin looked about, no one else was in the diner, and in the parking lot, there was only his car. He didn't reach for the paper she proffered.

"How the hell should I know, sonny?" She quipped, impatience and sarcasm colored her words. "Some dude with a hat pulled down over his eyes and who didn't look up gave me a buck to give this to you. So here it is." She dropped the note onto the table and walked away shaking her head.

Bergin reached for the note and unfolded the paper. The note was scrawled quickly in an untidy hand in pencil.

The stranger in Erdman's car is supposed to be in town tomorrow, coming to the Dance Hall, midnight. Take care or he will kill you as soon as look at you.

Bergin looked around again as he refolded the note and placed it in his pocket. Tomorrow night he would be at the dance hall and hopefully connect with this stranger who was in his brother's car the night Clara went missing.

Maybe then he could get some answers.

He finished his meal and drove back to the farm as dawn was breaking.

* * *

The day was clear and bright as Bergin worked along side of his father. He was exhausted from being out all night again, but didn't dare say a word about it to his parents. They had no sympathy for him.

As he was finishing in the barn, the clouds began to darken the sky. A cold wind had whipped up coming out of the north. It smelled of snow. He stepped out into the barnyard and looked at the menacing storm clouds that were gathering.

"No, not tonight, please," Bergin whispered to the skies. He didn't want to miss the opportunity to encounter this man he had been looking for.

His father came up behind him and he too looked to the heavens.

"Gonna snow. Better help get the livestock battened down

before it hits." He gestured to the pasture where the cows were grazing on the little stubble they could find.

As they forked the straw into the stalls for the horses, Bergin saw the first flakes begin to fall. With dismay, he watched as the flakes, full and moist, began to accumulate on the frozen ground. The temperature was dropping and the wind was gusting as the sun set, hidden behind a thick veil of clouds.

In the house, Bergin stood by the window and watched as the snowfall became a blizzard that obliterated everything, creating a soundless world of white. The house creaked against the strong winds, and the fingers of the icy currents of air clawed at the worn clapboards and whistled through the thin, un-insulated walls, chilling the house.

Bergin shivered and turned away from the window. He knew it was useless to try and head into town tonight. The snow was drifting and the roads would no longer be discernable. It would take them a while before they could even get to the main road if the snow continued to fall like it had been.

For now, Bergin had been forced to give up his search for the man no one seemed to know that Erdman had in his roadster that September night. He trudged up the stairs and fell into bed, too tired to remove his clothes. He fell into a deep, dreamless sleep.

The snow had come and blanked the land making the rural roads nearly impassable. Winter held the land in its frozen grip for the next few months, snow falling on snow, roads remained obliterated under the drifting whiteness that had transformed the familiar landscape to something strange, beautiful, and ruthless.

Bergin could only bide his time.

When the snow melted, and the roads were passable again he would take up his search for the mystery man.

CHAPTER 32

It was March.

A frosty chill settled about the awakening land as the sun set. No one stirred outside in the dark of the night. The worst of the winter was behind them and some little snow still huddled in the shadow side of buildings and in gullies. The earth was beginning to awaken to the rhythms of spring.

Erdman drove into the barnyard of his parent's home.

No one would see him; it was late at night, and they would all be asleep. He hid his Hudson in the barn. He didn't want to take the chance that anyone would spot it and turn him in. He was still worried that the sheriff would come after him about Clara Lindgren. He had to come back and see if the rumors he was hearing were true. He needed to know if Bergin was moving in on his territory, running his booze routes and hanging about in the dance halls and bars asking questions about a night in late September that he would prefer to forget.

Erdman hid out in the barn until he could be sure his parents would welcome him back home. He was hoping for a big welcome like the Prodigal Son he had learned about from the Bible lessons taught in Sunday school. After the letter he had sent as he left college, he could not assume that his folks would still love him or welcome him.

He also held back because he saw a newer automobile parked by the house and wondered about whose it was. The old Model-T was still there, so he knew his father hadn't gotten a new car. He also knew that the old skinflint wouldn't have bothered to buy anything new, he would have picked up some used piece of junk instead.

The roosters crowed as the sun was beginning to paint the sky in soft colors of peach and pink. Erdman stretched, he had not slept too well in the straw. He needed to relieve himself and he was hungry. Climbing down from the loft, he went into the horse's stall to take care of his most imminent bodily need.

He could smell the bacon frying in his mother's kitchen. He

licked his lips as his stomach rumbled. He stood half hidden behind the barn door and gazed at the house. Should he go in or not; he wrestled with what to do. He didn't think he could take it if his folks threw him out.

His father came out the kitchen door and was walking to the barn. It was time to do the morning milking. Erdman stepped back into a shadow as his father entered the barn and set the milking stool beside one of the cows. The straw made more noise than he would have liked.

His father's body tensed and he looked about warily.

"Who's there?" Mr. Halverson called out into the stillness. He listened, then slowly stood up and looked about. He reached out for the pitchfork that was leaning by the stall. "I know you're there, better come out and be seen, or you'll be skewered on this fork, by golly." The man's face was set in angry determination.

Erdman sighed; he had no other choice but to show himself. He stepped from a shadow into the light, his head down in shame.

"Poppa, it's me, Erdman," his voice was sullen and held none of the usual bravado that was his way.

"Erdman? Son?" His father said in disbelief. "You have come home? We never thought you would come back! Thank God you are home." He dropped the pitchfork in the hay and ran to embrace his son.

Erdman wrapped his arms about his father, knowing now he would be welcomed back into the fold. He didn't have to sleep in barns and fields anymore. He didn't have to look over his shoulder for fear that some small town cop might grab him and throw him in the clink until things could be sorted out with old man Lindgren. There had been a couple of reports of young men nabbed and detained because they looked like Erdman. That was one of the reasons he had laid low.

"Yes, poppa, I'm home if you want me," he tried to keep the joy from his voice.

"Want you?" His father stood back, holding Erdman at arm's length looking him up and down. "Your mother and I have been worried sick for you. We have never wanted you to go away neither. This is your home and always will be." He hugged his son to him again.

A self-satisfied smile spread across Erdman's face. He looked up and saw his younger brother standing in the doorway. He couldn't quite read Bergin's expression. He had never understood his brother in all the years they had been growing up, and he doubted that now he would suddenly be able to figure out this quiet, enigmatic little brother of his.

His father must have sensed something change in Erdman's body; he let go and looked behind him to see Bergin.

"Bergin, come and welcome your brother home! He has finally come back to us." He hugged his wandering son again. "I must tell your mother, she has been praying every day for you to come back to us, my boy!" He patted his son one more time, almost like he was afraid if he let go of him, fearing that he would disappear and it had only been an illusion he had seen.

"Hello Erdman," was Bergin's quiet reply.

"Come in the house, get washed up," Mr. Halverson said, smiling so that his cheeks were aching already. "We fix a special breakfast for you. What you want? Anything in particular? I tell your momma to fix it." Adolph Halverson almost skipped from the barn and across the barnyard to the house. He looked back over his shoulder once as he headed to the house to tell his wife their son had come home to them.

Erdman studied his brother before speaking.

"Little brother, aren't you going to welcome me home too?" He spread his hands in an innocent gesture.

"Welcome home, Erdman," his answer was succinct. "Go on in the house, momma will be wanting to see you. She has cried every night and prayed every day, hoping to see you again." Bergin walked past his brother and sat down at the milking stool to finish the work his father had forgotten in his joy at seeing Erdman. He placed the bucket under the cow, and pulled on the teats. The sound of the milk squirting against the tin of the bucket echoed about the barn.

Erdman wasn't ready to face his mother as yet. He wanted to know what all was going on in the area. He wanted to know why his brother had taken up his business in town. He wanted to know if the heat was still on from old man Lindgren about Clara. Bergin wasn't saying, so he would have to ask.

"It was silly of me to run off like that." He shoved his hands in his pockets and tried to laugh.

Bergin did not reply. He kept milking the cow, the rhythmic sound of the milk landing in the pail the only sound. The warm fragrance of it filling the barn.

"I guess I got scared. Lindgren was pretty hard on me." He walked over to where Bergin was working.

Still no reply from his brother.

Erdman shifted from foot to foot in a nervous dance.

"I wondered if you had heard anything, you know, in town, about me?" He watched his brother's back; he didn't miss a beat in the milking.

He still made no reply.

"Come on, Bergie, talk to me!" His voice had a whiny quality to it now.

Bergin stopped milking for a moment and rested his head on the cow's side. She shifted, and made a soft mooing noise.

"Where is Clara?" Bergin turned and stared at his brother.

"I don't know." He looked about the barn, unable to meet his brother's icy stare. His fingers twisted the fancy ring on his hand nervously.

"You heard about Lindgren's dream?" Bergin's voice had a menacing edge to it that Erdman had never heard before. It frightened him a little.

"It's all bunk. Just the ravings of an old man." He waved his hand through the air like he was swatting at something in front of his face.

"He has told the sheriff his dream," still the same cold tone of voice.

"So?" Erdman asked, finally meeting his brother's gaze. "What does it have to do with me?"

"I remember that you were writing her a letter the day before she disappeared." He sat up straighter and faced Erdman.

"And?" He shrugged his shoulders looking more like a turtle drawing in its head. "I wrote to her more than once you know."

"You were supposed to meet her that night. Her sister read some of the letter, Erdman." His expression was one of disgust.

"Clara was supposed to meet me, we had it all arranged. We planned to run off together." Erdman dragged his toe through some of the straw on the floor.

"What happened?" Bergin looked at his brother, studying him.

"She didn't show up. I don't know why not. I figured she went off by herself. You know, that she had taken up with some other guy, that's why I dropped her."

"Some other guy?" Bergin asked, hardly believing what Erdman was saying.

"Well, yeah. There had to be someone else, didn't there?" He shrugged a shoulder. "Sometimes it seemed as if there was someone else she really liked. I never knew who it could be. She must have been seeing him on the side. You know, cheating on me or something."

"There was no one else; I talked to her often when you were off flirting with the other girls." Bergin moved the milk pail away from the cow and stood up, turning to face Erdman directly. "There was no one else but you. It was always Erdman this and Erdman that."

"Then why didn't she meet me that night?" Erdman looked at the ground, now digging his toe into the dirt. "She must have run off with someone else."

"I doubt that. She was enmeshed in that sticky web you always manage to weave around women," Bergin's voice was touched with the anger that was growing inside him. He never said clearly what a cad his brother really was. That was when he dropped the bomb. "She said she was with child, and that it was yours."

"Mine? How could that be?" He staggered back a few steps, as he pointed to his chest. "No way." He shook his head.

"Don't play the innocent with me. I know you two were fooling around; I saw you one time," his voice was hard and his expression was something Erdman had never seen before. His brother seemed to be full of resentment and hate.

"You little spy." Anger flashed in Erdman's eyes.

"No, I wasn't trying to spy on you. It was time to get going, you had gone off into the fields, and were, well, you know." Bergin's stomach turned as he remembered seeing them like that.

"Then you know I couldn't have hurt her. I cared for her," Erdman pleaded. He knew he had to win his brother to his side. Bergin's obsession with the girl was clouding his judgment. Family is all that mattered, brothers should stick together, not be separated by some easy Rosie-Round-Heels like Clara.

"Cared for her? Really?" Bergin gave a harsh laugh.

"Yeah, you know I did." He looked at Bergin with a sneer of

disbelief.

"I know you called her a hick from the sticks when Manya, that tarted-up girl from Omaha asked you about her," he spat back.

"Compared to Manya, whom one never had to coax to do as I wanted, she was a bit of a hick," Erdman nodded, remembering the easy pleasures of the girl's body. Then it was just as quickly replaced by his anger.

"Manya was a sleazy piece of trash with the bad hair, who would spread her legs at the sight of anyone male and ambulatory. Don't think you were so special big brother. She offered herself to me plenty of times. I refused because I found her, and her well-trafficked body repulsive." He wanted to spit; the taste in his mouth sickened him as he mentally compared the two women. "Clara was worth ten of Manya. Even now the way you said her name, dismissing Clara like she didn't matter."

Erdman stood silent. He had no answer for his brother.

"Go into the house, Erdman, they are waiting to slaughter the fatted calf and welcome you home." He sat back down on the milking stool, dismissing his brother with a wave of his hand. "I have work to do and God knows you won't lift a finger to help."

Erdman stood for a moment, staring at his brother's back. He was surprised by how different he was. Bergin had always been so compliant, so agreeable to everything he had always done. What had changed him?

Erdman shook his head and walked out of the barn. It was something he would have to figure out later on. He would find a way to take care of Bergin. Right now, he was hungry, and wanted to know that he was still loved.

* * *

Erdman was happy to hide out at his parent's farm.

He still hadn't gone into town as yet. That day would come; he was sure. Soon enough, he would make his presence known in town. He felt it might be okay to reappear after his hiatus in a few more weeks.

There were places to go, girls to enjoy and parties to attend. He could pick up and run the booze again, make some more money like he was used to. He hated not having lots of cash to spend on the things he liked. He sure didn't find his pleasures on the farm.

At least his mother and father had made such a fuss over him that he knew it was safe to be home. His only concern was his brother. Bergin had avoided him whenever he was near. He figured his brother was sorry he had come back and taken away the farm from him again.

He shrugged it off, believing his little brother would get over it.

He had other concerns to deal with.

Erdman heard a little more about old man Lindgren from his father, that the old man had turned crazy, telling people about some dream where his daughter came to him and said she was dead.

"The man has gone mad, I tell you. Mad," his father told him with a bitter sneer tapping at his temple with a crooked finger.

"Good," Erdman said out loud as he smiled to himself as he polished his Hudson roadster. That old man had scared him when he came around the college.

He let his thoughts wander as he worked on the automobile.

Maybe Lindgren would get the message and quit making such a fuss over her. She was no great shakes anyway. She was easy enough to bed, but after getting what I wanted off of her, I was ready to move on to someone with a little more flair, who liked to have fun and drink, and let me take what I wanted when I wanted it.

"I sure could use a little of that sort of loving right now. It's been a while," Erdman sighed, his hand straying to his crotch.

CHAPTER 33

Frank De Boer sat at his desk in the sheriff's office looking across at Christian Lindgren again. The man had been in his office nearly every day for the last three or four months insisting that his daughter was dead, telling him that the law needed to do something about it. Lindgren had been to every lawman, every justice of the peace, every magistrate in the county, he had even taken his troubles to the County Attorney to solicit help for his plight.

It had done no good. He had told his tale to just about anyone who would hold still long enough to listen.

Everyone knew about his dream.

"Look, Christian, I can understand how you feel, your daughter's run off and not bothered to contact you." De Boer believed that the girl had gotten herself in trouble, and had gone off to deal with her shame in private. She would return when it was all over. He hadn't let Lindgren know that he believed the girl was pregnant when she went missing. He knew her father would never believe it. De Boer wasn't sure that it was really true, but he had heard it all through the ever-flowing veins of gossip that were part of the life blood of any small community.

He had also known that Clara Lindgren had been running around with the Halverson boy. That was where the problem lay as far as he was concerned. Erdman had always thought he was above the law and that the rules didn't apply to him. His parents were educating him so he could take over the farm. De Boer knew that Erdman had no real intention of farming. Rumor had it that he would sell the farm first chance he got after getting his hands on the property.

Erdman was the opposite of his younger brother, who was hard working, never in trouble and loved the farm. His parents should have nurtured Bergin, not Erdman. But that was his opinion. That and a nickel could get him a cup of coffee.

"No, she not run off," Christian Lindgren's Swedish accent was still thick even after more than forty years in America. It was always thicker when he was under stress and that is where he was right now, stress was taking its toll, and he was sounding like he just got off the boat last week.

His sentences were still imperfect, too. He had never seen the need to educate himself in grammar. He often shrugged and said: "I'm a farmer, what do I need good grammar for? You think the corn is gonna know the difference?" No one could argue with his logic on that point.

"Look, Christian, we've been all through this for months now," De Boer said, rubbing his chin. He wished there was something he could do. He was a small town sheriff without the resources to do much of anything when it came to crime in the area. Most of the time he only had to deal with petty theft, bar fights and the occasional horse thieves once in a while. Crime was low among the hardworking Swedes that farmed the land. It was how he liked it, too.

He thought about Lindgren's daughter. She was probably off having her baby. There had been other girls that had gone missing, only to return looking a little haunted and sad.

"Someone has killed her. This I know." Lindgren pounded his fist on the desk. "I tell you every time, I have a dream, she come to me and call to me, *poppa, I am gone, come find me*. Then she show me the grave, her grave. I am sure of this."

De Boer shook his head helpless to know what to do to help. Lindgren looked like he hadn't slept in weeks. His hair was a tangled mess, his clothes were rumpled and dirty and dark circles ringed his eyes. He had the look in his eyes of a man who was only going through the motions of living. The man had had most of the winter to stew about his haunting dream and his missing daughter.

De Boer figured that the only way to get Christian Lindgren out of his hair was to give in and do a search like the man was asking for. After all, it couldn't hurt. Now that it was spring, the snow had melted and the weather was a little more moderate, he might be able to get some help.

"All right, Christian, if we go take a look for your daughter, will you let it alone if we don't find her?" De Boer looked intently at Lindgren waiting for an answer.

"Yes." The first light of life began to glimmer in his dull eyes. He sat up straighter in the chair and looked eagerly at De Boer. "That is all I ask for, that we go look for my Clara."

"All right. Let me put together a search party, see who would be willing to come help, and plan something for later this month."

"I go ask my friends to help." Christian got up out of the chair less wearily than he had when he sat down. It was as if a great load had been lifted from his shoulders. "My son say he can get some men to help from the American Legion Post. You say the day; we will pass the word. They will come help." He extended his rough hand to the sheriff, a faint smile crinkled at the corners of his eyes.

"Let me know how many people you can round up then." De Boer shook hands with the man, pitying him a little for the pain he was living through.

CHAPTER 34

Bergin wandered into the barn looking for his brother. He knew that whenever there seemed to be work, his brother was not to be found. He climbed the wooden ladder to the loft and saw Erdman sitting by a makeshift table on a bale of hay drinking from a bottle of hooch.

"I thought I might find you here," Bergin said, shaking his head. Bergin had given into his brother's whining and pleading that he go get him some booze. He was able to track down one of Erdman's bootlegging buddies again, who sold him a few cases at a time. Bergin then doled it out to his brother one bottle at a time. He knew that his brother would guzzle the whole stash if he could.

Bergin had not been able to continue going into town as often as he had wanted to see if he could discover who the stranger was with Erdman that night Clara went missing. He had missed the stranger that night when winter had settled in about them and had not been able to pick up the thread again. He had tried to broach the subject with his brother, but all Erdman could do was complain about how Bergin had cut in on his turf, and taken over his means of earning a living.

Erdman had heard the story of Bergin's poker playing escapade, and had been enraged by jealousy, telling him that not one of those men had ever invited him to sit down and play poker with them. Erdman let his brother know that he resented that new car he had bought with some of the gambling money, but he didn't dare say anything about the money to his parents or they would find out that he, too, had been running booze to gamblers and the like.

It was after Bergin had tried to speak to Erdman about that night that his brother had taken to drinking in the barn. There were times when he wished Erdman had stayed away. He was still as useless and good-for-nothing as ever.

He wondered how his parents could still look on Erdman as their pride and joy as he sat up in the loft and got drunk every day, and never did a lick of work about the farm. Sometimes he hated his brother for being the favorite. Bergin hated his parents for treating him as if he was no better than a hired hand. Or worse, as if he didn't exist at all.

Erdman rose and tried to lurch over to where Bergin was standing, but unable to maneuver too well, fell back onto the hay.

"Bergin, little brother, did they send you looking for me? Or have you come on your own?" He saluted his brother with the bottle. "Have some?" He offered.

"No thanks. Not this early in the day." He placed his fists on his hips.

"Prude." Erdman took a deep pull on the bottle. Some of the booze dribbled from the side of his mouth. He wiped it away with the back of his hand.

"Erdman, they are going to search for Clara Lindgren on Saturday. They are asking for volunteers."

"So?" He shrugged his shoulders. "What's that got to do with me?" He was happy sitting in the barn hiding out from his father who wanted him to do some work in the fields. Spring was blossoming, and there were more crops to be planted in the coming weeks.

Bergin knew that the work would go so much faster with Erdman working instead of drinking. But Bergin did have an ulterior motive or two for keeping his brother inebriated. Bergin hoped that eventually his parents might see Erdman for the wastrel that he really was, and Bergin hoped that one day Erdman would tell him what really happened to Clara, and who the silent stranger was in his car that night.

"I am going to go help search for her." Bergin studied his brother's face. "I thought you might want to help, too." Bergin took the bottle his brother offered him. Smelled it and shook his head. He did not make any move to give it back to Erdman.

"Hell, no, little brother." Erdman sat back and put his feet up on the hay table and his hands behind his head. "She is out of my life forever." He smiled and fiddled with his ring, twirling it about his finger. It was something he did often whenever Clara Lindgren's name was mentioned. Unless, of course his hands were full, holding a bottle of booze.

"They are going to look for her up by the old Albertson place," Bergin said, watching his brother's face for any sign of recognition.

He had a feeling that Clara was dead and that his brother knew where Clara was. Over the weeks Erdman had been home, Bergin would mention different remote locations to Erdman, to see if his brother gave anything away.

"What?" He snapped back, wrinkling his brow. The color drained from his face. "Why there?" He tried to sound nonchalant, but his voice quavered, betraying the fear that welled within him.

"Why not there? It's as good a place to look as any." Bergin noticed the shift in his brother's attitude. Suddenly, he saw that Erdman was afraid. He narrowed his eyes at him, unsure of why he would be so terribly afraid. Maybe this was his secret.

"They should look for her in the city, I bet that's where she is hiding out." He tried to fight back the unsettling feeling in the pit of his stomach. He reached his hand out for the bottle. He needed a drink.

"Well, they are going to start at that old farm. I heard that it resembles the one her father saw in his dream about her." He squatted down in front of his brother, the bottle still in his hand.

"That dream is nothing, but pure garbage," he snorted in disgust. "Give me that bottle if you aren't going to have any." He grabbed for the bottle.

"Maybe, maybe not. But I will be there to help." He handed the bottle back to his brother. "I hope to God that they don't find her out there." He stood and looked down at his brother who greedily drank the liquid courage.

"Why should you care? I'm the one who had to screw her, remember?" He barked back at his brother, wiping the mouth of the bottle before taking another drink.

"It distresses me to hear you speak that way of that particular pleasure," Bergin shook his head as he looked down at his brother. "Clara was an exceptional woman. You should have treated her better."

"She was a pain in the ass," Erdman shook his head in disagreement. "A clinging vine who wanted me to settle down, get trapped into a life that I never want to live. Farming, wife and children. Ugh, it's so disgusting, so mundane. It's not for me."

"All parties and fun for you?" Bergin asked.

"Yes, for as long as I can." He swilled the booze into his mouth, letting it burn his throat on the way down.

"Well, if you get a conscience between now and Saturday, you know where all of us will be." Bergin looked down at his brother and shook his head knowing Erdman was never going to change his mind or his ways.

"Don't worry, little Bergie, you won't find me wasting my time looking for that stupid girl. I told you all, she went off with someone else." He let go a resonant belch.

"The man you had with you that night, did she go off with him?" He tried once again to get his brother to tell him who the man was.

"That's for me to know and for you to find out," Erdman's slurred words were almost indistinguishable from the alcohol.

Bergin turned to go. He knew he would get nothing more out of his brother for now. He would have to take another trip into town soon, see if he could find anything more on who that stranger was.

CHAPTER 35

Early on a cold misty morning in late March, Sheriff De Boer gathered a group of volunteers to search for the Lindgren girl. More than one hundred men had said they would help when he put the word out. It looked to be more like two hundred that had come out to help that frosty morning. That was no surprise to him. It was a closely knit community bound together by familial relationships that reached back to Sweden for many generations.

It was also a community that was worried for Christian Lindgren and was outraged that any young lady would be so used and abused by a wastrel of a man such as Erdman. They had heard the rumors and they had each in turn passed on some piece of the gossip that had spread like an infection through the community. It had managed to accomplish one positive thing, however. If the rumors were correct, it had trapped Erdman on his farm tighter than a stone wall. There was nowhere he could go now without being taunted for what he had done to Clara Lindgren.

He looked about at the number of men who had come to help. He was pleased that so many people cared enough about helping, but was somewhat saddened that they had not cared enough for her in life to have paid her court, or married her.

In humoring Mr. Lindgren, he agreed to have the men begin to walk through the fields on the hills just beyond the ruins of an old house that the elderly man said he had seen in his dream. Lindgren couldn't tell them anything more than the house was where he had been brought to at the opening of the dream, and then, after walking a distance, that he could not determine there would be another clump of trees. That was the place, he said, they would find his Clara in her long and narrow grave.

The weather had not cooperated. It was a terribly cold day. The land was blanketed in a thick foggy mist that bit into the marrow of a man's bones. These were the worst conditions to man an expedition. Sheriff De Boer had been trying to decide what to do next.

De Boer was about ready to cancel the search; the fog was so terribly thick he hadn't been able to see but a few feet in front of him on his drive in to his office that morning. Lindgren wouldn't hear of calling it off. He said it was foggy in his dream too. That it was a sign that this was the day they would find his daughter.

De Boer deliberated for a little, then with a curt nod of his head he ordered the searchers to assemble as instructed.

They all drove out to the place where Lindgren said they should begin. To where there was a crumbling ruin of a house that had once been the Albertson's place. It had been built of the stones found so abundantly in the fields in this area back in the 1870's when the farm had been prosperous. Around the turn of the century, Lars Albertson had flown into a drunken fit of rage and slaughtered his entire family, then killed himself. No one found them until weeks later.

Some said there was still blood that could be seen on the rotting floorboards. That the places where they had found the family were stained black and no amount of scrubbing could clean the stains away.

Others said they had seen the pale forms of what had been the family as they called out across the fields on cold, snowy evenings. Crying out for help and beckoning with hands of rotted flesh and bones.

That was the reason that some said the property was haunted. Maybe that was why the fields close to the old house were still not tilled. One story a farmer told was that he was tilling the soil near the house and saw old man Albertson's ghost come after him with a gun. He never went back, and the area gained an evil reputation.

That was the area that they were heading to for the search. Each man knew the reputation, but they had not let their inner fears stand in the way of helping Christian Lindgren look for his missing daughter.

The fog lay thickly on the land. The men assembled by the ruined house, each looking over his shoulder, a little afraid of what might be peering at them through the empty windows. Even the stirring of a torn lace curtain in a broken window set them on edge.

Their voices murmured softly in the mist, their words lost in its milky folds.

The sheriff gave the directions. They would spread out an arm's length apart. Each man would walk the field from west to east; a stick in their hands to test the ground if they turned up something suspicious.

Like a group of nervous horses spooked by the fog, the men cautiously began to spread out into a line. They measured out their distance, each laying a hand on the shoulder of the next man. No one too willing to stray too far from the next man for fear he too would be lost in the oblique whiteness.

No one said a word. Silence enfolded them as much as the fog. Not even the birds twittered in their nests that morning. The solitariness of the stillness made each man feel horribly alone.

De Boer looked up. The sun was little more than a pallid, frozen circle in the sky. He called to the men to begin. His words were lost in the swirling whiteness. But the men whispered to one another to begin, passing the command down the line in each direction away from the center.

They moved gradually, like a wave across the field.

The men walked slowly on their route unsure of what was before them. The mist was burning off slowly as the weak sunlight began to try to warm the day. Visibility was increasing, revealing a fairyland painted in frosted white; it clung to the trees, to the grasses, to everything. It was as if they were intruding on some other world where everything was insubstantial.

Slowly, the searchers moved forward into a place where the fog was thinner, and they could see a few more feet in front of them. Then it would close about them again, robbing them of their sense of direction and sight. Everything was clothed in the white, misty folds of nothingness.

They would try to shiver off their fears of the unknown.

The men would press on, hoping for another glimpse of the ground, of trees and one another. In a moment the fog again lifted, some of them stood in a grove of ancient oak trees.

Carl Peterson tripped on a tree root, and disturbed some of the soil. His brother, Fritz walking near and a little behind, saw that the soil was a little different in color, the way the earth looks after it had been turned. The rest of the soil around it was dark brown. This was a yellowish color. They all knew no one tilled the soil up here, so close to the old Albertson place.

"Here," Fritz called out, jabbing his stick into the earth. There was little resistance to his prodding, proving out that the soil had recently been turned. "Here, this must be it. The earth is soft."

His words were murmured up and down the line, as no shouting could penetrate the hush of the fog that enveloped them.

De Boer hurried to where Peterson had called out. He saw the tree root that Carl had tripped over, and the yellow-brown soil. He squatted down to take a closer look. A white, misty wisp of fog reached up and encircled his fingers as he touched the soil.

He pulled his hand back as if he had been bitten.

For the first time, he had a feeling that this was the place Clara Lindgren would be found. He realized that he hadn't really believed Christian Lindgren at all. He looked up and met the gaze of Christian Lindgren as he searched De Boer's face for an answer to his unspoken question. *Will you find my Clara, now?*

De Boer stood up and nodded to Lindgren. The older man could do nothing now but stare at the ground. A tear trickled down his cheek, and froze there. He did not wipe it away; he knew that, just as in his dream, this was Clara's tear.

The sheriff ordered some men to get some picks and shovels, and begin to move the scrub of broken branches and then to remove the earth cautiously. A frosty white tapestry of stubble decorated the ground. They removed the glacially pallid branches, piling them a few feet away.

The huge oaks stood like sentinels looking down on the work of the men.

They worked for hours.

They worked in silence.

The only sounds were of shovels on stone and earth, and even that was muffled by the cloying closeness of the fog.

Slowly they shoveled the soil and rocks away. It had not been an easy task to dig this grave. The rocky soil had been frozen, and did not give way easily. They used picks to break up the surface soil, and once below the permafrost, they used shovels.

It was not long before they uncovered the heels of some shoes.

The grave was not even two feet deep.

As they continued to excavate, an unpleasantly cold wind picked up, chilling the men to the core of their beings. The fog began to dissipate, and soon all that remained of its milky mantle was the frozen whiteness that still clung to everything like a shroud. A pale sun shone down weakly on the grave as they stood about it in silence; each man whispered a prayer from their hearts for the girl they had discovered lying there face down before them.

De Boer stood next to Lindgren. Lindgren was silent; tears flowed down his cheeks. De Boer thought he could feel the man's pain; it was so palpable in the air. He motioned to the men to remove her.

Gently, they took her from the shallow grave, placed her on the ground and turned her face up. A thin shaft of sunlight broke through the mist and clouds and shone on her face for the first time in six months, then it was gone, and the gray dimness returned.

She was as her father had described.

She was wearing her very best coat dress of cotton in the dark colors of fall; browns, greens, russet, and dark yellow. Over the dress was her best golden-brown, woolen coat. Her left hand was clenched in a fist and was at her heart, between her breasts. She also wore a pearl necklace, and a little purse hung on the belt of her dress.

There were leaves in her hair, and dirt on her cheeks.

It was a long narrow hole in the ground where she had lain these many months. It was all just as Lindgren had seen in his dream: just as he had described it to each one of them over and over so that they too knew all the facts of the dream by heart.

They looked on at Lindgren as he knelt by the body of his daughter, Clara, and wept. They wept with him.

* * *

Bergin Halverson stood in the folds of the fog and watched as they uncovered Clara's body. Anger burned in his chest as he stood there powerless to do anything. There were questions that he would ask his coward of a brother who he had left sniveling in the loft of the barn back home. He couldn't help but think that Erdman had something to do with Clara's being here in this terrible place.

* * *

By the time the coroner arrived, there were one hundred men standing silently around Clara's shallow grave. In a hushed silence, they had gathered boughs and branches and laid them about her out of respect.

The fog had persisted most of the day, but the cold wind had dissipated most of the mists, though some still clung to the lower-lying areas of the ground.

Night was coming on.

At the coroner's signal they lifted her up and laid her into a long, shallow, wicker basket that had been brought specifically for transporting her remains. They were careful not to touch her, or brush the mud from her clothes or her face, nor to remove the leaves that had tangled in her soft hair.

Some of the men checked the ground and gathered up everything they could find that had been hers; even a few pearls that had fallen back to the earth when they lifted her into the basket.

A half-dozen men stepped forward to carry her. Bergin was one of them.

In silence, the body of Clara Lindgren was gently placed into the back of the hearse. Her father stood and watched as the horse drawn carriage made its way slowly down the trampled path to the dirt road. A fine dust, disturbed by the wheels, curled up and about the hearse, like spectral figures of children playing behind the vehicle.

A light snow began to fall.

The men turned their faces up to watch the snow falling through the branches of the tall oaks that sheltered the grave.

The ethereal gloom of twilight was settling in around them. If they had looked beyond the trees, they could see the lights in the Halverson's farm windows; it was only a quarter mile away.

* * *

In the murkiness, as night began to settle in, a solitary figure stood looking in the direction of the searchers, wondering if they'd find his little secret.

He trembled not from the damp, but from the darkness in his soul.

CHAPTER 36

Adolph Halverson looked up to see his oldest boy walking past the barn. He had heard the rumors in town. He had heard the details of the dream, and that each detail was true, just as his neighbor Christian Lindgren had dreamed them.

That frightened him.

This girl had written to them months ago claiming that Erdman was the father of her child. He had not known her, but knew that the Lindgren's were good people, for the most part, and he wondered if his son had been less that truthful to them about this whole affair and his involvement with Clara Lindgren.

Though he didn't like to hear what Bergin was saying about Erdman, his favorite child, he could no longer shut it out. It saddened him that Bergin had turned out to be such a disappointment in so many ways. He didn't know why, but he had never really liked the boy. Ever since he was an infant crying incessantly in his mother's arms, he had taken a dislike to the child. It was why he had turned a deaf ear to whatever the boy had been saying to and about Erdman for a long time now.

He still didn't want to believe what he had been hearing about Erdman, especially if it came from a jealous little brother that he had no time for. There were some things that he could not shake loose from his mind about Erdman.

There were things he had been learning about his son that he never would have guessed were possible. He thought that he and his wife had raised their son to be a good, honest, sober, God-fearing young man. But, of late, his son had been completely useless due to his constant state of drunkenness. He didn't know where the booze had come from, but Erdman always managed to get his hands on a bottle and couldn't seem to leave it alone.

If he was honest with himself, his son now disgusted him. His wife still treated him like he was a little boy and refused to hear anything negative about him, and refused to hold him accountable. Maybe that had been their mistake. They had always bailed him out whenever he had gotten into a scrape of any kind.

He was resolved; if Erdman had anything to do with this disappearance and death of Clara Lindgren, he would not stand for it. He would no longer cover up for his son. He had done so once because he wasn't sure if it was an accident and preferred to believe his son when he wept in his arms and said he was so sorry that the gun had gone off by accident, and that he didn't know it was loaded.

Adolph blamed himself in many ways; he felt he had failed his son in not teaching him well enough about firearms. He had pleaded with the sheriff to rule it an accident; Erdman was young and had his whole life before him. The sheriff had given in. Now he wondered if he had done the right thing.

"Erdman," he called out from the barn. "Erdman!"

After a few moments, Erdman came into the barn and looked about.

Adolph beckoned him to come into the barn where he was repairing one of the horse bridles. He noticed that his son was sober at least. It was still early enough in the day. But the boy seemed to have a hangover. He had found Erdman passed out on the parlor floor that morning and had left him to lay there until he could come out of it and forage for some coffee and bread his mother had left out for him.

"I want to ask a question, my son." His father waved him to come over. Erdman came out of the bright sunlight of midday into the soft light of the barn.

"What do you need, Father?" Erdman asked, rubbing his head as if that could relieve the pain of another hangover.

"This girl, did you have anything to do with her disappearance and her death?" He asked standing defensively as if he was waiting to take the crushing blow the truth could deliver.

"How could you ask me such a thing?" Erdman stepped back and gave him a look of disbelief. His breath reeked of alcohol and stale coffee.

"I remember that night she was to have gone missing. I was up; I heard the chime clock ring out one in the morning. Then I hear you drive up and park your car." He put the awl down and looked in his son's eyes, hoping for the truth.

"That was not the only night I came in after one," Erdman's voice had a whiney quality to it presently. He fidgeted with the pocket on his overalls.

"Not right away did you come in the house, but soon enough you do, after fiddling with the car, I think. Then you come in the house and turn on the radio. I came downstairs to see if everything was all right. I see you eating a sandwich and reading a catalogue." He looked the boy over closely.

"Yeah?" He looked at his father, expecting him to say something more. He began to turn the ring about on his finger. "That may have been what I was doing that night. I don't remember exactly."

"I go back to bed and wait until I hear you come to bed a little later," he continued, noticing the discomfort Erdman seemed to be in as he spoke.

"So what? Are you spying on me now?" Erdman crossed his arms across his chest defiantly.

"No. I just remember because it seemed strange at the time." He shrugged and took up the awl again to continue his work.

"It was nothing," he dismissed his father's questioning look with an impatient wave of his hand.

Erdman walked away as Bergin curried one of the horses in the stalls near by.

* * *

Bergin had been working on the horses, when his father had called to Erdman to come into the barn. He stayed there, brushing the horse as he listened. He knew if he stopped currying the horse would snort and he didn't want to call attention to his presence so close by.

It was the first time their father had ever questioned Erdman. He wondered what the old man had seen or heard to make him question anything his perfect son had done. He listened with interest as his father asked Erdman about Clara, and then of what happened that night.

Bergin stiffened with the tension of knowing this was important to what he had put together so far. He needed to take some time and put it all together properly. He had been frustrated that he had not been able to do as much in town now that Erdman was home. Bergin no longer could use the excuse of doing something for Erdman, which had allowed him to head to town.

He wondered, too, why his father had never made a comment about the new car or the clothes that were delivered the next week after he ordered them. Maybe it was because he just hated to admit that Bergin existed.

He sighed as he heard Erdman tell his father "it was nothing" and begin to turn away. It was then he made his presence known in the stall, stepping out to curry the rump of the horse. Erdman had seen him, and paled somewhat.

Bergin even chuckled to himself about having to deal with more than one horse's ass at the present time.

* * *

Erdman resented his father's questions. He was supposed to believe in him, not question him about that stupid Lindgren girl. They had found her; she was dead, so why was he asking these questions?

He shot an angry glance at Bergin as he appeared from the back of a stall. That little creep always seemed to be lurking about listening in to everything. He crossed the barnyard and went into the house to get out of the warm sun.

He needed to think. He was worried.

What if his father had seen him come in late that night? He had been out, just as he had been out so many other nights. He had been to Council Bluffs for a while; there were people who could vouch for where he was. Murray down at the pool hall; he had offered the man a drink, and they killed off a bottle out behind the hall. Then he had gone to the Ogden Hotel to see if there was any action there. Sometimes some of his friends would gather in the bar. The twins had danced with him, but he soon got tired of their company and left. He had hung around in Council Bluffs to see if Clara would show up.

But she hadn't.

Clara Lindgren had not come to town. She stood him up. So he decided to call it a night and headed back to the farm. He did make one more stop on his way home. He had driven down the lane. . . but he didn't want to think about that.

And there was that man.

He shoved the thoughts aside.

He sighed. He hated what his life had become now, thanks to her.

He hated it that he was no longer able to attend college and sample the best of life, the girls, the sex, and the booze. That stupid girl had taken it all away from him.

He needed a drink.

It was time to go look and see if another bottle would miraculously appear in that special hiding place behind the barn. He kicked at the dirt as he walked, making a list of the people he could blame for his troubles.

He snorted an angry laugh.

He thought of his brother.

He hated the way his brother looked at him; it was as if little Bergin knew his deepest, darkest secret. He couldn't have that. No one must know his secrets.

No one.

No one at all.

Especially not little Bergie.

Bergie who was such a little goody-two-shoes.

He laughed as he thought of how he was the favored son, and how his little brother always caught the heat for what troubles he had gotten himself into. For years, he could always get away with blaming his brother for his misdeeds.

He stopped a moment and scratched his head. A nasty thought flitted about his mind. . . could he find a way for Bergin to take the heat with the Lindgren girl?

"If only," he said aloud as he turned the corner of the barn. "Somehow I don't know that it would work this time."

He began to search in the weeds that tangled in the ground on the back wall of the barn. No one ever bothered to mow them, so they were long, jumbled and a great place to hide a bottle.

"Okay, I know you're here little bottle. Come to Erdie," he called softly as he swept his hands through the tall weeds. "Ah! There you are my little treasure. Come to poppa and make me forget my troubles." He snatched up the bottle and kissed it with pleasure.

As he turned to go, he noticed the sun glinting off another glassy surface. He leaned over closer and saw there was another bottle hiding in the tousled, spring growth.

"What do we have here?" He looked around to see if anyone

was looking, then grasped the bottle and tucked it into his overalls.

"My fairy godmother of the booze must have heard my wish. A second bottle. Just what I wanted. Just what I needed." He flashed a smile of thanks to the sky.

He had two bottles now. So, he decided he was going to really get drunk. He headed off to climb up into the loft; hopefully, his father would be off doing something else, and his jerk of a brother would have finished with the horses by then.

He poked his head around the barn and looked in. It was quiet. He slipped inside and looked again. No one was around. He took his prizes up into the loft.

He took a long pull on the golden liquid.

"Wow. This hooch is pretty strong stuff this time," Erdman said to himself. He took another drink. It was hitting him hard, but that was just what he wanted. "Come, oh mighty veil of drunkenness, take away the memories that won't leave me alone." He hoisted the bottle to the roof before taking another swig.

"Get her out of my mind!" He took another swig and lay back on the hay. The world was looking fuzzy now.

Maybe he could get some sleep.

* * *

Bergin had placed a second bottle beside the one he usually left for his brother. Maybe Erdman could drink himself to death. He knew his thoughts were sinful, but he had come to loathe his brother and suspected that he was the one who had killed Clara and placed her in that shallow grave all because he wouldn't face up to the consequences of his pleasure-seeking ways.

He had seen Erdman head out of the barn, and heard him fumbling in the back looking for his daily fix. He finished brushing the horse, and found some excuse to get their father out of the barn so Erdman could secrete himself in the loft and tie one on.

The second bottle was in the hope that he could get him sufficiently drunk to actually confess to the truth of what had happened to Clara Lindgren. He knew his brother had something to do with it, and he needed to know exactly what it was.

Bergin had, in a way, fallen in love with Clara, and had never had the chance to let her know that she had truly been loved. It was a deep hurt that would not go away.

He would wait until he was sure his brother had guzzled enough of that rotgut to sufficiently loosen his tongue before he would head up to the loft and ask him some more questions.

CHAPTER 37

Sheriff Frank De Boer had asked that there be a team of doctors present to autopsy Clara's remains. There were too many rumors flying about, and he wanted to be sure that it would be a group of well-known and well-respected medical men who examined her, so there would be no questions and as few rumors as possible. Dr. Charles Burton, a professor of pathology at the university, worked along with the other two doctors from town, Dr. Meade and Dr. Watkins.

The only place available to them was the funeral home where they usually prepared bodies for burial. There was no hospital or morgue near enough, and neither doctor had adequate facilities to perform an autopsy.

As Clara's body was lifted from the wicker basket onto the table, a rapid-fire tattoo of sound echoed about the room, as the pearls from her broken necklace fell onto the table and then the floor, startling them all.

Dr. Meade picked them up, gently placing them into a little pan. Also, a small bottle of perfume fell from her purse, releasing a spicy, earthy fragrance. He took the vial and tightened the cap, also placing it in the pan. As they began to examine her clothing, tightly folded sheaves of paper fell from her bodice. Meade took a pair of tweezers and lifted them carefully, placing the wad of paper in another pan. They could see that there was something written on the pages in a purple ink.

They would examine it later.

Her clothing was carefully removed and placed on a nearby table. They recorded every detail.

They turned their attention to the body next.

Most of the soft tissue had desiccated below the skin, which had become like brittle, tanned leather. She was still recognizable in a frighteningly grotesque way. Her hair was still a soft brown, crusted here and there with the dried remains of body fluids.

The three men looked at one another and then with a slight nod from Dr. Burton they proceeded with the autopsy. Each man was aware of the feelings toward this poor girl, and the pain her father had been carrying. They all knew too well the dream the man had related to them also.

When Dr. Burton turned Clara's head so he could take a closer look, a large chuck of the skull bone fell to the table. He examined the damage to her head. The skull was crushed as if someone had hit her with something like the back of a shovel from behind. There were also fractures at the left temple.

"It could have been the one blow that killed her, or the combination of them all," he said, indicating the broken fragments of her skull.

"It didn't take long for her to die," Dr. Meade said as a statement more than a question.

"No," Dr. Burton replied.

The doctors continued to examine her body.

"There does not seem to be any rape here either." Dr. Watkins had delivered Clara, as well as most of the babies in the county over the past thirty years.

"Any sign of abortion?" Dr. Meade asked.

"Not that I can see," Dr. Watkins shook his head.

"They said she was pregnant," Dr. Burton stated the rumor he had heard.

"Shall we have a look then, gentlemen?" Dr. Watkins picked up a scalpel, but waited for his collogues to give their assent.

The blade cut through her leathery skin and was folded back to reveal the ribcage. Dr. Burton cut through the bones, and removed the sternum and part of the ribcage so they could examine what was left of the organs.

She had been killed late in September, and had lain undetected by the local vermin through the winter. Most of her body was intact, with little destruction by the infestation of bugs that are so prevalent in dead bodies. The organs had shriveled and were also somewhat leathery in consistency.

Carefully, Dr. Watkins then slit open her belly and peeled back the skin, shifted her desiccated organs and cut through the tissues of the womb to reveal the small body of a fetus that had been growing inside of her. He examined the small infant that had never had a chance to be born.

"This baby seems to be about six months along, and was a girl," Dr. Meade concluded upon closer examination of the small body resting within Clara's body.

In silence, they finished their autopsy and sewed her back together again. She would be readied for burial next. They covered her with a cloth, each of the doctors touched by the work they had completed.

"No one should have to die like that and be left alone in such a place," Dr. Watkins commented with a frown as he straightened the edge of the fabric that covered Clara's body.

Once they had completed their work, they invited the county coroner and Sheriff De Boer to come witness the opening of the wad of paper that had fallen from her bodice when they had first laid her on the autopsy table.

With tweezers, Dr. Burton carefully opened the papers, prying them apart; they were the pages of a letter written to Clara that was dated on the morning of the day she disappeared.

CHAPTER 38

The news spread quickly through the community. The body of Clara Lindgren had been found, just as her father had described from his dream. Immediately followed by the question, who would have done such a thing to her? Then adding that she was such a sweet girl.

There was a group of older women who gathered once a week to quilt. They sat around the walnut quilt frame with their latest project stretched across the boards.

"It was so sad to hear that Clara Lindgren was found dead," a woman spoke softly in thickly accented English. Like so many of her generation, the lilt of their native Swedish colored their speech.

"My Fritz was there, and he said that she was dressed in her best clothes." She fitted the thimble onto her finger and poised her needle, looking around at the others before making her first stitch.

"Her papa saw it all in a dream. I hear him tell it." Another woman bit off the thread from the spool and threaded the needle. She had been threading needles for so many years she didn't even need to look at it anymore.

"And there was a terrible cold mist that clung to everything until they found her. Then and only then, when they took her out of the grave did the sun break through the mist and shine on her face," a third woman added as she wove her needle in and out of the fabric quickly, each stitch small and evenly spaced from years of practice.

"Her papa cried like a baby there beside his Clara," the next woman said as she knotted off the thread between her thumb and forefinger.

"Who would have done this to her?" Deftly, the first who had spoken, said as she pulled her thread through the layers of fabric.

No one said a word.

The sound of their needles pulling thread through the cotton layers was the only sound in the room. Each knew the name, but no one dared to say it. Some of them were related to them by marriage or were very distant cousins.

"They say she was seeing someone," one of them said at last, her eyes darting from face to face still not able to say his name.

"Yah, we all know. I hear that she was with that Erdman Halverson boy," another said softly, her lips pressed tightly together after she spoke his name.

"I hear tell that when they took her to the funeral parlor for the Doctor to look her over, they found a letter," one of the women said with the tone of authority. Someone had let it slip out into the rivers of gossip that the letter had been found.

"I heard that too. A letter written in purple ink," she punctuated her words with a taught pull on her thread.

"Poor Clara Lindgren," a woman clacked her tongue.

They all nodded in agreement and turned their attention back to the work at hand. The quilt was a present for Mrs. Lars Hanson, who was expecting her first child.

CHAPTER 39

Christian Lindgren stood in front of the sheriff's desk. De Boer had offered him a seat, but he had chosen to stand. He looked a lot better than the last time he had been in the sheriff's office.

"You know what you must do, Sheriff," Lindgren said. "You must go and arrest that boy that did this to my Clara."

"Christian, you know I can't just go arrest him without some proof." De Boer leaned back in his chair and shook his head from side to side. The inquest had begun that day. The pages of Erdman's letter were pressed between two pieces of glass for all to see. Her sister Ingmar had identified it as the letter Erdman had sent to Clara that day, asking her to meet him.

"My Clara is dead; he was her young man, what more do you need?" He sputtered in anger. "You seen the letter."

"It's not that easy, Christian. I have to build a case so we can try him and send him to jail." He sat forward and spread his hands in supplication. "We have to follow the law. I'm confident the coroner's inquest will indict Erdman Halverson," he said, knowing full well he would like to go out there and grab the little punk and throw his sorry keester in the hoosegow for a while and make him talk. He rubbed his fingers over his fist, knowing that was how he wanted to speak to that rotten, little murdering rat, Erdman Halverson.

"So meanwhile he can go about living life, breathing the air that he took from my girl?" His voice was soft, resigned and full of pain.

"I know it's not the answer you would like, but believe me, I, for one, do not intend to let him get away with it." He looked at Christian, met his gaze and nodded. "I'm doing all I can to bring him to justice for what he did to Clara. Please believe me."

"Yah. I know you are a good man, and will do all you can." He turned and walked to the door. With his hand on the doorknob, he turned and spoke again. "We bury my Clara day after tomorrow from the church where she was baptized, confirmed and I had hoped she would have been married. Please come if you can."

CHAPTER 40

In a dark corner at the back of the pool hall, in the late afternoon, a man sat by himself nursing a beer. He fiddled with a three-stone diamond ring on his little finger, turning it around and around. It was a nervous habit of his. He had come back to collect a debt that was owed to him. It had taken him a little while to discover where the man lived so he could send him a message. He was not about to confront him on his own turf. He wanted the gutless wonder to come to him. He wanted the lily-livered jerk to pay him what he promised.

He took out a Council Bluffs postal card he had picked up of a man and a woman holding hands on what was called lover's outlook or some fool thing like that. They were standing atop an oddly eroded formation of one of the Loess Hills that were so prevalent in the area. He thought the image was apt, with everything taken into consideration.

He penned a message, and affixed the stamp. He would mail it as soon as he finished his beer. He knew it would arrive the next morning.

CHAPTER 41

The banner headline on the local newspaper that day announced that the coroner's inquest had indicted Erdman Halverson for the murder of Clara Lindgren. The paper related the details of the trial for the readers to devour, since there was not enough room in the courtroom for everyone to fit.

Death, for Clara, was instantaneous from a crushing blow to the back of her head from a spade or hammer.

They printed a copy of the letter that was found on her body at the autopsy. It was a crucial piece of evidence in bringing the indictment against Erdman Halverson. The paper related that Clara's left hand was clenched over her heart, as if to guard the letter secreted in her bodice and held it there. They also noted that the ink used to write the letter was purple.

Dear Friend,

I suppose you may be thinking that I have been awfully neglectful of you, but really, I haven't been at all. You see, the fact is that I have not been able to write to you at all. The reason for that is because I was in the hospital for a while. I had a couple operations. Now, I think it is the right time for us to show some sort of action.

Here is my idea for what we should do.

We should get away. But not for good. We should disappear for a while, you know, so I thought we could skip town for a couple of weeks. On our way we can go and get the ceremony over with. Then later, we can come back. Maybe a few weeks from now, to tell everyone, if they don't already know all about it. See about getting one of your brothers to take you to the dance in Council Bluffs later tonight.

I will meet you there.

Then we can get across the river to Omaha to take care of the things. Do not take any clothes or a suitcase. Just what you can wear. You don't want to raise suspicion. See if you can try to lay your hands on some cash. As much as you can. We will need it so we can have a comfortable trip. At least Omaha is a big town and we can holdup there for a little bit on whatever cash you can manage to scrounge together.

I plan to be in Council Bluffs between nine and ten o'clock. Look for me. And when you see me, come on out of the hall and walk up the road until I catch up to you. And remember, everything, everything must be kept on the QT.

Leave a note someplace where your family can find it in a day or so. Just say that you have gone away for a little while, tell them not to worry. Let them know you will be back as soon as you can. Remember not to tell them where you are going. And above all, do not mention my name to anyone.

I will look for you in town. But if that won't work, you can sneak out of the house sometime around midnight. Head out towards the road. I will look for you there. Just walk down the road until I can meet you. Be sure not to let anyone see you either. Follow my instructions, and all will be fine. One more thing, destroy this letter. Be sure to destroy all the letters I have written to you. Again, do not to mention my name to anyone at all.

One more thing to do, put on an act. If anyone mentions me, keep a hard attitude towards me to your folks.

Do everything just as I ask and it will all be okay. Because, if you don't do as I ask, your one chance will be gone and I will not be around anymore. So, if you wish to steer clear of humiliation, do as I say and keep it all mum. I will see you later tonight.

Remember, do as I have asked you, and destroy all my correspondence.

* * *

In the parlor of a farmhouse, a man read the letter as printed in the newspaper. His heart sank. He had been wrestling with the worst thoughts a parent can have about a child. Now he knew there would be no denying the truth. He might not be able to let anyone else know his true feelings, but in his heart he knew.

He knew the terrible truth that his son was a murderer.

Adolph Halverson knew that Erdman always used that purple ink in his letters.

CHAPTER 42

Adolph was working in the fields early the next morning. The pain he felt the evening before when he read the newspaper had turned into anger. He knew the best way to dissipate it was to get to work, and sweat it out. He was disgusted with his son, and had discovered, once again, Erdman had not come to bed that night. Adolph Halverson went looking for him. He found Erdman passed out in the barn, a bottle still clutched in his hand. The hand where he wore that fancy ring that made him look like some cheap criminal.

He took the bottle, poured out what little remained in the bottle and threw it in the trash. He wanted to shake Erdman, shake the boy hard so he would come out of this stupid place where he seemed to do nothing but wallow in self-pity. What could have been so terrible in the young man's life that he had to drown it so deep in alcohol?

He blamed himself, feeling that he had failed his son.

* * *

Bergin had finished the morning chores around the house. His mother told him that his father had gone out to the fields and would be back when he had calmed down. Bergin knew that meant he was to be left alone. He wondered what had upset him so; usually the man was angry at him for something. Bergin had not spoken to his father for a few days. That was not unusual at all. He didn't think he had done anything to incur the man's wrath.

Bergin stopped, his body tensed. He wondered if his father had found out that he was the one supplying Erdman with the booze? He shook his head and relaxed. If that had happened, his father would have come after him and beaten him senseless.

Bergin walked into the parlor. The room was never in any state of disarray, his mother wouldn't stand for any mess, in the case that someone may pay her a call. He saw the newspaper lying on the floor.

He picked it up and read the headline.

Letter Lured Clara Lindgren to Her Death
Last Tryst Note from Erdman Found on Body

Then he read the article and the letter. Like his father, he was filled with the knowledge of Erdman's involvement in Clara's disappearance and subsequent death. What other explanation could there be?

He knew his brother was a useless waste of human flesh, but could he really have killed Clara? It was a doubt that nagged at him. His brother had done a lot of despicable things, but could he kill a woman as simply as he had killed Tommy Stenns?

He folded the newspaper and headed up to his room.

Like his father, he needed some privacy.

* * *

Erdman stirred a little, coming to. The ground was hard beneath him. He figured he hadn't made it to bed again. Where had he ended up this time? His mother had allowed him to sleep on the parlor floor the other day. It had been where he had passed out, unable to make it up the stairs to his bed.

He reluctantly tried to pull open an eye. Matter had seemed to glue them shut. He rubbed at them, and when he was able to open them, he looked about.

"Hell, I'm in the barn still," he mumbled to himself. "Maybe no one noticed."

He tried to sit up, everything began to spin, or at least to tip sideways then crash back to level before tipping sideways again. He lay back down with a loud groan. He just was not ready to get up yet.

Soon he slipped back into an alcohol-induced sleep.

* * *

Bergin had tried to make a timeline of his brother's movements for Thursday, September twenty-fifth. The work around the farm was complete for the day, and the sun was setting by the time he had driven off to town. Bergin couldn't remember exactly what time he had gone. There was nothing to set the memory in his mind; it was so like many other evenings when Erdman headed off pleasure-bent for town.

Bergin had discovered that Erdman had been dancing with Christine and Marie in the dance hall until about ten or ten-thirty. Then he spent some time drinking with some friends, and had gone in the pool hall until about eleven-thirty. That was when the manager of the Ogden Hotel and the other man had seen a stranger climb into the back of Erdman's car and wait for him.

He had asked many people, yet, no one knew who the man was.

Bergin made notes on a scrap of paper, lining out the hours and events. He noted the gaps in the timeline.

Their father had heard Erdman come home after one in the morning, fiddle about with the Hudson Roadster for a bit before coming inside and fixing himself a sandwich. Erdman listened to the radio, and looked at a catalogue before heading upstairs to bed.

The next morning the Lindgren brothers had come over looking for their sister.

They had said something about Erdman's car having new tires that didn't look as if they had been used at all. He thought he had seen what could have been an impression caused by the car left in the dirt around Erdman's car. After the Lindgren brothers left, he spent a little time looking about to see if he could find any recently discarded tires for that automobile.

To his dismay he did find four tires, stuffed into a bin in the back of the barn. One of the tires had a distinct patch, just like the Lindgrens had mentioned. What that meant to him was, at sometime that night, Erdman must have been out to Clara's place.

Bergin sighed, hating himself for learning this. He really had hoped his brother hadn't had anything to do with this. He could no longer deny the ugly truth that confronted him. His brother was a killer.

Having had enough, he gathered his notes together with the newspaper and wrapped them in a cloth as he secreted them together in the loose floorboard in his room. He took the letters from the book where he had hidden them and placed them in there too. He had finally opened and read Clara's letters at last. She had let Erdman know of the child, and pleaded with him to do the right thing. Erdman must have known what the letters would say and that was why he hadn't opened them.

Bergin replaced the floorboard, and threw the little rug his mother had braided over it and headed out of his room. Like his father, he sought some work to allow him to burn off his anger.

His mother was in the kitchen as he headed for the door.

"Morning, mother," Bergin said as he passed her.

"Bergin, you go, get the mail. It just came," she always gave him her orders as if he were a servant.

Saying nothing, he headed out the door and walked down the lane to where the post box was attached to a fence. He pulled out the mail and sorted through it not really paying any attention.

Something caught his eye.

There was a postcard for his brother.

He flipped it over; the picture side was a man and woman on a well-known Loess Hill place for lovers. He turned the card over, since it was a postcard, he read the message. After all, everyone reads everyone else's postcards.

The message was cryptic.

Erdman Halverson,
Meet me at midnight tonight.
Back table Ogden Hotel Bar. I hear it is a favorite of yours.
I have come to collect what you promised.
As you see, I now know where you live.
Be there. You know what is at risk.

There was no signature. Bergin had a feeling he knew who it was from.

Bergin shuffled the postcard back into the rest of the mail, and returned to the house. He knew that his mother would leave it alone until his father could deal with it. Erdman was the only one who seemed to disregard this family rule, just like he disregarded so many other rules.

He would keep an eye on Erdman; see if he got his postcard, then if he went out later, he would follow him. He wanted to know who it was that had sent the card.

He knew that he couldn't allow Erdman to get so roaring drunk tonight. At least, not until he had gone to town. He felt sure Erdman would go. The note implied that this person would come after him if he did not.

Bergin walked back out of the house in search of his brother.

Bergin found his brother passed out on the floor of the barn. He nudged him with his foot to awaken him. Erdman sat up, and proceeded to convulse in dry heaves. He was disgusting. Finally, he managed to get to his feet and stagger to the house.

He watched as his brother nosed through the mail.

Erdman flopped down onto the bench in the front hall as he read the postcard, the color drained from his face as he read, then looked around to see if anyone was nearby. He stuffed the card into a pocket and headed for the outhouse.

Bergin checked later and saw that there were torn bits of what had been the postcard at the bottom in the muck. He waited and watched to see what his brother would do. He had already informed his mother that he might need to head to town that evening, just in case he needed to tail his brother.

Erdman never left. He cowered in the barn.

Bergin wanted to make sure that Erdman wasn't going to sneak out later, so he provided Erdman with a bottle before he headed to town. Bergin knew his brother would get drunk and pass out somewhere while he drove into town. Bergin wanted to see who it was that demanded to meet with Erdman.

* * *

That night, Bergin drove into town. His thoughts raced about, wondering who had written the note. He had checked on Erdman before he left. He was happily drinking the hooch in the barn loft. When Erdman wasn't looking, he had placed another bottle near him. He was sure he would find it soon enough. He knew that Erdman would not be driving to town that night.

He snorted a little laugh of disgust, leave it to Erdman to hide behind a bottle and not keep the appointment with whoever wrote the note to him. Whoever this was, Erdman was afraid of him. Bergin had seen a look of terror on his brother's countenance when he read the postcard.

Bergin patted his pocket, checking again to be sure the brass knuckles were still in his pocket. He wasn't going to go without some form of protection. He knew Erdman packed a gun when in town, and Bergin had come to know why. The company Erdman kept was a pretty dangerous pack of hoodlums.

Bergin entered the old Ogden Hotel. It had been a fine hotel for many years, but it was beginning to show its age. It had been built in the 1870's and newer hotels had claimed the quality travelers now. The hotel had become a destination for illicit alcohol and roaring parties. He walked into the bar and took a quick look around. The bar was not as busy as he had expected it to be.

"Mr. Halverson," a voice called out to him. He looked about, searching the back corners first, then to the bar where a man was smiling at him. He walked over to the bar.

"Yes," Bergin replied, looking the man over. He was a squat man with thinning hair, rheumy eyes and heavy jowls that quavered when he spoke.

"Oh! For a moment I thought you were Erdman, but you're his brother, aren't you?" He said in a voice maybe a little louder than necessary. His eyes darted nervously from Bergin to the shadows of the room. "Can I get you anything, sir?" His laugh was forced, as he tried to look calm, but failed. Beads of sweat formed on his face.

Bergin heard but did not see the sounds of someone getting up and, after taking a few steps, opening a door, and it closing softly behind them. He had searched the mirror behind the friendly man for any movement. All he could make out were dark shadows moving against an even darker backdrop. The momentary glint of faceted stones flashed from the darkness where the figure departed.

After the door closed, the man sighed deeply and relaxed.

"Who was it that just left?" Bergin asked him.

"You don't want to know." The man's eyes flitted about the room; he wouldn't look Bergin in the eye.

"That is why I came here, to find out who he is. I have been looking for him for months." Bergin had grabbed the man by the lapels of his cheap suit and pulled him up on tip-toe. The man began to sputter.

"Please, you don't want to know him. He is a murdering swamp rat," the barman whispered, his eyes darting back to the doorway in the shadows. "Just know that I have saved your life."

Bergin slipped the brass knuckles onto his hand and pressed them into the man's cheek. He hadn't gotten this close to allow the information to slip away.

"Talk," Bergin demanded in a low, menacing tone. "Who is he?"

"Oh, hell!" Beads of sweat appeared on the man's forehead and he began to tremble. "His name is Johnny "Sparky" Mann. I don't know if it is his real name, they say the prison system let him go because he had refused to be killed when they put him in the electric chair for killing six men and women in cold blood," the man's words now poured out of him like a torrent and there was no stopping him.

Bergin let go of the man's lapel, and lowered the hand with the knuckles, replacing them in his pocket.

"He was here looking for your brother, and since I knew him, I was to point him out to Sparky, you know, be sure it was the right man. Evidently he has heard talk of how much you two look alike. He said he had no traffic with anyone but Erdman. So, I had to let him know you weren't Erdman, or he would have killed us both." The man's whole body began to shake.

Bergin nodded and stepped away from the man. He didn't want the man to see him trembling. This Sparky had even spooked him more than he wanted to admit.

"If you see him again, let him know I would like to speak with him," Bergin said in a hushed voice before turning to leave the bar. The man had eluded him. He would have to find another way. At least he knew who the man was.

CHAPTER 43

Something woke Bergin from a tenuous sleep. It was late. Bergin listened; he heard some strange, terrifying sound coming from the barn. He lit the lantern and headed out to see what it was. It sounded worse than one of the pigs in labor.

In the barn, he heard it again.

His anger flared. It was Erdman drunk out of his skull.

He climbed the ladder to the loft. Erdman was sloppy drunk, and the sound had been his attempts at singing. Never a pleasant sound when Erdman was sober, tonight it was a shrill squealing now that he was inebriated.

"Erdman, shut up," he scolded his brother.

"Why should I?" He looked in the direction of the voice, but was unable to focus.

"Because you'll wake up mother and father, that's why."

"Let them wake up, they can come join the fun." He hoisted the bottle in salute before swilling down another sip.

"You are such a selfish and inconsiderate sod, you know that?" Bergin sneered. He had had enough of his brother. Bergin had left the second bottle the other day hoping to get some coherent confession out of him but it had not worked. Erdman had simply passed out before he had finished the second bottle.

"Me, selfish? Hell, no. Not me," Erdman laughed, weaving from side to side as he sat in the hay. "I am loved by one and all. I am known for my generosity," he slurred his words.

"No one loves you any more." Bergin crossed his arms over his chest.

"I'm sure dead little Miss what's-her-name does, wherever she is." He hoisted the bottle in the air in mock salute to her.

"Yes, and her name was Clara, Clara Lindgren," Bergin said, pressing his lips tightly together, fighting his anger.

"The little witch won't leave me alone. She keeps dogging my footsteps. That bitch keeps me from sleeping," Erdman said, looking about as if there was someone else in the loft with them.

"Could it be that she haunts you because you are guilty?" Bergin asked softly, uncrossing his arms. Maybe he would be able to get the truth out of Erdman.

"Guilty of what?" He looked surprised.

"You killed her, didn't you?" His voice was hardly audible. For a moment he wasn't sure he had said it aloud.

"Know what? I'm gonna come clean with you, little brother." He wobbled as he sat on the floor. "I'm gonna tell you all about it." He took another pull on the bottle.

Bergin froze, afraid to move for fear his brother would never tell him what he wanted to know. His attention span was short when sober, and even shorter when tanked up on booze.

"I was angry with her. She was supposed to meet me in town. Keep it all quiet, you know. But the little bitch made me come to her." He drank again from his bottle. "I went by their place, see if she would be there. See if she really was telling the truth about the kid and all." He swayed from side to side, his eyes unable to focus clearly.

Erdman looked down at the bottle in his hand and his finger traced around its contours. The facets of his fancy ring glittered in the light.

Bergin wondered if his brother would say anything more. He was about to say something when Erdman started talking again, going on with his recollections.

"Well, there she was, come out of the house when she seen the headlights. I turned them off, didn't want anyone to see I was there. She hopped into the car and off we drove. She told me that she knew I would come, can you believe that? She went on to tell me that she was so pleased that I still loved her. God, I wanted to smack her right then and there. I never loved her. She just had something I wanted, and once I got it, I didn't care anymore. She didn't know how to make sex fun. She just lay there like she was made of wood," Erdman shook his head and made a sour face as he recounted making love to her.

Bergin stood looking down at his brother, his rage growing.

"We were driving for a bit, and then she took my hand and placed it on her belly." Erdman shuddered at the memory. "She said it was mine. Hell, I knew no one else would have had her, so it had to be. I was terrified by the thought of a child. I didn't want it. I didn't want her either."

Again, Erdman fell into silence before speaking again. Bergin waited.

"We were close by the Albertson place when I stopped the car. I needed to get away from her, so I got out and she followed me. She dogged my footsteps; she wouldn't even let me walk around to the back of the car to get a drink without hovering and chattering about doing the right thing by her." He drained the last of the booze from the bottle, then tossed it aside. It skidded across the loft boards and crashed to the floor below.

"Then what happened, Erdman?" Bergin's voice was soft, but it seemed so loud in his head. His heart was beating fast now as he waited to hear what else his brother would have to say about that night.

"It happened. Yep. She got cracked in the skull with the crank for my car. She had to die because she wouldn't let me go. She expected me to marry her. Her! Gads, she was the last female on the planet that I would ever want to marry. She was so dull, so annoying, such a lousy, stinking hick, and one hell of a lousy lay," he spat into the hay, the venom of his words hung in the air.

"So, you ended it by killing her?" Bergin's voice was but a whisper. He was horrified by what his brother had said. He had wanted the truth, and now that he had heard it, he was sorry to possess such knowledge.

Erdman was not his brother anymore.

"Nothing else for it. She wouldn't stop clinging to me, begging me to do the right thing. Women are so stupid. They think if you screw them that you're gonna have to marry them. When I marry someone she is gonna be a lot better than that stupid country bumpkin."

"You selfish bastard," Bergin's voice was full of menace.

"Oh, I forgot, you liked the silly cow," Erdman snorted a laugh. "Would you really want some female bitch that I had already used and threw away like garbage? Well, then you're welcome to the trash little brother," Erdman began to laugh hysterically. He was too drunk to control himself any longer.

Erdman didn't see it coming; Bergin's fist smashed him in the face.

"You lousy bastard. She was worth fifty of you any day!" He

pummeled his brother as hard as he could.

"Hey, quit!" Erdman yelled at his brother as he tried to shield himself from the angry blows that reigned down on him.

Bergin did not stop.

His anger had finally broken loose, and he was not willing to stem the vitriolic tide of his wrath for his brother.

* * *

The man had gotten the warning that the person who had come in the bar was not the one he sought. The resemblance was strong, but the barman had warned him in time. He had slipped out the back door in the bar and waited in the street. The man was his prey's brother. He didn't want to bother with anyone else but Erdman Halverson. He would be sure to get the man another notice of his demands. This time he wouldn't rely upon the postal service to deliver his message.

He waited in the shadows for this brother to drive back to where they lived. He had a feeling he would find the brother he wanted hiding out on the family farm, cowering behind his mother's skirts probably.

Johnny "Sparky" Mann followed Bergin back to the farm. He had doused the headlamps of his car so Bergin wouldn't know he was being followed. Halverson's car made enough noise to cover the quiet roar of his own engine.

When Halverson drove down a lane to a house and parked the car, Sparky drove a little way past the drive. He killed the engine. He would wait, be sure all was quiet before he made his move. He fiddled with his diamond, pinky ring, thinking about what he would do to Erdman.

He must have dozed in the car; he didn't know for how long. He sat up listening to a terrible sound that carried across the farmyard. He saw a lamp light and someone come out of the house and into the barn. The noise stopped. He couldn't figure out what it was, but it was terrible.

Then he heard voices, two men yelling at one another from what he could tell. After a while, the man with the lantern came back out of the barn and headed for the house. All was quiet in the barn. He figured that was where Erdman was hiding out. Sparky Mann opened the glove box and took out the flashlight he always kept there and began to walk up the lane to the barn.

CHAPTER 44

DeBoer had driven out to the Halverson farm to bring in Erdman after he had been indicted. He wanted to be sure that Erdman Halverson didn't run away again.

Adolph Halverson met him with an angry expression, carrying a pitchfork in his hand.

"I've come for Erdman," De Boer said, wary of what Halverson might do. He knew that Erdman's father was fiercely protective of the boy no matter what he did. Mr. Halverson had placed ads in the newspapers telling his son to come home so he could fix everything. De Boer had also learned that Adolph Halverson had sent some money to his son while he was on the lam.

"He's not here," Halverson glared at the sheriff.

"You can't protect him for long, Halverson, you know that. He has been indicted; he is a wanted man now." De Boer placed his hand on the handle of his gun to show he meant business. "Mr. Halverson, you don't want to run afoul of the law yourself now. Tell me where Erdman is."

"I don't know where he is." Adolph glanced at the pitchfork, and thrust the tines of the pitchfork into the ground.

"You tell him to come in quietly and it will be a lot easier for all of you out here, understand?" De Boer moved his hand away from his gun, and rested his fists on his hips.

"Yah, sure, we do that," Mr. Halverson spit at the ground still defiant.

Bergin came out of the house to see what the sheriff was going to do. He knew the man was looking for his useless brother.

"Bergin," the sheriff called to him. "You know where your brother is?"

Halverson shot his son a threatening look, Bergin seemed not to notice as he walked over to where the men were standing.

"No, sir, I don't know where he is right now. I haven't seen him for a while." He met the sheriff's gaze steadily.

"You'll be sure to get word to me where he is when he turns up, won't you?" De Boer studied the younger Halverson's expression for telltale signs of any falsehood or misdirection. He knew Bergin to be a man of his word.

"I'll do my best, Sheriff," Bergin nodded, then looked over to meet his father's angry scowl, then back to De Boer. "Erdman comes and goes as he pleases, but we do not see him at work much, we could have used his help."

"That's none of your concern what your brother does," Mr. Halverson snapped at Bergin in a menacing tone.

"Sheriff, could I ask you something?" Bergin turned away from his father and faced the sheriff.

"Ask away," De Boer shrugged, not sure where Bergin was going with his question. Obviously, it was making his father a little nervous.

"Have you ever heard of a man named Johnny Mann?" Bergin took a quick look at his father whose expression changed from menacing anger to puzzled confusion, touched with relief that he was not going to say any more about Erdman.

"What do you want to know about that cankerous piece of garbage for?" De Boer was surprised by the question.

"So you have heard of him?" Bergin repeated.

"Sure, every lawman in the Midwest has heard of Sparky." De Boer rubbed his chin. "Why do you ask?" He furrowed his brow.

"What can you tell me about him?"

"He is a vicious sewer rat that would as soon kill you as look at you. He went on a killing spree a while back in Missouri. Supposedly, someone owed him some money and didn't want to pay him. So, Mann hunted the man down, and only after killing the man's family one by one, doing despicable things to them as he killed them real slow, only then did he come after the man himself," De Boer paused still wondering why someone like Bergin would ask about such a man.

"Why do they call him Sparky?" Asked the senior Halverson.

"He was caught, tried and found guilty of killing those six people. 'Sparky' Mann was sentenced to fry in the electric chair. The chair malfunctioned somehow. It had been tested earlier and was working, but when they strapped him down and threw the switch, there was no juice. So they undid him, ran a bunch of tests and it worked just fine again. So once more he was strapped into the chair, and nothing happened," De Boer shook his head; his disgust was plain for all to see. "An old tradition that goes back to the days of the hangman says if the method of punishment does not work, the condemned is pardoned."

"Did they let him go?" Bergin asked, horrified.

"He escaped," De Boer's mouth twisted into a tense knot. "Why do you ask?" He leveled a piercing gaze at Bergin.

"I think he was in town the other night. That somehow, my brother may have crossed paths with him."

"Erdman and Sparky?" De Boer looked from father to son, his expression now one of concern. "Then if and when Erdman turns up, you best let me know. If he is tangled up with this 'Sparky' Mann, his life may not be worth a plug nickel."

"This man would hurt my boy?" Mr. Halverson asked in a fearful voice.

"He sure would, depending on how mixed up Erdman is with Mann. If you'll excuse me, I need to go send a few telegrams. If Mann is anywhere around here, we want to catch him."

* * *

Erdman was frightened. For the first time in his life, he didn't have any glib answer to make it all go away. He woke up, hung over again, and saw something that scared the liver out of him. He saw a note pinned to the board in the barn, by where his head had lain the night.

It had been pinned with a knife.

It was another demand that Erdman come see him. It also stated that he didn't want him to send anyone in his place. He demanded to meet that night in town, or the next time the knife would simply be in his neck. It had been so close, what was a few more inches? This time he signed it *Sparky*.

Erdman trembled. Mann knew where he lived for real. Erdman knew that Mann would kill him if he failed to meet him again. The man was a vicious killer, and from what Erdman had learned, Sparky Mann even enjoyed his work.

To make matters worse, that morning Sheriff De Boer had come to the farmhouse looking for him.

His father had lied for him. Evidently, Bergin had as well.

Erdman had made himself scarce, taking refuge in the barn when the sheriff asked to look around in the house. He knew that his bed hadn't been slept in for days now, since he had been passing out anywhere but the bed. He hadn't even changed clothes for days either, so his room would look deserted. He hoped.

He couldn't stop trembling.

He watched as the sheriff got in his car and drove back down their road.

"You have to help me, Bergin." Erdman pulled his brother into the barn. His eyes were darting about, looking for the law behind every post and tree. "I have to get away." He wasn't going to tell him everything about Sparky.

Bergin looked at his brother, not sure if he should really assist him in anything more than his drunkenness. Erdman was sober this morning for a change. Maybe the beating had done him some good.

"They have nothing to tie me to her," Erdman hissed. He was fiddling with the fancy ring on his hand. The diamonds glinted in the sunlight.

"But you wrote to her. They have the letter; it was identified by her sister," Bergin answered. He remembered that Clara and Erdman had written back and forth to one another. He had seen the letters; Erdman had tossed them at him one day saying something smug about being adored by so many women he didn't really know what to do with them all.

"I made her burn all my letters," he said, his face a little too close to Bergin for his comfort. His brother's breath reeked more than usual. "She was always so obliging and did just what I wanted her to do."

"You killed her?" Bergin stepped back, looking his brother in the eye wanting to see if he could tell the truth now that he was sober. He didn't trust his brother's drunken blathering.

This time Erdman had gone too far. He couldn't just toss this off as if it were nothing. Their father could not protect him from the charge of murder. Not this time. The coroner's jury had indicted him. This morning, the sheriff had been out there looking for Erdman, to arrest him and take him to jail.

Erdman Halverson was a wanted man.

Bergin could feel a cruel smile play at his lips.

* * *

Silence hung between them as Erdman fought to keep the terrible thing he had done buried deep within himself. He didn't like to think about it. But she had given him no choice. It had to be done. She was the last woman he wanted to marry. After all, there were still too many good times to enjoy before he was saddled into marriage, the farm and some children as his parents had planned for him. It was not the life he wanted, not by a long shot. He wanted to party, drink more wine and screw more women. He wasn't finished tasting the pleasures of this life.

"You were always fond of her, weren't you?" Erdman asked his brother.

"Yes. I thought she was a wonderful woman," Bergin said as he remembered Clara. "She was a really nice girl, until she met you."

"Me? What did I do to her but show her a good time?" He couldn't believe that his brother could say something so mean.

"She wanted love, marriage, and a family. You only wanted a good time. I don't think you ever cared for her at all." A flash of anger glinted in Bergin's eyes.

"I did, at first, sort of. Then she began to be a clinging vine. I needed my freedom." Erdman squirmed with the memory of her that last night grasping at him, clinging to him. And of the thing that writhed in her belly.

"But you still seduced her, made love to her and got her with child," his tone was flat and showed no emotion.

"I told you it wasn't mine," he protested. "She was the one who couldn't keep her hands off of me, little brother. I do seem to have that effect on woman." He tried to let it roll off his back like it was nothing.

"I know she had given herself to you, and only you, trusting that you would do the right thing."

"Well I did what I had to do," Erdman shrugged his shoulders as if it didn't matter.

"You killed her," Bergin's voice was no more than a whisper.

Erdman studied his younger brother's face. He had never seen him look like this before. There was a darkness in his eyes that made him a little nervous. He looked away. He stared at the ground for a little while before he spoke. Then he inhaled deeply and looked up at the rafters of the barn.

"She had to die," Erdman nodded.

Bergin sighed.

He had one more question for his brother.

"Who is Johnny Sparky Mann?"

All the color drained from Erdman's face, his eyes widened in terror and before Bergin could catch him, he fainted.

* * *

When Erdman came to, Bergin was sitting beside him. Silence hung between them, each waiting for the other to speak first.

Erdman had no more words. He wouldn't tell him anything about Sparky Mann.

Bergin had so many questions, but didn't know where to begin. Finally, he broke the stillness and spoke softly to his brother. Bergin knew what he needed to do. If what the sheriff had said about Sparky Mann was true, then he had to get his brother away from the farm. He didn't want anything to happen to his parents, nor himself because Mann was tracking Erdman.

"You will need to get out of here." He couldn't look at Erdman. Not now. Maybe later after he had dealt with the anger that raged in his heart that Clara was dead at his brother's hand. He had confessed it in his drunkenness, as well as in his sobriety. He knew it was not a lie Erdman could tell. "De Boer is sure you killed her. You know that he will be back for you soon. He will find you if you remain here."

"You'll help me, won't you?" Erdman begged.

Bergin turned to look at Erdman. His gaze was stony and he could see Erdman blink in surprise at Bergin's coldness. Part of him wanted to beat his brother senseless for what he had done, the other part wanted to turn him over and let DeBoer have him so Erdman would have to face the consequences of his actions for once in his miserable life. He took in a deep breath and let it out slowly before he replied.

"Yes," Bergin nodded slowly. "I'll help you."

"Where should I go?" Erdman grasped his brother's arm like a lifeline. His voice was a whine now, filled with fear and uncertainty.

"Leave that to me." He pulled free of his brother's grasp. He had always been treated like the stupid little brother who was so pathetic and useless. Erdman had always lorded it over him that he wasn't going to inherit anything from their parents. Now it looked as if Erdman had been wrong.

"I don't want to go to prison. I couldn't take it. I would rather die than be in jail," he sniveled, tears coming to his eyes as he tried to reach out for Bergin again.

Bergin moved away from his brother's touch and wouldn't look at him anymore.

"Don't worry. I'll be sure you don't have to go to prison," his voice was a soft whisper, but had a hard, cold edge to it. "Looks like I get to clean up another one of your messes, big brother."

"I'll make it up to you, I promise. I have lots of cash stashed away. You know, the profits from my bootlegging. There is more than fifty-five thousand dollars hidden under the seat of my car. I'll share it with you; make it worth your while to help me get away," Erdman whimpered. "You can have this ring too; it's worth a lot of money."

"I don't want that ring or any of your money. Leave it where it is for now. We can get it later," Bergin shook his head, disgusted. "Just get some things together. Take what you want from here, because you will not be coming back."

"Never come back?" Erdman asked in disbelief.

"No, never." Bergman finally looked at Erdman. "You understand that you can't ever return, don't you?"

"But, maybe after all this has blown over," Erdman suggested, as if he could make a deal with Bergin. "Maybe I can come back. The farm is supposed to be mine."

"No, you can never come back here, ever. You are wanted by the police. You are also wanted by Sparky. Get it through your thick skull that you can't come back. Ever," Bergin stressed his words one by one as he worked to suppress a wicked smile that played at his lips. "You will forfeit the farm and all claims of inheritance. It is my price for helping you."

"We could get some good cash out of it if we sell it," Erdman begged, still showing plainly what a selfish brat he really was.

"Erdman, you have always been so good at bragging, but you never have been one to face up to the realities of life." Bergin was disgusted with his brother's sniveling. "Well it's time for you to take a good, hard look at what you have done and pay the piper for your actions."

Bergin instructed Erdman to keep himself hidden in the old Albertson house and he would meet him out there later, after dark, and be sure to get him away, so the sheriff wouldn't be able to send Erdman to jail. Erdman nodded eagerly like a drunk agreeing to anything so he can get that next drink and headed out of the barn to collect a few things and to say goodbye to his parents.

* * *

Erdman was in tears as he entered the kitchen. His parents were sitting silently at the kitchen table. His father looked up at him when he came through the door.

"Don't cry, my baby boy," his mother said, reaching out to hug him.

Erdman wiped away the tears with the back of his hand and avoided her embrace.

"So, what we gonna do now?" His father demanded.

"Bergie is going to help me get away," Erdman sniveled.

"He is?" Mr. Halverson said, astonished that the younger boy would do this for Erdman. "I know he went to town a number of times to do some things for you, but I didn't know he would help you get away."

"He did," Erdman replied, wondering why Bergin would have done such a thing. He chuckled softly as he recalled one of the stories he'd heard about Bergin taking his place with the bootlegger. "A lot of people thought he was me, well, at least for a while. Funny, I never thought we looked so much alike."

His father stood up and looked him over closely. "And you say he will help you get away?" An idea seemed to be taking hold in his mind.

"He did," Erdman replied, confused at his father's demeanor.

"Then, I tell you what we must do," Mr. Halverson nodded, looking back and forth between his wife and his son. "It will demand you do something terrible, son. But if you are to live a long life, it must be done. After it is done we speak of it no more." He drew them in closer and in a whisper explained what he saw needed to be done.

It was the only way he assured them.

CHAPTER 45

It was late; mist swirled in the air as the spring fought to claim the season from winter. Two men had managed to meet at the place where Clara Lindgren had lain in the earth for many months. The makeshift grave was an open chasm that yawned up at them. They paid little attention.

Night closed in about them as they argued in the fading light. Their voices carried across the fields as another man approached them unseen.

CHAPTER 46

The dawn was clear and bright with the sweet sunlight of early spring that swept across the land. The earth was fragrant with scent of new life quickening in the soil, and the promises of an abundant harvest to come that fall. The birds twittered in the trees and brush, in a hurry to build their homes for the young that would soon fill their nests. Their songs carried on the soft breezes that caressed the earth. The fruit trees were in blossom and the grasses were sprouting in the fields.

Christian Lindgren had finished the morning milking and was walking back to the house. Today was the day he would place his daughter's remains into the earth. The Coroner's Jury had come back with an indictment for Erdman, but it did not ease his pain or make him feel any better about losing her.

He had heard, late last night, that the boy had disappeared again. The sheriff told him that they were putting out wanted posters across the country. He had nodded his head and thanked the sheriff. He doubted that Erdman would ever be caught.

Christian looked out at the western horizon where he saw some dark, angry clouds forming. The wind began to shift direction coming out of the northwest. It brought the scented air of winter.

It smelled of snow.

The temperature dropped as he stood there.

He looked out across the fields where the delicate crops of corn, wheat and beans were just beginning to push up through the soil seeking the warmth of the sun. He knew that if it snowed, it would cover the delicate crops, protecting them from the frosty temperatures that were chilling the air. As he watched, the skies clouded over into a dark and turbulent slate hanging low over the earth.

Winter was not quite ready to give way to the spring.

He headed into the house for breakfast with his family.

The morning that looked so full of the promises of spring had changed quickly to the leaden skies of winter within a half hour. By the time they had finished breakfast it had begun to snow and the temperatures had dropped into the twenties and the wind whipped across the prairie. The dark clouds were heavy with precipitation. Thick globs of snow fell quickly covering everything in whiteness.

In a few hours, they would lay Clara to rest in the cemetery behind the church. Christian Lindgren looked out at the thick layer of snow that had already accumulated and decided it would be best for him to hitch up the horses to the old sleigh to drive over to the church with his family.

* * *

"Just where do you think you are going?" Mr. Halverson demanded of his son, Bergin.

"I'm going to Clara Lindgren's funeral, poppa," Bergin replied as he climbed into the small sleigh. The horse whinnied knowing it was about time to go somewhere.

"Get down from there; you have no business going there," his tone was harsh.

"Clara was a friend of mine. I happened to have cared for her, and I will not insult her family or her memory by staying away." Bergin took up the reigns in his hand, but didn't urge the horse to move as yet. He knew his folks blamed Clara for their troubles, just as his stupid, weak brother had done. Snow was falling about them, muffling their words.

"I said get down from there," Adolph Halverson shouted to Bergin. "I won't have you going to pay respects to a girl that ruined your brother's life." He took hold of the reigns and the horse started a little.

"Ruined his life? Poppa, you have to be kidding me?" Bergin was not about to keep silent any more. He had heard enough insults and shifting of blame onto Clara for the last few weeks. When would his parents come to their senses and realize that his brother was a louse and a user? "She lay dead in some shallow grave for months while Erdman pretended that he knew nothing, when all along he knew exactly where she was because he was the one who put her there."

"I will not believe it," Mr. Halverson shook his head in denial. "I can't. That is not the son I raised."

"Well, maybe you better give it a try, because that is the truth," Bergin allowed his anger to come through as he spoke to his father.

"How can you speak against your brother like this?"

"Because he told me that he was responsible," Bergin sneered; knowing it was the one and only time his brother had taken the responsibility for something.

"Impossible!" He shook his head again a sour look on his face.

"Yes, poppa, he told me one night when I caught him out in the barn boozing it up again. I asked him point blank and he confessed to his dirty little secret. Face up to it, your son, your precious and most beloved son, Erdman Halverson is a murderer," Bergin realized he was yelling.

Halverson let go of the reigns and took a step back, placing his hand on his heart, his mouth gaped open, but he could make no sound.

"Don't pretend to be shocked, poppa," Bergin said in a hushed voice. He could see the pain in his father's eyes, an ache that told him that his father knew he was right. "You have always known that Erdman was not the paragon of virtue you wanted him to be. Admit it, you knew that he was a louse, a user and could never live up to the man you had hoped he would become."

Adolph could only shake his head. The snow that had accumulated in his hair fell to his shoulders and the ground.

"I'm going now, poppa. I'm going to pay my respects to Clara Lindgren who was a good, honest woman who trusted the wrong man. My brother." Bergin took up the reigns again and snapped them together against the horse's back. "I will see you at supper," he said as the horse pulled the sleigh forward through the thickening layer of snow.

If he had looked back, he would have seen that his father stood rooted to the ground like an old, broken tree, the snow accumulating on his head and shoulders.

* * *

As Christian drove his family to the church, the snow continued to come down, silently engulfing them, blanketing everything. Silence hovered over the land as only happens in a snowfall. No one spoke, not wanting to break the tranquility that embraced them.

It was snowing heavily. He could no longer see the horizon. He remembered a snowfall about a year and a half ago when his Clara had gone to a wedding. It was in the church hall, at the reception that she had met that young man that was to eventually take her life. Christian silently asked God to forgive the thoughts of revenge that ran endlessly through his mind.

He pulled into the churchyard where a few others had already arrived. He didn't expect there would be very many people willing to come out on a snowy day like this. His wife and children went into the church to be sure all was in readiness.

Lindgren stood at the top of the stairs of the church. He looked out on the land that he was about to place his beloved daughter. He watched as some cars drove up and parked. Others came in sleighs as he had, knowing that a spring snowstorm can cover the ground quickly. So many were coming; it touched him deeply.

He turned and walked into the church. In the sanctuary near the altar was the gray casket that held all that remained of his favorite child. No, that wasn't quite true; he still had his memories of her tucked away in his heart. A tear welled in his eye, and fell onto her coffin. He placed his hand on that tear, and with a caress wiped it away.

His wife came to stand with him; she slipped her arm about him. She too had tears in her eyes.

"I know we shouldn't love one child more than another, but I always loved Clara the best," he admitted.

"I know," Bertha nodded. "She was so very special." Tentatively she reached out to touch her daughter's coffin. It was cold under her fingers.

* * *

They stood by Clara's coffin with their children and received the condolences of the people who had come to pay their respects to Clara. Lindgren was moved by the number of people who had braved the bitter cold and deep snow to be there.

Five hundred people came to Clara's funeral. Five hundred people huddled close about them as they lowered her coffin into the ground. Lindgren took a handful of dirt mixed with the snow and dropped it onto the coffin. A hollow thump resounded back from her grave from that clot of earth.

Ingmar dropped the bouquet Clara had caught at the wedding onto the coffin. The dried flowers shattered into a flurry of creamy petal fragments. The falling snow covered them over, like the waxed flowers Clara had hoped to wear at her own wedding.

A silent shroud engulfed the land, silence that muffled the moans of those weeping for Clara and her family.

* * *

Ingmar was silent, afraid that if she moved she would never stop weeping. She missed her sister, but had found some small comfort in Bergen. She was pleased to see him there at the funeral, but she was also a little surprised, considering what his brother had done. Bergin was not his brother, and she had always known they were two very different men.

As Bergin stood before her and her family he had tears in his eyes for Clara. She had not known it, but he had loved Clara, too.

After the graveside ceremony, he had gently taken Ingmar by the elbow and guided her to the sleigh where her family was waiting. She had looked up in his eyes and had seen something there she had never expected to find. She had whispered to him to please come and call on her, if he would.

He nodded and told her that he would be honored.

* * *

Bergin had not expected to be so kindly received by Clara's family, especially her little sister Ingmar. He had broken down and cried in front of them, embarrassing himself. However, Ingmar had taken his hand in hers and squeezed it, saying thank you. There had been something in her smile that had encouraged him, something in her demeanor that seemed to say that she thought well of him.

As she was about to leave the reception she had whispered to him to please come call on her. He had tried to keep the somber expression as befit the occasion of a funeral, but nothing could have pleased him more. He thought back to the night of the wedding and how he had wanted to dance with her.

He had backed away when his brother had started to see Clara;

he had hoped his brother would grow bored and forget Clara, and then he could come see Ingmar if she would allow it.

He had smiled, and whispered back that it would be his honor to call upon her.

Bergin stood and waved goodbye to them as their sleigh pulled away in the deep snow. She looked back to see him standing and waved back. A ray of sunshine broke through the grayness for a moment before slipping back under the cloud cover.

He climbed into his own sleigh and contemplated the events of the last few days. Things would never be the same now. Erdman was gone, Clara now rested in a proper grave and he had permission to call on Ingmar. He hoped that after all the terrible things that had happened, this would be something good.

He snapped the reigns and plodded slowly home, smiling all the way. It had been so long since he had smiled and it felt good. Bergin knew there was something he needed to take care of before he could leave the past behind. He needed to meet with Sheriff De Boer to let him know what had transpired the night that Erdman planned to run away. Then it would be up to De Boer to deal with it as he saw fit.

BOOK THREE

CHAPTER 47

For more than thirty years, no one had seen or heard from Erdman. It was as if he had disappeared through a break in the fabric of the universe, for no trace of him was ever found.

Right after Clara's funeral, Erdman's father had put out a letter in a few news-papers asking his son to come home, that he would stand by his son knowing that he didn't have anything to do with the girl's disappearance. In this letter, he added that Erdman's mother also believed him innocent of any wrongdoing and instructed Erdman to try his hardest to get in touch with him, and he would do the rest no matter how black it may look; he would fix things.

There was never any reply to that notice in the papers.

The body of a young man was fished out of the Missouri River. Rumors spread quickly, speculating that it had to be Erdman. That he had taken his own life, rather than face the law. However, they were all wrong. The body was not that of Erdman. His father looked relieved and pained as he walked out of the morgue. It was someone who had drowned upriver, and was eventually claimed by a grieving young wife who said he had gone fishing one morning and never returned.

The gossip soon died down about Erdman having run off because he had to be guilty. Stories surfaced once in a while about some of his escapades; of his running liquor and keeping company with fast women.

Soon his memory faded from all but a few who still spoke his name on occasion.

Within a year after Erdman disappeared, his mother's health began to fail. She had said that she saw no purpose in life without her beloved boy. To her last dying breath she never believed anything ill of her pride and joy, her son, her only son worthy of her love, Erdman.

She died that summer and was laid to rest in the same cemetery as Clara.

Bergin worked the land with his father until Mr. Halverson was killed two years later in a farming accident. The accident had unnerved Bergin in a strange way. He wasn't really sure it had been an accident. His father was not accident prone, and this had been a silly error of judgment. For months afterward, Bergin looked back over his shoulder or jumped a little too quickly at some sudden sound.

Bergin was the only one who stood at his father's graveside to say goodbye. His father's inability to accept his older son's faults had cost him many friends over the years. Bergin was all he had left, though he never spoke to him unless it was to tell him what to do on the farm. Adolph told Bergin that he only had enough love for one child, and Erdman was the oldest, and had taken all he had to give.

Bergin stood there alone in the warm sunlight by the man's grave and whispered to his father the question he could never ask when he was alive.

"Why wasn't I enough, papa?"

Bergin and his father never spoke about Erdman since the day of Clara's funeral. Adolph refused to accept or believe anything that would make his favorite son a murderer. Neither did he change his will; he left everything to Erdman. They had always hoped Erdman would return and wanted to be sure he would be able to get his full inheritance, just as they had always planned. There was no mention of Bergin in the will at all. It was a blow that cut him deeply to the bone.

It had always been Erdman and no one else.

Erdman never wrote, never called when telephones were at last installed in the country. Bergin knew Erdman would not. Bergin knew that Erdman could never come home again.

Some speculated that Erdman had gone to Chicago or New York. Some said he had enlisted and died in WWII.

Only one person really knew where Erdman was, but would not say.

Without telling his father, Bergin purchased the old Albertson's place with some of the money Erdman had secreted away in the car. He had a small cabin built some distance away from the crumbling, old Albertson's house. His father never knew he had purchased that place. Adolph Halverson's only comment was to ask why anyone would ever want that useless farmland. The ground was considered to be cursed. Bergin had his reasons for buying the land.

Bergin worked his land, as well as his father's after the man's death. He carried on, working both farms until he could have Erdman declared legally dead and take proper possession of his parent's farm after his father's death. It took seven years until the courts could declare Erdman Halverson legally dead.

By then hardly anyone remembered who he was. The depression had hit people hard, and many had lost their farms and were forced off the land. Others left, selling out and heading to the cities, no longer wishing to be farmers.

Bergin managed to make it through the hard times. He worked hard to become a wealthy man.

The years passed, and soon Clara and Erdman passed from memory of all but a few people.

* * *

Bergin had called on Ingmar just as she had asked him to do. He had done it to be kind, and to keep contact with the family of a woman he had loved. He didn't think that Ingmar would really be interested in him as anything more than a friend of Clara's. Bergin was pleased to discover that he was wrong. As he would visit with Ingmar, he found that he was falling in love with her. Falling in love with her with a deep and abiding passion. His love for Clara, though ever-present, was never as passionate as his love for Ingmar. She returned his affections, confessing that she preferred him to all the boys in the county that were still pursuing her.

One soft, summer evening, Bergin asked Ingmar to be his wife, and she accepted him. They shared a bond that no one else had or ever could share; they had each loved Clara in a special way.

Ingmar and Bergin were married in the fall in their church. Christian and Bertha Lindgren were pleased with their son-in-law. They were deliriously happy with their grandchildren as they came along. Christian could tell that Bergin loved his youngest child with tenderness and affection. He also came to learn that Bergin had loved his Clara.

A few years after they had been married, Christian's heart gave out as he was working in the fields. He died as he always said he wanted to, while working the land. When they would try to make him take it easy, he would tell them that he wanted to wear out, not rust away slowly.

They buried him next to his beloved daughter. Eight years later his wife joined them in the eternal slumber.

CHAPTER 48

It was late in the season; the harvest was in, the evening lingered warm into twilight in the late September dusk. The trees had bedecked themselves in the gaudy colors of fall. Bergin and Ingmar's oldest daughter had come home for a visit with her two boys, Carl and Peter who were now seven and eight.

The children were playing with their cousins, little Christian and Olav, up by the old Albertson's place. It seemed to be a rite of passage to go up there and scare the liver out of each other, telling stories and daring one another to enter the crumbling house where that crazy man had killed his family and where some woman had been buried in a shallow grave in the grove of ancient oak trees.

The land had been cursed for so long, no one living could remember when it was not under some shadow. Maybe it had been cursed, even in the time when the Indian tribes wandered the area. The children told stories of ghosts, and dreams that had only a shred of truth to them after all the years of telling them.

The old place was rotten with age and lack of care. The roof had collapsed long ago, and the ceilings and floors had rotted away. Only the crumbling stone walls remained upright. As some of the boys were coming through the front door into the ruined hall, a beam collapsed, crashing to the ground, scaring them so that they all ran screaming for the shelter of the grove of oak trees nearby.

"This is as good a place as any," little Christian said to his cousins. He knew the stories the best of them all. He had been named for his great-grandfather who had died.

"Yeah, this will do," Peter said, pointing back to the ruins. "We can see the house from here, see if the ghosts come out."

"Yeah, it's too dark to see if the blood is still on the stairs," Carl stated as a matter of fact, standing as tall as he could for all his eight years would allow. "Not even the flashlights will help. It's just too dark."

"It's there." Christian pointed to the rocky ground.

"How do you know?" Peter asked, staring wide eyed at the

silent, stony ground.

"I seen it the last time I was up here with my big brother and his friends. Seen the ghost too," Christian said.

"Cool," Carl whispered, a little fear trembled in his voice.

"This was the place they found the body of that woman," Christian informed them as if he was the local tour guide.

"Really?" Peter's eyes widened a little with a fear that was creeping about him. He didn't dare chicken in front of his cousins.

"Yeah, it was right here that they found her dead and rotting corpse," Olav spoke up for the first time.

"What?" Carl squeaked.

"About thirty-five years ago they found her somewhere around here," Christian said in a hoarse whisper, sweeping his arms wide to encompass the area around them.

"Is she still here?" Peter asked hesitantly.

"Nah, they took her back to town and buried her," Olav replied.

"Was she dead?" Carl asked.

"Of course, stupid, she had been buried out here for six months," Christian laughed at Carl.

"Where did you hear all this?" Peter asked, not so sure he should believe what he was hearing.

"Yeah, where?" Carl added, feeling braver now. "I don't believe you."

"Well, you better believe it. I even went to the library and read about it in the old newspapers," Olav replied, looking from Carl to Peter and back again.

"Tell us! And don't leave out a word," Peter demanded.

"Back in the old days, when our folks were a few years older than we are now, there was a woman named Clara, who had gone out of her house one night and disappeared into the night . . . " Olav retold the story of Christian Lindgren's dream and the discovery of Clara's body. One of the boys, listening carefully to the story, dug about distractedly in the soft soil that had once been her grave. His stick caught on something. He pulled at it, and a piece of cloth came away. When they all saw what was in the folds of cloth they screamed.

Much as they wanted to run, they were paralyzed with fright.

"She's still here!" Peter screamed.

"She can't be!" Christian said shaking his head.

"Well, someone is!" Peter replied pointing to their discovery. "Look!"

The boy shone the flashlight beam onto the place where he had been digging. He swept away a little more of the soil. Part of a skull had been exposed, the empty eye sockets gaping and the jaw slacked open as in a grotesque laugh.

They all screamed again and ran, this time as fast as they could move.

CHAPTER 49

The next morning the sheriff, Bert Kunkle, came out to the place where the hysterical children had said there was a dead person. Growing up, he too had heard the stories of the Albertsons and of Clara Lindgren. He also knew that there were no bodies left around the area. The Albertsons had all been laid to rest together and Clara Lindgren reposed in the church cemetery.

He was hoping that if there were really bones that they would be of some animal that had died up there. Often people mistook animal bones for human remains. The children had pointed to the general area, not wanting to get close to it again, in case a ghost would reach out to grab them for disturbing their rest.

Kunkle circled around the long narrow trench, before squatting down so he could brush away some of the dirt.

He sighed.

The boys were right; it was a human skull. He would guess that there would be more bones in the grave, as sure as General Douglas MacArthur declared he would return to the Philippines during the Second World War.

Kunkle stationed a few police around the bones to be sure no one came and messed with the site before he could get the thing fully excavated and out of there. He called in the coroner, Frank Landry, to have a look and take care of the formalities.

Landry and some men dug in the earth and discovered it was a full skeleton.

"I wonder who the hell this is?" The sheriff scratched his head.

"No telling, Bert. Better get the bones back to the morgue so we can take a better look. Anyone missing in the last five to thirty years?" The coroner asked, hoping to prompt some recollection of who this might be.

"Not that I know of, Frank," the sheriff shook his head. "It's probably some vagrant came up here and died." He hoped that would be the case. Because he had no clue about anyone being missing from the county, at least not on his watch and he had been sheriff for the last fifteen years.

"Then who buried him?" Landry asked as he carefully cleared dirt away from the remains. "People don't usually lie down, pull up a little dirt and bury themselves."

"Another vagrant?" He shrugged his shoulders as he looked down at the coroner transferring the bones to a box so he could take it back to the lab for analysis.

"I don't envy you this case to solve." He carefully picked up the skull and looked into the gaping eye sockets. "I can tell you this person was a male, probably between the ages of nineteen and thirty. Does that help any?"

"No," he replied back. He really didn't want a case like this on his books.

"Well, I'll see what else I can come up with for you." He smiled, knowing he was frustrating the hell out of the sheriff. They were good friends, and poker buddies.

"It's got to be some transient died and his buddies buried him here," Kunkle stated again, agreeing in his mind with the coroner, that he didn't have a clue how he would solve this case.

Landry placed the skull in the box. Kunkle watched him as he worked unearthing more and more of the skeleton.

"Somehow I don't think he was a transient." He carefully picked up a group of bones that formed one of the hands with his trowel. "Look at this."

"What 'cha got?" He leaned in closer to see what the coroner was talking about.

"He is wearing what looks to be a gemstone ring, a pretty nice one, too." He pointed to a heavy gold band set with three faceted stones still on the finger of the skeleton.

"Damn." The sheriff shook his head. "Definitely not a vagrant."

CHAPTER 50

The newspapers ran the story about the skeleton of a man found in the grove of ancient trees in a shallow grave that had once been the place where another body had been found back in 1925. The story of Clara Lindgren's murder was once again headline news. There was a photograph of the grave and an old picture of Clara that had been her high school graduation photo. Someone had found it on a hunch in the photo morgue of the paper's basement.

There was also a photograph of the ring that was found with the body. Anyone with any information was asked to please come forward and help with the identification of the man found in the grave. The story even ran on the television newscasts of the Omaha stations.

What they did not print in the papers were the other items found with the body. It was speculated that the body had to have been there for more than twenty years since there was so little that remained of clothing. There were buttons and coins found in the dirt. The coins were a quarter, three nickels, two dimes and seven pennies. All had dates that ranged from 1919 to 1925. The buttons were of metal and some of bone. It took a little more work to get the information about the metal buttons; they had rusted badly, but were still able to provide some information. They were finally traced back to the Levi Strauss & Co. and were made for their *koveralls* in the 1920's.

The sheriff sat at his desk and looked at the reports from the coroner and research assistant from the library who had researched the information about the buttons for him. His deputy, Max Porter, came in his office and handed him a cup of coffee before sitting across from his boss.

"Well, it looks like we have an old murder that goes back to sometime in the mid-twenties." Bert Kunkle took a sip of the coffee. "You find anything on any missing persons from back then?"

"Cripes, that was near to thirty-five years ago. Them old records were all destroyed when the basement flooded in nineteen hundred and thirty-two. Whose gonna remember back that far?" Max shook his head and held up his hands in a gesture of helplessness. "Whose gonna really give a flying, red rat's ass about someone been dead that long. Don't you think that if someone gave a damn they would have been in here over the last thirty-five years askin' about where was Joe Blow, here?"

"You have a point. However, we should still make every effort to find out who this is before we pack him into a box and let him collect dust in the evidence room," he had to agree with the futility of identifying the body so many years after it had managed to get itself buried in that grave. "Maybe that ring will bring someone in. Those stones are diamonds, and diamonds are worth a pretty penny." The jeweler had verified them as the genuine article and stated that they were worth many thousands.

"That's true," he too nodded in agreement, and then took a sip of his coffee. "How many karats did they come up to?"

"The large stone was two karats, and the stones on either side were each a karat." Bert read from the report on the ring.

"Them's worth a lot a cabbages. If'n anyone knows about it, they will be in if nothing else for the dough them are worth," Porter said, his mouth gaping open like he wanted to catch flies.

"Yes, it is worth a great deal of money, and is probably a collector's item," Bert said to the deputy.

"Oh? How so?"

"It was made by the famous jeweler, Cartier." Kunkle sipped his coffee, looking over the rim of the cup at his deputy. He knew the man was not the brightest bulb in the pack, but he had proven himself useful at times.

"Never heard of him."

"Someone has." He placed his coffee cup on the table as he thought about the bones found in the shallow grave. "Someone knows who this is, and I hope like hell they come in and tell us."

"Be nice if they'd a come in and confess for us." He snorted a laugh, knowing it was not likely to happen.

"See if you can't get old man Halverson to come in and talk to us. After all, the skeleton was found on his property. Plus he grew up here and may have been around when all this came down. Maybe we can coax some information from him."

"I'm on it like white on rice, Sheriff." He bounded out of the seat and through the door like a heat-seeking missile.

CHAPTER 51

Bergin sat alone in the dark wondering what he should do. The Sheriff had called him and asked him to come in to see if he could help them sort things out.

He was probably the only one who knew whose skeleton they had unearthed up in the old grove of oak trees. He had kept the secret all these years, what good would it do now to let them know who they had found.

It came on the soft breeze like a caress. A fragrance he had forgotten long ago, yet once knew so well.

He closed his eyes.

He remembered her. She had always worn that scent.

He felt that it was a sign.

He felt as if she had come to tell him to let them know who the bones belonged to. He sensed that it would help her to rest in a way she hadn't been able to. That she too wanted to be free of the past.

That maybe if it all finally came out they could all rest easily.

"All right, sweet girl. I'll do it. For you," he said to the darkness, for no one else was in the room with him. He was alone in the house.

Or was he?

He felt a gentle touch on his cheek, and then the fragrance was gone.

CHAPTER 52

Ella Watson tapped at the sheriff's door.

"Yes, Ella, what is it?" He asked. He was always amused at how timid she was when she would knock on his door.

"There's someone here to see you." She looked about like a trapped mouse. "He says he might have some information for you about the man found in the grave."

"Show him in, Ella. By all means show him in." Bert gestured in a wave as if to call him into the room.

She stepped back and gestured for the man to come into the sheriff's office.

"This is Mr. Bergin Halverson, Sheriff Bert Kunkle." She looked back at the sheriff before slipping from the doorway to make room for the man to enter.

Bert stood up to greet his visitor. He knew the Halverson family had been farmers in the area since the late eighteen hundreds when they had emigrated from Sweden. He also knew that Halverson's brother was the one suspected of killing Clara Lindgren, but knew little else about him. Rumor had it that the brother had run away and years later he was supposed to have been killed in WWII.

"Sheriff, I'm Bergin Halverson." He extended his hand. The sheriff shook his hand and offered him a seat.

Bert was surprised at Bergin Halverson. He was a tall slim man whose blonde hair was beginning to turn gray at the temples. His face had a few lines in it, but he looked much younger than the fifty-seven some odd years he was purported to be. The man was simply dressed in a dark suit and conservative tie.

"What can I do for you Mr. Halverson?" He sat back in his chair waiting to hear what the man had to say about the body.

"Your man asked me to come in and see if I couldn't shed some light on the identity of the person in the grave on my land." A distant look played in his eyes. "This is not easy for me, Sheriff."

"Sit down, Mr. Halverson." Bert gestured to the chair across the desk from him. He waited while Halverson settled into the chair, and wrestled with his thoughts. "I asked you to come in here, because I believe you may be able to help us in this inquiry." Bert reached into the drawer and placed the ring on his desk.

Bergin made no move to pick it up.

* * *

"Yes, I think I can help you identify the remains your men unearthed the other day," Bergin sighed.

"Oh? And who do you think he may be?" Kunkle had already been inundated with crackpots and crank callers about these bones. Now across the desk sat what he thought was a respectable looking man claiming to know who the dead man was. He had asked Halverson to come in to see him.

"I know that the man in the grave was my brother, Erdman," he said in a gentle voice as he looked down at his hands in his lap.

"What makes you think that, sir?" He would be glad to know who the stiff was so he could get it cleared off the books. The guy didn't look like a nut case.

"This ring that you found with the body," he asked, looking up for a moment to meet Kunkle's stare. "Back in nineteen-twenty-four my brother bought himself a three-stone diamond ring set in a heavy gold band as a reward. He had just cleared a couple thousand dollars from his bootlegging operation, and wanted to let people know that he was making plenty of money. He bought himself a gambler's ring. That ring," Bergin laughed a little as he remembered his brother's bravado.

"What makes you think that this ring is his in particular?" Bert asked. He would have to make sure before handing over such a valuable item and he needed proper identification of the bones. "Can you tell me anything that might help make an iron clad identification of the ring?"

"It was four karats total, a two karat in the center flanked by one karat stones." He paused a moment as if trying to remember something else. "Oh yes, and was made by Cartier. It was quite a ring."

"So, you think the ring and, subsequently, the body could have been your brother's then?" Kunkle asked, looking the man over. He needed to be sure before he could go on. He also would need to know how the body came to be in the grave.

"Yes. My brother disappeared shortly after he was indicted by the Coroner's Jury for the murder of Clara Lindgren. He had run off once before when he thought her father was going to have the old sheriff, Mr. De Boer, run him in for questioning," his words came slowly as he remembered the events of those years past. His eyes had a faraway look to them. "Erdman came back again, he was not one to hide out or rough it for long; he was too accustomed to the easy life, and his bankroll of cash was hidden on the farm. He was killed the day before we buried Clara and he was put into Clara's old grave. It's a little ironic that he lay there in Clara's grave for so long and no one found him for nearly thirty-five years, don't you think?" Bergin smiled a little.

"Did you kill him, Mr. Halverson?"

"No, sheriff. I didn't kill him," Bergin shook his head.

"All right, for now," the Sheriff studied Bergin Halverson. "Then tell me, is there anything you can remember about your brother, besides the ring that might help to identify him? Old bone breaks, fillings anything like that?" The sheriff prompted as he reached for the autopsy report done by the coroner on the remains. There were a few distinct things about the skeleton that were unique. This Erdman was a pretty slippery character from what he knew about him, and he could have slipped the ring on the hand of someone else and disappeared into the night, becoming someone else entirely. It was a lot easier to do back then.

"Let me see, this all was so long ago, and I've not thought of my brother or our childhood in years." His soft blue eyes looked into Bert's. He took a deep breath and let it out slowly as he cast his mind back to his youth. "There was something that might help. When he was about fifteen, he had been playing around when he should have been working, and fell out of the hayloft and broke his left arm pretty badly. Our father set the bone, and mother wrapped it with a splint. It healed pretty well too; he never seemed to have any trouble with it at all after that," Bergin laughed again. "Erdman always made the most of it; he would claim it was bothering him if there were chores to do. It never bothered him when there was fun to be had. Oh, Erdman was such a fool."

Bert let Halverson drift off into the past with his memories before speaking again and calling him back to the present.

"Do you know any reason someone would want him dead?"

"Of course I do." He looked at Bert with a surprised expression. "He was the reason Clara Lindgren was dead. He was the one who buried her there."

"You know this for certain?" Bert raised his eyebrows and picked up his pen to make some notes on their conversation.

"Yes, he told me all about it before he ran off, the day before her funeral. He was such a coward. There were a couple hundred people who wanted to see him get what he deserved. You see, Clara Lindgren was beloved in the community back then. She was a very special girl." That faraway look came into his eyes again as he remembered her and their lives back then.

"It sounds like you were a little in love with her, yourself," Bert said, his voice soft. He remembered his first crush, she could still bring a smile to his lips.

"Yes, I believe I was in love with her in a way back then," Bergin's smile was wistful as he spoke about her.

"Love is a strong passion, makes us do some crazy things," Sheriff Kunkle studied the man across the desk from him as he nodded thoughtfully, but made no reply. There was something the man still had to say. It might be something to do with the dead man, it might not. He called it his cop instinct. He could be patient and see what else the man had to say.

Bergin shifted in his chair, he cleared his throat but still said nothing.

The sheriff allowed the silence to persist. To him it looked like Bergin was wrestling with some long-kept secret. Slowly, Bergin looked up at the sheriff and gave him a sad smile.

"May I tell you something, Sheriff?"

"Please do," the sheriff replied. Now it would come, he thought, that which this man has held to his heart for so many years. At last he can speak about it, let it go.

"Each one of us wants desperately to be loved. We try to get love in many ways, some people have to take it, and others think they have to have it all so there is none left for others. I was the second son, and was totally eclipsed by the bright, shining perfection of my brother. My parents could not see what I saw. They showered him with all their love, all their support and all their affection while I stood in my brother's shadow and went unnoticed for so many years," Bergin paused a moment then asked a question. "Do you have any idea what I am talking about, Sheriff?"

"I think I do, I was a second child myself, you kind'a get overlooked."

"I felt as if I didn't even exist for my parents. Everything was always about my perfect brother. He could do no wrong, and when he did get in trouble either I was the one who got blamed, or they would simply deny that he could do anything wrong.

"I could see what they could not. My brother was a lazy, good-for-nothing waste of human flesh. He used people, and if they got in his way, challenged him in any way or refused him anything that he wanted, he destroyed them. He would use any means available to get what he wanted. He was a grasping, greedy young man, but no matter what he did, my folks turned a blind eye to his misdeeds." Bergin took a deep breath and let it out slowly.

"He used Clara in the worst way," Bergin sighed. "He took advantage of a vulnerable girl who wanted so much to be loved, to be married and have a family. She wanted what everyone else seemed to have. He used her desires as a weapon against her. He seduced her. And when she wrote and let him know she was carrying his child at first he denied knowing her, then he tried to say her dates were wrong or even that it had to be some other man's child. At one point, he might have tried to blame it on me. I never touched the girl, much as I might have liked to back then." He looked up at the sheriff again, and his cheeks colored to a deep crimson.

"I know what you mean," Kunkle smiled and nodded slightly as encouragement for the man to continue with his story. Much of this was part of the legendary folklore of the area, and he was getting to hear it from the one person still around who was in the midst of it all.

"After they found Clara's body, and he was indicted for her murder, my father covered for him, still unable to get it through his thick skull that Erdman, his precious son was a murderer. But I knew. Erdman knew that I knew, and that was what frightened him. That is what put my life in peril."

"Did he threaten to kill you?" The sheriff asked. His cop mentality was beginning to create a scenario in his mind that spelled trouble.

"Not in so many words, it was what I saw in his eyes that day when he begged me to help him get away. It was a look that told me if I helped him he would do all he could to keep me silent, to keep me from ever being able to divulge his secrets. You see, I knew only too well all that he had done and even what terrible things he was capable of doing. I was the invisible son; I was the child no one paid any attention to. Even my brother treated me as if I wasn't around most of the time, unless I could be of use to him." The bitterness of his memories was evident in his words.

"I had said that I would help him get away. We had planned to meet up at the old Albertson place that night. It was supposed to be haunted, so no one went there. It was also very near there that Clara's body was found. Erdman hid out in the old house until I could get there. Our property is not far from there. I had taken the car over earlier and parked it near the old house, then I walked over to meet him after dark. I was nervous in that I did not trust my brother."

Bergen began to tell the story of what happened that night as Sheriff Kunkle listened and took notes. At first it was hard for Bergin to let go of these memories so tightly held, buried so deep within his being, but soon like the crack in the dam, the memories breached the walls of the silence imposed upon them for so long, and broke free into a flood of words, memories and emotions that filled the space around him and cast him back into the darkness of that night.

CHAPTER 53

Bergin watched as his brother headed into the house to gather a few things together. He moved like a hunted animal. In some ways, that was just what he was, a hunted animal. The sheriff was looking for him, and De Boer was not a man to give up on a matter of the law.

Bergin sat in the shadows of the barn and thought about the dirty deal he had just entered into with his brother. He did not like it, and he would have to find a way to extract himself from the arrangement. He was lost in thought when he heard the screen door of the house slam shut.

Erdman emerged from the farmhouse, and stood in the barnyard looking about as if he were taking mental inventory of all that was the farm. He twirled the fancy diamond ring on his hand, a nervous habit of his. Flashes of light glinted in the stone as it turned and reflected the bright sunlight.

It alerted Bergin that something had changed.

Erdman stood like he was master of the world, not a sniveling killer seeking to run off and hide. Erdman walked out onto the yard and headed over the pasture that was adjacent to the Albertson land. He did not look back; he did not look around. He no longer had the look of the hunted.

Bergin also noticed that his brother had not packed anything. He carried no suitcase or bundle of clothes under his arm. He was still wearing the flannel shirt and *Koveralls* he so hated.

Something had changed.

"But what?" Bergin whispered into the cool darkness where he sat.

His eyes wandered over to look at the back door of the house where Erdman had just exited.

"What happened in there?" He whispered to himself as a feeling of dread began to circle around him. His thoughts nagged at him as he turned his attention back to what he had been doing.

* * *

It would be a while before he could head over to find his brother. There were chores to finish before he could even consider it. He would be missed if he slipped away too soon. He had seen his father once in that whole time and the man had simply looked at him for a moment and, shaking his head, had hurriedly walked away.

After a few hours, he realized it was getting dark, and he might be able to meet Erdman as they had arranged. He was going to let Erdman take his car, since the Hudson would be too easily spotted. Too many of the area police were familiar with his car from his bootlegging days. He managed to slip away for a little while to drive the Chevrolet up to the Albertson place, parking it by the road to use later.

He planned to walk over the fields between their places to meet Erdman as it got dark. When he returned from delivering the car, he took care of a few things Erdman would need for his escape. He had to do them between his chores so his father wouldn't yell at him for not tending to the farm.

He had wrapped up the cash his brother had asked him for and placed it in a small carrying case. He had never seen so much money at one time. There were thousands, maybe even a hundred thousand dollars, his brother has secreted away. It made him wonder what other illicit activities his brother had been involved in. Bergin's mind turned to Sparky. He had gotten some intelligence on the guy in that he was a small-time hood who had killed people for the fun of it. He didn't even want to contemplate why Erdman was mixed up with such a man.

Twilight was always a magical time, neither night nor day, but rather a place where things are seen that are not real, and imagination blossoms into strange and ethereal apparitions. He walked across the field and up the hill to the place of their appointed rendezvous. A soft mist was forming in the deeper hollows of the ground and began to reach up to touch him as he walked through the semi-darkness to their meeting place.

The moon had risen in the east and hovered close to the land, glowing a golden orange as the last embers of day began to fade from the sky. The birds chattered in the trees as they settled in for the night, while others did their night flight before retiring. Some bats swooped silently in the trees, preparing for their evening foray.

"Bergin," Erdman's whisper was constrained and carried on the growing mist of night like a spectral thought itself.

"Erdman," he heard someone reply in a hoarse whisper, the voice more substantial, though tinged with the color of growing fear. "Where are you?"

Bergin searched for the source of the voices. He wasn't expecting anyone, and the other voice, though decidedly other male did not sound like his father. He felt a tingle of fear prickle through his being as he recalled earlier how Erdman had seemed so confident, so sure, no longer afraid after he came out of the house. He hung back a little way, not willing to walk into a bad situation.

Maybe the sheriff had discovered that Erdman was planning to run off and was here to make sure he didn't get away again.

As the twilight began to fade to night, the moon rose higher, lustrous above the trees, casting its strange bluish light on the scene below. It looked more like a landscape pulled from the imagination of a dreamer than that of reality.

Erdman appeared in the crooked doorway of the ruined house like a menacing shadow. Something in his hand glinted faintly in the pallid moonlight.

Bergin moved a little closer to have a better look, the hair on the back of his neck began to prickle. His body tensed. The mist began to rise from the earth, curled about his feet and tangled about his legs, holding him motionless.

Someone came out of the shadows, twigs snapped as they approached Erdman.

"Bergie?" Erdman called out and started to walk toward the sound. "Come out where I can see you." The metal flashed again in his hand.

"Thought you could get away from me, did you Halverson?" The man's voice was rough. He was not clearly discernable in the fading light since he was wearing all black clothing.

"Sparky?" Erdman's voice took on a terrified tone.

A menacing laughter emanated from the darkness where the man crouched in the weeds. Stealthily he closed in on Erdman.

"How did you find me?" He looked out into the gloom like a blind man searching for something, his eyes opened wide in fear.

"I followed your surrogate," his laughter was cruel. "You

shouldn't have sent someone instead of you to meet me. You know I don't like that. When I does business with a man, I want to know who it is I'm working for." He pulled a gun out and made sure Erdman could see what it was, the glint of a barrel catching in the moonlight.

"I didn't send anyone to meet you." Erdman stepped back into the shadows a bit, his eyes riveted on the gun.

Bergin realized this must be the man, Sparky, who sent the postcard to his brother. He decided to say nothing for the moment, but crept in a little closer.

"Sure you did, your kid brother who looks like you come into the Ogden and was looking around. A stoolie of mine gave him away. And I might add that's what saved his hide that night. Instead of slitting his throat, I let him go so he could lead me to where you was hiding out."

"You followed him to the farm?" Erdman's voice cracked. He took another step back. "Is that how you found me?"

"Yeah, let's say I had a tour guide to lead me there. He didn't see me neither, but if you recall I left you a little something," Sparky's laughter was a low rumble.

"The note with the knife," Erdman whispered. He looked around for a means of escape.

"And so, here we are tonight, just us, and you thinking you was gonna go on the lam and not tell me where you was goin?" He smiled, a gold tooth glinting in the little shreds of moonlight. "Well, you done made a big mistake. You know that me and my associates would be able to find you no matter where you think you're hiding. We can come after your family, too, if I don't get what I want. It could take years, but we will hunt them down and kill them all. Do you understand what I am telling you, big man?"

"No, no! I can still pay you. I have the money coming to me here. My brother will be bringing it with him," Erdman's voice betrayed his fear.

"You do still owe me for whacking the broad, sure. But now the juice on this deal has increased the amount substantially." Sparky was standing close enough to Erdman now that they could have touched.

Bergin took a step back, drawing in his breath. He thought he just heard the man say he had killed Clara. He had heard enough slang from his brother's associates and friends to understand that *whacked the broad* meant the man had killed the girl. And Clara was the girl.

He must have made too much noise, for Sparky turned around to see who else was there and called out into the darkness.

"Show yourself," Sparky demanded, waving his gun in the direction of the sound he had heard. "That you little brother? Coming to save your brother?"

Bergin made no sound; he tried to breath through his mouth to keep as quiet as possible. His heart pounded in his chest, and hoped they could not hear it.

Erdman took a step forward, taking the distraction as an opportunity to take a swing at his adversary while he was momentarily distracted. Sparky was too fast for him. He saw that Erdman was coming for him, and took a step to the side, avoiding the blow aimed for his head. Instead Erdman's blow connected with the gun in the man's hand. A shot tore through the night as the gun misfired, and flew off into the tangle of weeds in the distance.

"You's gonna pay for that, little man," Sparky hissed at Erdman, pulling a knife from his pocket. He flashed it at Erdman to be sure he would see it. The pale blue of the moonlight glinted off the blade. "For that, I'm going to make sure you, and your whole family gets whacked. Got it?"

"Don't hurt my folks, please," Erdman whimpered. Fear hung in the air like a foul stench emanating from his body.

"I'll take special care with them, and will let them know how much you cared." Sparky swiped the knife at Erdman. He laughed at his adversary's retreat.

Erdman took another swing at Sparky.

Sparky ducked out of the way.

Erdman spun about; trying to regain equilibrium, he had not expected to miss, or to have the man retaliate. Sparky moved like a wild thing. He socked Erdman in the gut. Erdman doubled over from the blow, grunting as the air was expelled from his lungs. Whatever weapon Erdman had been holding in his hand clattered to the ground. Sparky kicked it away and pounded Erdman on the back of the neck.

Erdman fell to the ground and began to whimper in pain, begging for mercy.

Sparky kicked him in the side and laughed.

"You useless piece of garbage," Sparky taunted Erdman, dealing him blows as he circled about him. Erdman writhed in pain on the ground. "No one welches on me. Well, at least no one that lives to tell the tale." He flashed the knife in the air so Erdman could see how he was going to die.

Sparky crouched over Erdman and held the knife at his throat.

"Please, don't hurt me. Let me live," Erdman was crying and begging Sparky.

"Time to meet your maker, little Erdie. But before I cut you up, tell me where the dough is, 'cause I know you got it, and maybe I will not kill your folks or your brother if you tell me real nice like. Okay?" He laughed again. "And if you don't tell me, I will be sure to come after them until I do get it. Understand? I will keep you alive long enough to tell me where it is, but until you do, I will deal out the pain real slow like, cause I love to hear you scream and beg."

The man must have started to cut Erdman's flesh because he screamed now in pain and thrashed about trying to escape the sharp knife blade that was so cool on his skin. The blood was warm in contrast as it burst from his severed flesh.

Erdman was making so much noise that Bergin was able to pick up the weapon that Sparky had kicked away from Erdman after disarming him.

Bergin, motivated by his brother's terrible screams came up close to Sparky and struck a blow against the man's head. He heard a disgusting sound as the man's skull cracked, and he fell to the side of his brother and grew still.

Bergin rushed to his brother's side. The knife the man had wielded had been thrust deep into Erdman's chest as he fell off of him.

Erdman was bleeding heavily.

"Erdman," Bergin called out, tears coming to his eyes. He was surprised to feel so much love for his brother; he didn't want to lose him. All the anger and resentment he had held over the years dissipated in an instant and he wanted his brother to live.

"Bergie," Erdman managed to say, his voice gurgled. "Forgive me?" He looked into his brother's eyes, pleading for that last release.

"For what?" He sobbed, confused by his jumbled emotions.

"For killing Clara?"

"I didn't kill her." His eyes fluttered closed for a moment. "Sparky did."

"What?" Bergin tore at his shirt, pulling it off and pressing it onto the wound in his brother's chest. He was afraid to remove the knife for fear it would only make him bleed all the faster.

"I hired him to do my dirty work," he whispered. "I am so sorry." He blinked back the tears that welled in the corners of his eyes.

"We have to get you home." Bergin pulled the shirt away from the wound, but the blood had soaked through the fabric.

"No. I'm not going to make it." Erdman tried to shake his head, but winced in pain. "You have to forgive me."

The mist began to deepen. It reached out and touched them both as they spoke. Neither paid it any attention.

"Erdman," he started to say, but he was cut off when his brother spoke again. What he heard chilled him to the bone.

"I wasn't supposed to be the one to die here tonight. You were," his voice was getting weaker, his strength seeping out onto the ground with his thick, warm blood. It looked black in the moonlight.

"Erdman, what are you saying?" He sat up straight, looking down at his brother, not believing what he had heard.

"You are the one who was going to disappear tonight, little brother," he struggled to say. "I was supposed to go away for a little bit, and then return, but it was not as Erdman that I would return. You can't have failed to notice that we resemble each other a great deal now, have you?"

"You were going to kill me?" Bergin could hardly believe what Erdman was saying to him. "And take my place? Live my life?" He stood up and took a step away.

"Right, little brother. You catch onto things pretty quickly for a farm boy. Yes, after a little while I was to come home as Bergin. I had gone off to search for my brother, the best man in the world, but failed to find him. It's all so sad."

"No," Bergin looked into his brother's eyes, and replied.

"Oh, yes, little brother, I was planning it all with poppa in the house before I came out here. I had to. I had no choice anymore. See, I hired that man to kill Clara, and he would have tracked me down no matter where I would go or where I would hide. He had to believe that Erdman was dead and I had to become you. He was a man not to give up."

That was when it happened. He saw his brother look over at something.

A film of vapor was moving toward them.

Erdman gasped, his eyes wide.

The mist coiled about them both, closer, cold. Bergin thought he saw something too. A haze, like a shroud enveloped Erdman's body. He gurgled, blood came from his mouth, and his eyes looked as if they were following something.

Some *thing* that had taken form in the mist.

Something that looked almost human.

He was stunned as he watched, not believing, not wanting to see what was there. In the mist a form began to take shape, at first transparent, then growing more substantial, taking on form and shape, until it could be discerned what he was seeing there; the wraith of a woman standing quietly waiting for the mists to gather sufficiently to give her mobility and voice.

Then there was a fragrance in the air that wasn't there before.

Bergin closed his eyes and inhaled the scent. He knew it was hers.

He opened them again and now could see her pale skin and soft dark hair that framed her stunning green eyes. He shook his head to clear the visage, yet his eyes could not look away. His gaze was held fast by her stare. She began to walk to the two of them. Closer she came, reaching out her pale hands and long, white fingers. They seemed to elongate and entwine themselves about Erdman.

Erdman tried to squirm away from the thing that was wrapping itself closer and closer about him, the cold misty air choking him; he couldn't get sufficient breath. His eyes had a frantic look of terror in them as he gasped for the breath that would not come.

"Help me!" Erdman managed to say, frightened of what was happening. "Clara, no!" With the last of his strength, he clawed at the mist, but his fingers could find no purchase. He fought his insubstantial foe in a vain attempt to break free.

Bergin was paralyzed by the visage of the scene before him. He didn't believe in ghosts at all. He wanted to scream, to run, but his whole body had gone rigid with fear.

Erdman didn't stir. He was still.

Bergin watched as the mist that clung so tenaciously to his brother began to dissipate and fade to nothingness as he struggled to move his body once again. The paralyzing terror seemed to melt away from him, freeing him. He knelt down by Erdman's still form. In the moonlight, he could see that his brother's eyes no longer held any life. He touched Erdman's neck for a pulse and found none.

Erdman was dead.

He sat back on the blood soaked ground and began to weep.

The fragrance began to fade, and a night breeze dispersed the clinging mist.

"Erdman! No!" Bergin cried out against the night. He sat back and cried for the loss of the brother who had caused him so much pain. Even though he had been a wastrel and a cad, Bergin realized that he still had loved him. He was, after all, his brother.

Bergin wasn't sure what to do next. A new terror grabbed at his heart.

Erdman had confessed that their parents expected him to be the one who was lying dead in this place, not Erdman. His father would surely kill him if he let him know what had happened. His father would never believe some thug had killed Erdman.

Bergin looked around and realized where he was. The pit where Clara had been buried was still there, no one had filled it in. He was desperate; he hauled his brother's body over to it and dumped it in the hole.

"Forgive me, Erdman. You and poppa left me no choice," he said to his dead brother as he scraped the dirt around him, and covered him over with it. He hoped no wild animals would dig him up, so he placed some rocks and the boughs they had used for Clara over the grave.

He stood and looked down at the makeshift grave. Once again, someone he loved rested there.

Bergin had one more thing to deal with.

Sparky.

He went over to where the man lay, afraid he might wake up and kill him too. He had taken the knife that had killed his brother in hand, and walked cautiously up to where the man lay.

He need not have worried. The man looked like he was dead. The blow to his skull must have killed him.

"Now I have done murder," Bergin sighed. "God forgive me."

He decided to dump the body in the nearest creek. It took him a while to haul the body down to his car, but he managed. He almost forgot the case he had packed for Erdman with the cash. He didn't want anyone to find it, nor did he want anyone to discover his brother's grave. At least, not yet.

No one was around to see as he dumped the man's corpse onto the riverbank. He figured someone would find it and begin an investigation. He pushed the body down the slope, it rolled to the edge of the river, a dark shape against the fractured moonlight that played in the ripples of current along the bank.

Bergin was dead tired when he returned home well past midnight.

CHAPTER 54

He was still numb from what all had happened that night that he had forgotten the dirty little deal his brother had made with his parents. When he returned from the river and went into the house, his father, who was sitting at the table, jumped up when he came in the door.

"Erdman," Mr. Halverson said with a smile, arms widening as if he would hug him.

Bergin turned and looked at his father, remembering with horror their plan.

He watched as his father's expression changed from joy to anger. The anger was directed at him.

"Where is Erdman?" He demanded scowling at Bergin. "What have you done with him?"

"He couldn't go through with it, poppa," Bergin lied, trying to think up a plausible story that the man would believe.

"Go through with what?" His father plopped back down in the chair. It was the first time Bergin had ever seen his father afraid. "I don't know what you are talking about, boy." His mouth pulled into a taut line.

"He couldn't kill me, like you planned with him." Bergin turned to face his father, leveling an icy stare at him. "He always was a yellowbelly, and he couldn't do it."

"Then where is he? Where is your brother?" He bellowed, spitting out a rapid-fire of questions; it was his only defense. "Why are you so filthy? Where is your shirt?"

"I had to change a tire on the car on the way back from town. I took Erdman to the train station in Council Bluffs and dropped him off. He won't be coming back. Ever," his voice was cold and hard.

"What are you going to do?" His father sensed there was something different in his youngest child.

"Nothing," he said, his lips pressed tightly together as he tried to keep his anger in check. His own father had plotted to kill him. Maybe that was where Erdman had gotten his mean streak. "For now."

His father still looked at him with a terrified look in his eyes. It reminded him of the way the cow's eyes look when too much exposed white shows their fear.

The old man simply nodded, unable to reply.

"I will say this, nothing better happen to me just in case Erdman surfaces again. Do I make myself clear?" He no longer trusted his father. He wasn't too sure that his father wouldn't do him harm in the night out of spite. He had to protect himself. "I will be heading back into town now, I might even let the sheriff know what you planned to do to me, so that if anything happens to me, they will come looking for you."

Bergin didn't wait for his father to reply, but headed out the door, and drove away from the farmhouse, wondering if he really would have the nerve to let DeBoer know what had happened.

It was something he could decide in the morning.

CHAPTER 55

"I buried my brother there in that grave he had made for Clara," Bergin said with a sigh. "Maybe I should have told someone, but I did what I thought was right at the time." His lip trembled as he fought back the fear that wrapped around him as he relived his memory of that night.

Bergin fell silent.

Kunkle didn't speak either.

"I didn't kill my brother, Sheriff," Bergin said at last. "However, I did leave him there. I knew if he was found I would have been the one to get blamed. My father would never have believed it was an accident. Especially after the plan he and Erdman had cooked up so Erdman could go on living as if nothing ever happened. It was a bitter pill to swallow that my father and brother could have plotted to kill me, and allow him to take my place, take my name and never face a consequence for what he did to Clara. I knew if I had gone home and told my folks what happened that they would have made sure I was tried and convicted for depriving them of their favorite child. So, I buried him in Clara's grave," he sighed as if a great burden he carried for years was at last relinquished.

"What did you tell your folks? They must have wondered why you came home." He narrowed his eyes at Bergin.

"I told them Erdman had decided to go into hiding after all. That he and I had made a deal," his laugh was bitter. "They believed me, or more they believed that their beloved son really couldn't hurt his little brother." He fell silent and wiped at his eye.

Kunkle shifted in his chair and put down his pen on the pad where he had been taking notes.

"For nearly thirty-five years I have been waiting for someone to find him," Bergin said shaking his head slowly. "Erdman's shadow has hovered over me all these years. I'm glad it's over. I'm relieved that he has been found at last." He rubbed his hand across his face, and his eyes.

"But you kept silent for so long. After your parents died,

couldn't you have done something then? Said something to someone?" The sheriff sat forward in his chair, the leather of his belt creaking.

"There was one other part of this story that not even my wife knows about." Bergin looked at the sheriff, his whole body growing tense again.

The sheriff saw the look of terror that flitted through the man's expression. He wondered what more there could be to this story that still gripped the man with fear.

"It was a number of years after my folks had died, and I had been thinking about how I might let someone know the truth about Erdman. Ingmar and I had been married and the children were going to school. One day my daughter who was about seven at the time, came home with a note pinned to her dress." Bergin fought back his emotions as he remembered that day. "I recall it was a sunny, warm day, everything had seemed so green and lush. Little Irene came walking up the drive, and I remember seeing the note, and at first not paying it much attention, as I thought it was something the teacher might have sent home. Something made me stop and go to her. I asked her about the note, and she said some funny looking, old man pinned it to her dress and said that daddy would understand what it was about." Bergin's hand began to tremble as he reenacted his movements of that day. "I unpinned the note from her dress and read what it had to say."

"What did it say?" The sheriff's mind was racing trying to guess what it may have said.

"It was not so much what it said, it was who it was from," Bergin swallowed hard before going on. "It was from Sparky Mann and all it said was that he was still looking for Erdman. It also stated that if he didn't find him soon he would be back to deal with us all. It was a threat to all of us, to all our lives. If he could get to my child…" Bergin trembled trying to shake off the feeling of terror that still gripped him as he remembered reading that note.

"He was still alive then?" The sheriff raised his eyebrows.

"Evidently. I thought I had killed him," Bergin replied with a frown. "I dumped him by the river. I didn't wait to see of he went into the water. It was too dark to see where exactly he landed."

The Sheriff nodded.

"That he could get to my children so easily scared the hell out of me. I couldn't let anyone know where Erdman was, you see, I was afraid that Sparky would come after me, after my wife and children if he found out Erdman had been dead all these years. I wasn't about to take that chance." Bergin's hands tumbled around each other as he battled with his old fears. "So I let it go, soon no one asked about Erdman anymore, and I ignored the rumors about him. He was forgotten. Though I could never forget."

"Then you bought the Albertson place?" There were many questions that he wanted answers for. He may never get another chance to find the truth and put the old rumors to rest.

"I did," Bergin nodded slowly, a funny smile played at his lips.

"Where did you get the money to buy it? It was the depression as I recall. I am sure that the land was not cheap. No matter about the house falling down, that was some good acreage of farmland."

"Yes, that's so true, though back then no one wanted to touch that land. I bought it cheaply, and I paid cash. You see, I had no idea that there was so much money hidden under the seat of Erdman's car until that night when I packed it up to bring to him. I thought it only fitting that I use that money to buy that land, and keep that grove of trees and his grave undisturbed as I worked the rest of the land. I didn't know what my parents had planned for the farm with Erdman gone. I never seemed to matter to them. I needed a place to live, and needed to earn my living too. I had a wife to support."

Once again, silence settled about them like the mist that had gathered that night so long ago.

"What about this Sparky Mann? Did you ever see him again or get any more notes from him?"

"Just a postcard a few years later, about the time my daughter came home with his note on her dress. It said he would never really be far away. Then, a few years later, I heard something about him being caught."

"Oh?" Bert sat forward, interested.

"He was found, but as they were going to bring him up on charges, he slipped away from them. I never really knew what happened to him, but for many years after I looked over my shoulder. I did suspect he may have had a hand in my father's death. That accident just seemed a little staged to me," his shoulders sagged as he spoke. "What will you do about Erdman now, Sheriff?"

"As far as the death of your brother, I believe I will rule this as an accidental death. I won't be pressing any charges. It is a closed case now." He didn't have any proof of foul play from the autopsy to build a case with either.

He felt a little sorry for Bergin in that he had lived with such a terrible secret all these many years. That had been a greater punishment than anything he could hand out.

Bergin simply nodded.

"I will have you sign some forms and you can take possession of the remains for burial, and the ring is yours, too." He stood up and walked over to the door. Opening it, he called to his secretary.

"Ella, would you get the forms we need for me to release the remains and other items into Mr. Halverson's custody."

"Oh, yes, Bert, sure. Does he know who the man in the trench was?"

"Yes, he says it was his brother."

Ella's reply was only simply a sudden intake of breath.

Bert came back and sat down again. He looked at Bergin. The man seemed to have aged in the time since he had arrived. He wondered what the man was feeling now.

"Ella will get some forms ready for you to sign, and we will release the body and other items into your care."

"Thank you," Bergin said. He still seemed far off in the past somewhere. "Thank you very much."

"Is there anything I can do for you, Mr. Halverson?"

"Would you be able to have the body delivered to the funeral home? I don't think I want to see him." He shook his head. "Not like that."

"We can do that for you."

Ella tapped at the door and came in to hand the forms to Bert. She snuck a glance at Bergin as he sat quietly in the chair.

"I'm so sorry about your brother, sir," she said to him before stepping back through the door.

Halverson thanked her in a soft voice. He signed the papers and handed them back to the sheriff. Then he lowered his head and stared at his hands clasped tightly together in his lap.

Bert picked up the ring and looked at it for a moment. He then placed it on the desk in front of Halverson.

Bergin raised his head and gazed at the ring for a moment before he picked it up and looked at it, turning it about. The light glinted off the diamonds, scattering little rainbows of fractured light on the wall. He slipped the ring into his pocket.

"You know, I still have his car in the barn where he left it the last time he came home. It was a nineteen-nineteen Hudson Speedster. He loved that car more than anything else in the world." Bergin rose slowly from the chair and reached his hand out to the sheriff. "Thank you, Sheriff Kunkle. I best be getting home now."

Bert shook his hand and walked him to the door.

"I sure would love to see that old car of your brother's some day," Bert said, not sure what else to say to the man. It seemed that Bergin had been waiting for someone to accidentally find his brother after all these years. Maybe keeping his car was an act of devotion in a way.

"Maybe some day, Sheriff, maybe some day, if I ever decide to uncover it and have a look myself." Bergin gave him a wistful smile.

Bert watched as Bergin nodded goodbye to Ella and slipped out the door into the sunlight.

CHAPTER 56

"Ironic that Erdman ended up in Clara's makeshift grave," Ingmar said to her husband when they were seated in the living room after supper that evening.

Bergin sighed as he reached in his pocket and took out the ring that had been his brothers. He put it in her lap.

"What is this?" Ingmar looked at him quizzically, picking it up and looking at it.

"Erdman's diamond ring," he replied. "It was in the grave with him."

"What are you going to do with it?" She looked at the ring, then at her husband, then back at the ring. She turned it and the facets of the diamonds sparkled, creating little rainbows on the wall. "It's beautiful."

"I don't want it." He dismissed it with a wave of his hand. "You do what you want with it. Reset the stones, sell them, it makes no difference to me. He is not someone I want to be reminded of," his words were bitter.

"Was he really as bad as you see him? He did a terrible thing in killing my sister, but was he really beyond redemption?" She asked, looking over at Bergin.

"I don't know how to answer that." He had never told anyone that Erdman had hired 'Sparky' Mann to kill Clara. He didn't think it would make much of a difference if people knew. Clara was still dead. "You know when he was a child he killed another boy he was playing with. The boy had dared to challenge Erdman's version of the truth. Poppa got him off, insisting it was an accident. But I knew better. I saw what happened, but no one wanted to listen to me. I knew the truth. Erdman never could face the truth." He touched his wife's cheek with his fingertips. She had always been such a beautiful woman. She was like Clara in many ways, and in others they were the complete opposite.

"Try and forgive him, Bergin. I have, years ago. Let go of the old pain and anger. He can't hurt you any more." She put the ring on the table beside her and reached for his hand.

He took her hand in his and smiled at her.

"I will try." He knew she was right.

CHAPTER 57

The sun was bright that day as they stood by the grave of Erdman. A small stone marker with his name marked the spot. Bergin and Ingmar had buried him in a private ceremony in the churchyard beside his parents. Bergin had written a letter full of all his anger, pain and resentment that he felt for his brother. He placed it in the grave with the coffin.

He hoped it would be enough. Or at least that it would be a good start in letting go of the past, of Erdman and even of Clara, and reclaiming his life.

Bergin put his arm around Ingmar and led her away. They paused for a moment at Clara's grave. Ingmar stooped down to clear some weeds that had sprouted. Bergin touched the headstone gently.

For a moment, he thought he could see Clara standing before him, smiling. He blinked not sure of what he was seeing.

Then there was a fragrance that hung in the air.

He just stared.

Then the illusion turned and faded into nothingness.

"Maybe she was there that night," he said in a hushed tone more to himself than for anyone else to hear.

"What, dear?" Ingmar stood up and looked at her husband.

"Nothing, sweetheart. Do you know that I love you?" He smiled at her, feeling as if he had released a great deal of the past, and that he too had been released by that past as well. It was an odd feeling and it made him a little restless.

"I love you, too." She smiled back at him.

"Let's go home now," Bergin caressed her cheek with his finger. "I think I may invite Bert Kunkle over for supper, and then go take a look at that funny old car in the back of the barn."

"Are you boys going to fix up that old piece of junk?" Ingmar laughed.

"Maybe." He wrapped her into an embrace and kissed her. "Maybe I'll just let Bert haul it away and do what he wants to with it. I really don't care anymore," he laughed.

Across the graveyard laughter was heard, it was the laughter of a young girl. It resonated with a long, forgotten memory that both Bergin and Ingmar held in a special place in their hearts.

It sounded like Clara's laughter.

Author's Notes

In 1925 there was a woman named Clara who fell for a man named Erdman. When she went missing, her father was haunted by a prophetic dream that eventually led to the discovery of her body in a shallow grave.

As anyone who has written a book will tell you, there are so many people who help make a book become a reality. I thank my many friends who have helped, encouraged, critiqued, taught and listened to my joy, pain, frustration and excitement, but mostly all those who gave me their loving support and encouragement over the years.

Special thanks to the following:

Rick A. Jorgensen of the Golden Era Automobile Association for his expertise and advice about a fast car for Erdman. Don Murphy, for helping in my research. Pam Flint who read, corrected the manuscript and made suggestions and provided great encouragement. Helene Trottier for the final proofread and encouragement and for her gracious support for many years in my life. The cover art is an original water color by the author. Last, but not least, to Mike Simpson and his crew for being willing to take on *Clara's Wish* and get it published!

Special thanks to Drue Powers, Chief of Police for the city of Red Oak in Montgomery County, Iowa. He was always willing to discuss police procedure, and encouraged me to keep writing. Best of all was the day we discussed another story and planned the murder of a character in a future book.

About the Author

S. M. Senden was raised in Winnetka, a north shore suburb of Chicago. From an early age reading and writing were passions as was travel. Senden has studied, lived and worked in the USA, Europe, the Mid-East and Africa, spending a number of years as an archaeological illustrator for various expeditions. S. M. Senden earned a Masters Degree and has studied creative writing, play writing and screenwriting.

Publications include *Christopher's Egg* in the anthology *Change is in the Wind* published by Second Wind. Articles and mediations in both *The Clergy Journal* and *The Word in Season* and a number of ghost stories in various magazines.

S. M. Senden currently resides in the greater Omaha metro area and is working on another historical mystery *Under the Anheuser Bush*, as well as a modern day series involving forensic artist, Dr. Kate Ashton.